CRITICS
THIS 4-STAR

"Smart and sexy! Fritscher Fiction starts in your head and works its way down..."

"*CORPORAL IN CHARGE* is a **wonderful book**, full of **careful writing** and a fine sense of words...compassion and humor...full of hot, horny fantasies...surging with lyricism and insight....erotic dreamer, daddy, brother, shaman...**Fritscher writes with a gorgeous pen**. The story 'Caro Ricardo'" is an a clef memoir of Fritscher's relationship with his bi-coastal lover, **ROBERT MAPPLETHORPE**. "...a **tender, surreal** story of a desperate search for personal meaning, of being together and alone in the frenetic glitz of New York obsessions." —**THE ADVOCATE**

"*CORPORAL IN CHARGE* is a collection of **21 assertively sexual and imaginatively arousing pieces. Some are stories, some are true-sex adventures, others are elegant fantasies, some are rough-and-tumble orgies of the mind**. The title tale is actually a 20-page torrent of wordplay. Author Jack Fritscher's prose is **stark, subtle, smooth and suggestive, richly erotic** because it leads the way into a fantasy world...Best of the good bunch: 'Hustler Bars' and 'Earthhorse: Harvest,' a **stunning political sex fable** about an s/m future." —**RICHARD LABONTÉ**, *In Touch for Men*, A DIFFERENT LIGHT BOOKSTORES, NY, LA, SF

"*CORPORAL IN CHARGE* is the **best book...graphic, explicit...and unabashedly romantic in a truer sense than are most other books aimed at gay audiences**...a collection of short pieces which deal with s/m and **individual consciousness**. Like **GENET'S WORK**, these are essentially masturbatory fantasies...about the actual fantasy of romance....and **gay men love to read about romance...**" —**MICHAEL BRONSKI**, *Gay Community News*, BOSTON

"Fritscher is the **sole demiurge...of a cock-stiffening domain...a jittery stylist with a kinetic verbal sense**...stream of consciousness... Fritscher's...**writing...works spectacularly**...he celebrates gay fantasies of working-class men...In a story called 'Silver Screen Castro Blues' there's **enough ghettoized angst to keep the Manhattan literati wired for months.**" —**STEVEN SAYLOR as AARON TRAVIS**, *DRUMMER*

JACK FRITSCHER, like **ANNE RICE**, famously crosses genres—erotic with literary—and emerges as a cult best seller with work published in 30 gay magazines, a dozen anthologies, plus more than **100,000 copies sold of his books and 250,000 copies sold of his videos. CAMILLE PAGLIA** uses his writing in her *Vamps and Tramps*, and *The New Republic* compared his novel *Some Dance to Remember* (epic gay history: 1970-82) to **GORE VIDAL** and **JAMES BALDWIN**.

"Like **RECHY**, Fritscher joins words in powerful couplings that enhance eroticism...He is a poet of erotica."   —Joseph D. Butkie, *BAY AREA REPORTER*, San Francisco

"Fritscher's writing is fragile...mesmerizing, shocking, and **a cool book**."
—T. R. WITOMSKI, *CONNECTION*, New York

"In this long-awaited anthology...a wealth of new material fills these covers. Fritscher has a **wonderfully particular style and rhythm to his writing**.... Fritscher's **imagination is endless and totally without remorse**. What may really surprise readers is that amid the graphic descriptions of eros, there are **actual ideas** here."
—JOHN W. ROWBERRY, *DRUMMER*

"Fritscher's gift for language in *CORPORAL IN CHARGE* made me think of the POET **DENNIS COOPER**, and as in Cooper's work, there is a strong element of romanticism.... These are true erotic fantasies...that straddle the borderline between inventive eroticism and the phantasmagoric....Fritscher loves words as well as what they describe–which makes this **one of the hottest books in a long while**."
—IAN YOUNG, *THE BODY POLITIC*, TORONTO

"*CORPORAL IN CHARGE* is **literate, honest, funky, and even funny by intent**... freewheeling...**a good read**....Devotees of the darker side of the leather subculture will find a lot to like in this book."   —*NBN*, St. Louis

"In *CORPORAL IN CHARGE*, Fritscher is a **master—even perhaps a genius—of gay prose**...who knows how to write, and understands very well how an erotic writer plays with the brain, man's most accessible sex organ. The several leathersex stories are so lovingly rendered that **vanilla readers will be swept up into the performance art**.... The best piece is the title story, written in dialogue...is a like wonderful cinema verite."
—Q, *PHILADELPHIA GAY NEWS*

"**Spend your money on** *CORPORAL IN CHARGE*...celebrates the possible pleasures between men...Fritscher is at his best in his erotic inventive use of language."
—Thor Stockman, *GMSMA News*

Reviews
www.JackFritscher.com

Chris Duffy, Mr. America   Video: *Sunset Bull*

Corporal
in
Charge
of Taking Care of
Captain O'Malley

Stories for Bears,
Daddies, and Leathermen

jack fritscher

PALM DRIVE PUBLISHING
SAN FRANCISCO CALIFORNIA

All *inquiries* concerning performance, adaptation, or publication rights should be addressed to Publisher, Palm Drive Publishing, Mark@PalmDrivePublishing.com. Correspondence may be sent to the same address. Send reviews, quotation clips, feature articles, and academic papers in hard copy, tear sheets, or electronic format for bibliographical inclusion on literary website and in actual archive.

For author history and literary research:
www. JackFritscher.com

All photographs, including cover photograph, shot by and ©1995, 2010 Jack Fritscher
Cover design realized by Mark Hemry
Cover ©2010 Jack Fritscher

Published by Palm Drive Publishing, San Francisco CA
EMail: correspond@PalmDrivePublishing.com

Previously published: Leyland Publications, ISBN 0-917342-45-3, 1984
Library of Congress Catalog Card Number: 99-67126
Fritscher, Jack 1939-
    Corporal in Charge of Taking Care of Captain O'Malley and Other Stories / Jack Fritscher
    p. cm.
    ISBN13 978-1-890834-34-0
    ISBN 1-890834-34-3
                1. American Literature—20th Century. 2. Masculinity—Fiction.
        3. Homosexuality—Fiction. 4. Gay Studies—Fiction. 5. Erotica—Gay.
                6. Popular Culture. I. Title.

Printed in the United States of America
First Printing, 2000
10 9 8 7 6 5 4 3

www.PalmDrivePublishing.com

For Mark Hemry,
editor, producer,
lover.
We are friends together.

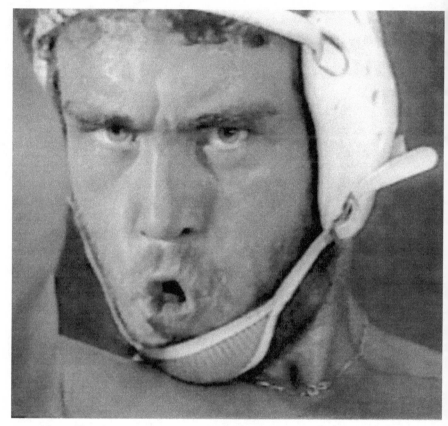

Steve Thrasher   Video: *Thrasher: If Looks Could Kill*

Contents

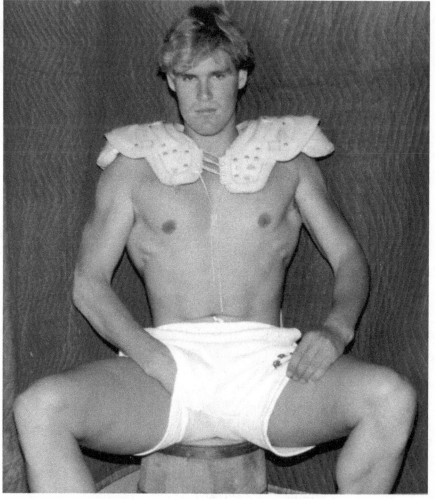

Lifeguard   Video: *Young Muscle*

That Boy
That Summer

In his eighteenth summer between senior high and college, Engine remembered, he had beat off exactly 358 times for an average of nearly four loads a day. Early mornings he woke with a pisshard that wouldn't go away. He walked to the bathroom, down the hall flooded with the early dawn light of summer, with his dick big and hard and bobbing in front of his young belly. The weight of it felt as good, cantilevered out over his big balls, as did the heat of it in the cool morning air. In the john, he stood sleepily over the toilet, holding his large meat in his hand, aiming his rod down at the bowl. His piss was slow in coming. His hand felt good on his cock. His mind darted, waking up, to the kind of stuff he had plotted to dedicate his summer vacation to: he intended to beat off as much as he could everywhere he could, thinking about and spying on, well, not spying actually, more like watching, no, studying, yeah, that was it, studying the guys he couldn't wait to rub shoulders with in the locker room come the fall semester.

Engine had scoped his plan, start to finish. He knew what he wanted. He knew what he liked. He had, that summer, not yet let any man touch his dick. At the Y, and in a couple of gas station restrooms, and in at least one highway rest stop, men had taken a gander at the meat Engine flipped out of his jeans. They had tried, some of them, to cop a feel of his sizeable rod. He let them look. He even let one or two of them kind of kneel in front of him while they looked at his dick and rubbed their own cocks.

Engine liked that. He liked the way grown men knelt to worship dick. The couple times that he had stepped back from the porcelain urinal, he turned with his dick hanging out of his fly and stood with his booted feet slightly apart. He noticed that as soon as the other man knelt down in front of him, his own cock started its launch from its long, low-slung hang, filling up with a tidal flood of hard, swelling meat stretching the rosy pink skin of his young dick tight around the thick shaft that curved ever so naturally off to his left.

He liked to watch his prick's no-hands rise to fullness that flushed the thick mushroom head.

He was surprised the first time that a man kneeling on the hard tile floor in the gas-station john moaned at the sight of his big tool. He stepped back half a pace when the man bobbed toward his meat. A thin strand of pre-fuck juice, clear as crystal, started as a big drop forming at the slit of his dick. His step back caused the drop to fall in a slow stretch of juice that the kneeling man wanted. But Engine wasn't offering that. No touch. Not yet. Not until he was ready. He wasn't prick teasing. He was totally focused on what he had to exchange at the moment. He was okay in his head with men looking at his dick close up, but he wasn't ready, at least not yet, not until he had beaten off enough by himself to let another man touch him, lick him, tongue him, suck him.

Engine knew about all those things. No one told him. He just knew. He was born knowing. His secret knowledge he kept to himself. His plan was to act on what he liked when he got old enough. What he liked was older men. Older men, to him that summer, were the guys on Freshman College Varsity. His plan was never to be touched until he was touched by one of them. He was satisfied, all the way up to the fall semester, to hang out near where these guys played summer ball, to park his old car near their van at the drive-in movie, and to strip off his own teeshirt and jeans close by the lockers where they peeled down and horsed around snapping each others' butts with towels while their dicks and balls flopped in their wild grab-assing before they headed down to the beach.

He beat off in the bushes watching them sweating in a fast and furious hardball tournament that lasted all summer.

He beat off in his old car at the drive-in movie staring into their van where they guzzled beer and smoked dope and made dirty jokes about the stuff on screen.

He beat off in the locker room sniffing their socks and smelling the sweat in the pits of their white cotton teeshirts; he searched their white jockey shorts, dropped, in their messing around, carelessly on the floor, for that special bit of skid-mark that only the crack of a ripe sweaty butt can blot into a trace of guys who are really hot shit.

He studied the way the college guys moved and found his own moves were already as sure as theirs. He studied the way they cut their hair and discovered his own natural bent in grooming matched theirs. He studied their cocks and balls. He inventoried the variety of their upperclassmen bodies. He liked what he saw. He liked the look, when he was alone, in his room laid back naked in front of a mirror, of his own body and balls and cock. He knew he would fit in okay. He could hardly wait for the fall. The thought of walking into the senior locker room, stripping down, playing a little ball, and showering all together in a tiled room echoing with loud shouting gave him a bone on. He could hardly wait to show off his dick, his sizeable big dick, to these guys.

He figured it might never happen, but he liked to think about standing with them all in a circle jerk. He knew they had done it. He had seen them, late one night, half-drunk and very stoned, standing stripped from a midnight swim around a small warming fire kindled on the sandy shore of Twin Lakes. They started out laughing and taking bets on who could last the longest or shoot the fastest or who had the biggest dick versus who had the smallest gun; but the longer they stood in the circle, the closer they moved. The laughing stopped. Their individual energies seemed to combine into one group energy. There was no touching. Only the movement of their arms stroking their hands up and down the shafts of their hard cocks. There was no embarrassment. No shame. They were buddies, all of them, together all the time, each one of them thinking, in the quiet of the summer night, mesmerized by the firelight, their own private thoughts, jerking off together as naturally as every other sport and pleasure they shared.

Engine could hardly wait to be part of a group of men like that. Dick in hand, he beat off thirty or forty times thinking about how they had looked, each and every one of them, standing around the fire, their faces and chests and bellies and cocks lit from beneath by the orange-and-shadow flickering in the soft summer night air. He knew all his life he would remember this summer of purposeful waiting. He even laughed at himself for holding out, acting almost virginal, until he could do it with the right upperclassman in the right group of men. Until then, that summer, he kept his dick to himself.

One thing Engine knew for fucking sure. He might be a "technical" virgin because he'd never done it with anybody else, but he was not gonna be any slouch. He knew when he finally hit the sack with the right man at the right time, he would know precisely what moves to give and take. A guy doesn't jerk off a couple thousand times thinking about all the things two men can do without getting pretty good at basic pleasure.

Engine figured it took a lot of nerve for a guy to go out and make love to somebody else unless he had made pretty good love to himself first.

He liked to cup his hand around his cock and balls and move it slowly to his face. He held his palm and fingers steady and lobbed a nice-and-nasty wad of spit into his hand. His big cock kind of rolled expectantly over on his left thigh. His dick liked stroking. His hand liked his dick. His head knew the right rhythms. His mind unreeled the right movies. Everything came together when his wet hand wrapped around the hot head of his dick and slid down the heavy shaft to his cockroot at the top of his tight balls. He liked to feel the hose-thick vascularity of the big vein that ran up the underside of his dick from his nuts to his cockhead. He was always rock hard.

That summer he played with himself in constant anticipation of the first man he would have and of all the men he would have after the first. He was absolutely and totally clear about the downright righteous encounter of man-on-man pleasure. That summer with 358 cumings under his belt, he developed a taste for his own cum, and through his own cum, a taste for the cum of the college guys he would soon join. He licked his own hand. He wanted to know for sure what his load tasted like so he'd know exactly how he tasted to the guys when they came back in the fall from working on construction jobs and from playing ball and from their own secret pleasures.

He had big hands. He had big cock. He had big plans.

He loved that summer when he had teased himself with total anticipation. He remembered all those private young loads he had shot on his own belly. He recalled how perfectly that summer had set him up for all the man-to-man fucking and sucking to come.

Sometimes, later on, pile-driving his dick, face-fucking some guy in a roadside toilet, he knew he'd think back on that summer when he had heated himself up to a hot, fevered pitch that would spur him on for a fucking lifetime!

Larry Perry   Video: *Naked Came the Stranger*

**When foreskins dock
through the Gloryhole of Love...**

A Sucker
for Uncut Dick

B-L-I-N-D M-E-A-T makes me crazy. I love big, thick, juicy, *uncut* dick. I love it clean and washed with the smell of fresh soap rinsed around the head under the big jacket of foreskin. I love it sweaty and cheesy with the honest smegma of a big working dick that hasn't had the time to strip its roll of lip back to wash its ring around the collar. I confess I spent half my time in high-school study hall flipping through my Funk & Wagnall's getting a hardon looking up words like *foreskin*, *smegma,* and *prepuce*. A barbaric word like *circumcision* gave an instant soft-on.

The other half of my time in high school I spent secretly cruising the locker room counting off my buddies who were cut and uncut. I saw a lot of "forbidden" meat in those sneak-n-peek days, and the most beautiful dicks I ever saw were the big, thick, chunky cocks that hung long and strong, with the heavy-veined shafts helmeted with a juicy fold of skin.

Any man who loves dick has a special place in his heart for the way a cock fills out a foreskin. An uncut dick rides different than a piece of meat that's been sliced. Uncut meat has secrets. Uncut meat doesn't show its crown right off. Uncut meat keeps its glistening wet head thick and full of jutting promise under cover of the rich roll of foreskin. Uncut meat looks different, smells different, and tastes of special secret man-flavors. Uncut meat feels like a full fucking handful when you grab ahold of it. Uncut meat offers that special little pucker right at the wet tip where the skin all folds down to a fleshy little iris that begins to open so easily, so smoothly, when coaxed by a hot and hungry tongue.

When that foreskin, lipped into foreplay, starts pulling back, as the ripe, juicy dickhead starts its launch out from its protective skin-sheath, some special kind of lube seems to sweeten the slick taste of the cock slipping out of all that uncut darkness into the light and air. Uncut meat juts out of its foreskin in a way that demands attention. And gets it. Check out any swimming-pool shower room. With all the cut meat scrubbing and soaping itself, what you see is what you get. A sexy guy scrubbing down his own crotch has to take a long deliberate time to wash his uncut meat inside and out. Under the thick foreskin that you see lies that super-sensitive prick that you might get a good gander at if you hang around long enough to watch him strip it slowly back with one hand while he soaps up the emerging head with the other. Guys with foreskins have special moves the way they lovingly take one finger, and lick it, and insert it under the fold of skin, and rub it gently around the hidden head of their sweet, moist meat.

Even when I watch a well-hung guy jerking off his own uncut rod, I notice a definite difference in the longer stroke he gets because of the extra skin that slides like a slick piece of heaven up and down his shaft. It's fucking magic to watch the appearance and disappearance of his dickhead in and out of his heavy-duty foreskin. Even the sound of uncut dick is different. A wet hand sounds wetter as the skin of the hand slaps the foreskin, itself like some kind of sexy chamois over the head, slipping back down the shaft of cock. Nothing looks better than light glistening through a big drop of clear seminal juice hanging right out of tongue's reach on the rich skinfold of a big, thick foreskin.

I've sucked a lot of dick. I believe in disconnected dick. I mean, I believe in dick for its own sake. I study dick. Who it's attached to can make a difference, for sure. But let's face it. There's probably hardly a man on earth who hasn't fallen on his knees at the sight of a big, healthy, juicy, uncut piece of hardening cock stuck frankly through a gloryhole. It's Seventh Heaven and Cloud Nine to grab ahold of a Ten like that and feel the thick shaft growing thicker, watching the head start to slip, marinated, in its own juices, out from its tight fold of foreskin. Any dick coming through a gloryhole is fine; but an uncut piece flopping manfully through and hanging expectantly while it begins its own hardening rise like some Titan missile rolling back its protective silo-covers is heaven on wheels.

Sometimes I feel like a Bounty Hunter trying to find uncut cock in an asswipe society that cuts the fringe benefits off most of its baby boys before they even get a chance to have any say about whether they want to keep their foreskin or not. Some uncut guys, while they're still real young, sort of feel out of place in school-gym showers; but after they gain a little outside sexual experience and find out how much cut guys prefer their humpy foreskins, they change their attitudes and start to flaunt the gift that was not cut away from them. I figure there's nothing hotter than a man with an uncut dick who likes to strut and swing his big, blind stuff!

Probably the most important and memorable experience I've ever had as a collector of uncut meat happened in an honest-to-god motel in Oceanside, California, where a nineteen-year-old Okie Marine with *acne vulgaris* and the biggest piece of unsliced bologna I've ever unbuttoned, stood opposite me with his blind meat sticking out rock hard after his weeks of basic training at Camp Pendleton.

He had a great nine inches pointing right at me. Big length. Big circumference. Foreskin as heavy as wet dreams are made of. My own cut cock responded in kind: hardon and right at him. We stood facing each other: cut to uncut. He looked down at our two throbbing cocks, kind of smiled, and with his hands still waxed from his obstacle course rope drills, took hold of my dick, and aimed my cockhead straight at his folds of pink, blind foreskin.

I couldn't believe the fuck of what was happening!

With his other hand he fingered open ever so slightly his tight foreskin. But instead of stripping it back and pulling his own dick out, he guided the dry head of my cock straight on inside his hot, wet foreskin. I felt the warm fold of it wrap around my skinned dick. I felt uncircumcised inside his foreskin. He guided me in deeper. The generous lip of his tip was maybe a couple inches over the head of his nine-incher. Two inches of my dick were slipped by this young Marine into the inside interior of his dark, wet foreskin before the tip of my dick touched the hard crown of his cock.

Once we were docked, like two spaceships in midflight, he wrapped his hand tight around the connection and began a stroking motion with his hand and a fucking motion with his muscular hips. He watched intently what went on down below and between us. Only once did he look up to see in my face the reaction I must have been showing. He was a kid who knew the value of being thick and uncut. He was man enough to share back the incredible experience of having manskin folded like a holster over a hot gun. He massaged our two dicks together, head-to-head, inside his deep foreskin. He kept up his rhythmic cadence. The hand-pressure, the heat and juice and excitement of fucking up inside his uncut foreskin made me detonate my load buried in his slick-lubed tube. As soon as I started to shoot, he increased the rhythm of his hand on our paired cocks, and pumped his own load into the hot mix of our mutual jism blended in his deep foreskin.

So what more can I tell you about my dirty thoughts, except that in my dirty life, I've found that you have to be real careful what you hunt for, because sometimes you get what you're looking for and then some. I'm not exactly playing "Can You Top This?" But I can tell you for fucking sure that since then I've not looked at an uncut piece of fresh, blind meat without thinking of fucking up inside that young Marine's tight, hot, wet, and juicy foreskin. *Semper Fidelis* to Uncut Meat!

**Fetish hunter raids gym,
tries on men's clothes...**

Big Beefy
College Jocks

Tempting. The taste for Big Beefy College Boys with built chests, hot nipples, big dicks, sweaty buttholes, daddies' money, fast cars. Fuck-crazy. Gloriously golden. Untouchable. Forbidden. Tempting. Stealing sniffs and whiffs off their gym gear dropped in wet piles on the dirty floor in front of their lockers.

Sometimes stealing a worn-torn teeshirt. A lot of times stealing a couple of their jockstraps. Inhaling hot elastic smells through the warm crotch cups. Breathing so long through their sweaty pouches that all my life's breath was totally filtered through the wet web of their moist jockstraps. Eating the coarse curled pubic hairs. Biting the hairs between my teeth. Sucking the sweat juice from the jockstraps. Scared shitless of getting caught, beat up, punched out, laughed at, kicked around. Those big, wet, wide feet stomping out of the shower. Big toes. Thick-haunched legs. First-string players. Wet, white towels dropping carelessly off their hard athletic butts.

Trying to tie my own laces, bent over, eyeballing their stud equipment. Big nuts. Big dicks flopping, curving left or right, betraying the hand the guy had for years beat his own meat with. Some pud thick-veined, long, and uncut. Some dicks thick, fat, juicy.

Big hands toweling dry big bodies.

Muscular arms raised, buffing the towels across broad shoulders beaded wet with shower spray. Armpits rampant. Fresh and dripping. Powerful arms rooted in thick shoulders crowning strong chests and staunch backs. Naked. Horseplay. A flurry of white towels snapping across the benches at bare butts: big hands cupping dick and balls for protection. Jumping. Laughing. Grab-assing. "Cut it out, asshole!" Bullshitting in the locker room. Wild. Fuckcrazy.

Studying how the biggest of them all takes longer drying his dick and balls separately and carefully. Quieter than the rest. His own man. Captain among the male animals. Big. Healthy. Strong.

The locker-room air warm with their heat, thick with their smells. The way a big, thick, perfectly formed foot plants itself square on the blond, wooden bench to be dried toe by toe by toe by a big, thick, perfectly formed hand rubbing foot and calf dry, dropping the towel like some carelessly forgotten gift that falls minutes later wet and smelling into my own casually open gym bag.

Touching with open palm the heat of their feet and butts stored in the warm wood of the bench.

The slow pulling on of clothes. One puts on his gray wool socks and sits naked, lost in thought, his dick, hanging lower than the bench, only slightly covered by his hands hanging from his forearms resting on his open thighs. Hulking. Severe. The kind of player with an aggressive attraction to opponents' groins and eyeballs. One who seems always to be standing, talking, unselfconsciously, stripped next to the bank of gray lockers with only his soggy towel wrapped around his neck, over his shoulders, and down off his big pecs. He's one of the Ball-Scratchers. Can't keep his hand from sort of lifting his nuts and pulling them around while his mouth moves and makes easy laughs that blend with the noise of wet males satisfied with their game and chomping for fun. One who fingercombs his wet hair, walks in his jeans, stripped to the waist, big arms slick-combing back his wet hair. His mirrored reflection lighting the rippled moves of his arms connecting to his chest. Tight hairy belly of a born jock. Easy smile. White teeth thick as picket posts. Predatory All-American chin. Aggressive stubble. Good moves. Captain's best buddy.

Slam of metal locker doors. Towels tossed in the direction of the heavy duck canvas bin. Coarse, white, cotton teeshirts tight across big bulked shoulders and tight around huge biceps. Loose-fit hang of teeshirt off the ledge of pecs over the jock bellies.

The sound of a long, heavy, thick, rich piss from the locker-room urinals. "Shit. That feels so good," he says. His big paw hits the flush valve. His other shakes his massive dick. He turns still tucking his meat into his white jockey shorts and jeans. The urinal porcelain, cool and white and curlicued with a harvest of perfect pubic hair. Perfect for a good licking. Nothing too extreme to connect with the essence of well built college jocks.

Gathering up their stuff. Taking home what they've forgotten. Saluting it: dick in hand. Cuming in it. Returning it washed to the pile of their clothes days later. Waiting for semester's end when the college gym manager opens up all the lockers these guys never bothered to empty. Not completely. Waiting for him to pull out the used jocks and socks and shirts and shorts and shoes and sweat-crusted salty gloves. Waiting for him to throw them on the locker-room floor. Unclaimed. Waiting with an empty gym bag. Waiting for him to disappear on other duties. Waiting to pick up in one final harvest the feel and smell and taste of all the sweaty guys watched all semester long. Waiting to fill my bed with all their worn-torn gear. Waiting to bag it and get it on home for the Ultimate Clothes Fantasy.

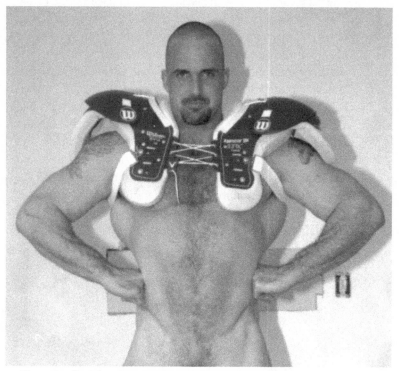

Chris Duffy, Mr. America   Video: *Sunset Bull*

**Now that it's finally years from then,
and you're speaking of it,
you can be kind...**

The Princeton Rub

Once upon a decade in a time-warp far away, guys in cotton polo shirts—nubbed with the deep pile of a hundred fresh washings—cruised carefully, eyeing the khaki-chino baskets pulled tight against inseams that shot down slack-legs with creases carefully ironed into place, right down to the pegged cuffs. They checked, with guarded sidelong glances, the Ivy-League straps buckled in the center of the small of the back, right above the rise of undergraduate butt that showed twin mounds when first one foot, and then the other, was raised up, putting the Blue Suede Shoes up for a brushing on a campus bench.

BLOND SWIMMERS
Men maybe never looked better than they looked around 1960. A check through old mags like *Tomorrow's Man* and *Sports Illustrated* is a hardon reminder of what us kids back then wanted to be like when we grew up. Olympian Don Schollander had the original blond swimmer's body: thick-shouldered, deep-chested, all white-teeth-and-big-smile in baby-blue nylon Speedo briefs. Schollander himself confessed to *Time/Life* that he shaved his body hair—all his body hair—to cut its slowing pull in the pool.

JOCKS AND JOCKSTRAPS
There was something in the air in those days before liberation: a delicious secret quality that dared not scream its name. Guys looked at each other maybe more than they touched; but finally when they worked their careful way up to touch, the touch meant something. Not that those days were better. They were

just different: more innocent, more ...more...sniffing, yeah, more sniffing around the pertinent edges. More excitement wondering if anybody else felt like you did. Wondering if your best friend—and all our best friends were team captains and class presidents—would blow the whistle if you told them all that you dreamed about some of them at night, but that the dream was okay, really, since you didn't dream about any of them completely naked (because that was the sort of stuff queers did), but you dreamed about a lot of them exercising wearing JOCKSTRAPS!

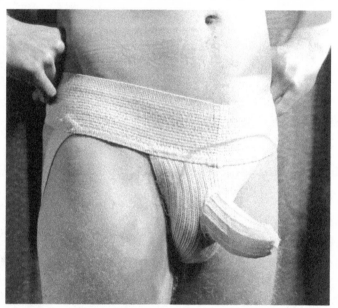

Popular culture ad, 1978, James Ltd. Author's Collection

JOCKSTRAPS! A word calculated to turn the softest dick hard. JOCKSTRAPS! Getting a hardon reading the Bike Athletic Supporter ads in *Boy's Life*. Looking up JOCKSTRAP in Webster's Dictionary during study hall and getting a roaring bone on. Hoping none of the other guys would notice the bulge in your khakis. Hoping Kenny Kehres wouldn't notice how you sort of leaned in toward his gym-locker with his JOCKSTRAP hanging at your eye-level as the green metal door swung past your face, and he turned fullchested and naked to you and said, "Excuse me," sort of absently flipping his dick up off his balls, and reaching close to your face with the smell of his privates on his hand to take his JOCKSTRAP off the door and pull it up first one leg and then the other, carefully straightening the flat rib of elastic—so white against his berry-brown tan.

Then alone, late one afternoon, finding his JOCKSTRAP lying forgotten on the locker-room bench. Alarmed by it. Staring at it. Getting hard looking at it. Not daring to touch it. Almost cuming in your pants at the excitement of seeing it—and the fear of being caught standing stock still alone and staring in a locker room empty except for that white cotton JOCKSTRAP.

SEE YA LATER, ALLIGATOR

Grooming then was a high art. Saturdays, every week, called for a trip to the barber who carefully clipped and trimmed your Brylcremed hair with medium sideburns and a long sweep back both sides to the slightest suggestion of a DA that drove school teachers mad.

Saturdays you could feel the white shaving lather dabbed hot around your ears, followed by the scrape of the straight edge stropped on a well-worn length of leather, and then the slight shaving of the hair around your ears and down the back of your neck.

You knew the nape of your neck had to be perfectly cut to look good against the blue oxford-cloth button-down collar of your open-neck sports shirt with the inexplicable loop right between the shoulder blades and over the pleat that ran down to where the shirt tucked into your slacks. You wanted your hair to look like Ricky Nelson, or like Troy Donahue, or, if you sneaked looks into bodybuilder magazines like *Iron Man*, then like the incredible Jim Haislop, or best, like the classic chiseled blond Tab Hunter incarnated in the movie *Lafayette Escadrille!*

1957 CHEVY BEL AIR

Sex, when it happened, was sometimes no more than buddy-talk after a double-date ended up (after the dates were delivered back to their front porches with the lights on), sidling into a double jerkoff, talking about the hard time we had getting the dates to put out and how we were, like man, so horny, and wasn't that a couple o' nice pieces, and, jeez, I'm so drunk I got a lover's nut that won't go away, and, shit, man, you tell me what you think about the other one, and we'll just sort of each take matters into our own hands, and, you know, without touching or anything, sort of cool down a situation too hot to ignore, and, cripes, we'll have to use the towel you got in the backseat to wipe up all this, jeez, fuckin' load, so fuckin' big it's a good thing I never got to home plate or I'd be somebody's daddy nine months from tonight, cuz look, man, both our loads are about the same caliber shot, and, hey, yours stays harder after you shoot, but mine's longer before and after, and I don't give a dip-shit if yours is thicker.

And all the time sitting there together in the 1957 Chevy Bel Air, you were sure that you might get fercrissakes *caught!*

PRINCETON RUB

Going all the way with your best buddy wasn't something you exactly talked a lot about. Buddy-rubbing was sort of what happened when some hot summer afternoon found you both alone together at his house with his parents gone, the air conditioner humming, and the transistor radio counting down the Top Ten.

You both smelled like chlorine from the swimming pool in the park. He was pink with sunburn and, sort of for a joke, showed you where his tan line left off and asked you if you wouldn't maybe rub some Coppertone over his shoulders.

You guessed it made sense when he dropped his Speedos and walked bare-ass to the window and snapped the venetian blinds closed. He turned around and his naked hardon greeted yours bunched up in your trunks.

"Come on," he said, and he lay down on his single twin bed, not even bothering to pull the shiny bedspread down. He tucked his dick into the bed and spread his legs, lifting his tight swimmer's butt into the air. His wet hair was fresh cut on his neck. The sun-heat rose like a sweat-vapor from his trim body. "Are you going to?" he asked.

"I'm coming," you said.

And you both meant the Coppertone-rub and something else.

Face down, he forced no look back at you. Only your swim trunks and jock stood between your hardon and his skin. You had no question about anything except lying down on top of his sunburned body, straddling his legs, dropping your cock between his thighs, feeling his legs closing in on your dick, his well-muscled thighs tightening around your prick with perfect control.

The slick of suntan oil, greasing your rod, moved you slow through the soft hair of his inner thighs, dragging the top of your shaft along the rim of his moist crack, not daring to be so bold as to brown him, thinking about touching the head of your dick to his hole, then thinking politely better of it, pulling back, slipping your dick into place between his legs, feeling the moves of his warm cheeks against your lower belly, riding the smooth rhythms of his legs flexing around your dick until his rhythms became your rhythms, and together you moved, long and leisurely, through the Princeton Rub until you both came and messed up the shiny bedpsread, which seemed to matter so much later when you tried to clean it up to cover the evidence of your pecker-tracks from his hawk-eye of a mother.

Now that it's finally years from then, and you're speaking of it, you can be kind about it all—with maybe no more than an ache in your dick for times when so little could seem to be, and really was, so much.

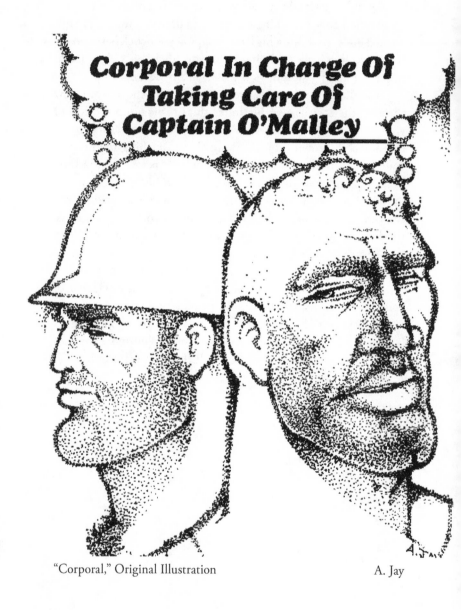

Corporal In Charge Of Taking Care Of Captain O'Malley

"Corporal," Original Illustration

A. Jay

Performance Art Screenplay...

Corporal in Charge of Taking Care of Captain O'Malley

Interior: Night. Wardroom of USMC Barracks. CORPORAL POWELL, 22, *powerfully built and hung, lies stretched back in a bunk, his booted feet spread wide, his USMC fatigues dropped down around his calves. He jerks his cock in close-up as the scene opens. At the* SOUND OF KNOCKING, CORPORAL POWELL *is joined by* CAPTAIN O'MALLEY, *his superior officer.* CAPTAIN O'MALLEY *is 32, handsome, husky, muscled, and very well hung.* O'MALLEY *is a Marine career man who knows exactly what he wants and, more exactly, how to get it. The camera moves in slowly, tighter on* CORPORAL POWELL.

POWELL: *(Softly, jerking himself)* Ahhh, sucking those guys off today. Jesus. In the fuckin' john. Ahhh. I been thinking about Weiser for a long time, man, uhhohh, fuckin' Goddamn, ohh. *(Loud knock at door)* Who is it?

O'MALLEY: Captain O'Malley.

POWELL: *(To himself)* Captain! Oh God. the Captain! *(Out loud) Just a* second. *(More loud knocking)* Yessir!

O'MALLEY: What's going on in there, Corporal?

POWELL opens the door

POWELL: Captain O'Malley, *Sir,* yessir.

O'MALLEY: Why do you have the door closed when the barracks is empty?

POWELL: I don't know, Sir. I usually just close the door, Sir.

O'MALLEY: At ease, Corporal.

POWELL: Thank you, Sir.

O'MALLEY: Have a seat.

POWELL: Thank you, Sir.

O'MALLEY: Corporal Powell, are you surprised to see me today?

POWELL: Yessir. You're not usually here at night, Sir.

O'MALLEY: I came to talk to you about something I received in my office today.

POWELL: Yessir.

O'MALLEY: I have a report on you from the Colonel.

POWELL: Sir?

Long pause as CAPTAIN O'MALLEY
circles around CORPORAL POWELL

O'MALLEY: The report says that you've been hanging out in the latrine. You hear me? *Hanging out in the Latrine, Corporal! Corporal Powell...*

POWELL: Yessir.

O'MALLEY: And sucking cock in the latrine, Corporal Powell.

POWELL: Uhhh.

O'MALLEY: Corporal Powell, speak to me when I talk to you. I'm your Captain.

POWELL: Yessir.

O'MALLEY: Captain.

POWELL: Yessir, Captain, Sir.

O'MALLEY: Are you a cocksucker?

Long pause

POWELL: Uhhh, nossir, I ahhhh, I've sucked a few, Sir, but... I'm not...

O'MALLEY: You're not a faggot?

POWELL: Nossir, nossir.

O'MALLEY: That's good news. But I'm a little disturbed about the report. The Colonel wants me to report back to him on this. So that's why I came to see you.

POWELL: Sir, I don't want to get kicked out of the Marine Corps, Sir. I love the Marine Corps, Sir, and the Honor Guard.

O'MALLEY: You'd better love the Marine Corps, you fuc kin' jarhead.

POWELL: I do, Sir.

O'MALLEY: But you're a cocksucker. You been sucking Marine cock...

POWELL: Yessir.

O'MALLEY: You suck only Marine cock?

POWELL: Yessir.

CAPTAIN O'MALLEY studies
CORPORAL POWELL up and down

O'MALLEY: I think I'll keep this report locked in my desk and not pass it back to the Colonel. You understand, Corporal Powell?

POWELL: *Yessir.*

O'MALLEY: I expect to get something out of this.

POWELL: Yessir.

O'MALLEY: I expect to get something out of this. Do you read me, Corporal?

POWELL: Not exactly, Sir.

O'MALLEY: I want you to suck my cock.

POWELL: Your cock, Sir?

O'MALLEY: *My cock.* The captain's cock. You see that thing hanging down in the pants?

POWELL: Yessir.

O'MALLEY: The pants leg?

POWELL: Yessir.

O'MALLEY: You see that big fuckin' cock through there?

POWELL: Yes, Captain.

O'MALLEY: You think you can suck that big piece of meat?

POWELL: Yes, yessir.

O'MALLEY: You better check it out. You better take it out of my pants. You better take a good look at it. (CORPORAL POW-ELL *kneels and unbuttons* CAPTAIN O'MALLEY's *fly*) You like the Captain's cock?

POWELL: *Yessir!*

O'MALLEY: Captain's Marine cock?

POWELL: *Yessir!*

O'MALLEY: Alright, Corporal. Wrap your lips around the head of that big dick.

POWELL: Yessir.

O'MALLEY: See what you can do. (POWELL *makes sucking and moaning sounds*) Suck that thing right. Get down on it and swallow that thing. Swallow that fuckin' Captain's cock.

(CAPTAIN O'MALLEY *slaps* CORPORAL POWELL) *Eat it!*

POWELL: Yessir.

O'MALLEY: I didn't hear you.

POWELL: *Yessir!*

O'MALLEY: Captain wants a good blowjob.... The Captain wants a good blowjob, you fuckin'.... Corporal Cocksucker, suck that big prick, Corporal. Corporal Powell, suck it. Uhmmm.

POWELL: *(Choking sounds)*

O'MALLEY: The Captain likes the Corporal's mouth wrapped around his big prick. You hear that?

POWELL: Yessir!

O'MALLEY: Captain O'Malley likes that big cock going in your mouth, sucking me off. Yeah, suck that big cock, Corporal. Come on, Corporal Powell. Come on, Corporal Powell, suck that big fuckin' cock, that big fuckin' Marine cock, slidin' up and in your mouth. (POWELL *sucks harder*) Yes, you like that don't you? (CAPTAIN O'MALLEY *slaps* CORPORAL POWELL) Speak when I talk to you.

POWELL: *Yessir!*

O'MALLEY: Alright, suck. Big fuckin' Marine cock. You got yourself a big fuckin' Marine cock now. No little.... You got yourself a man's cock. Yeah Ahhhnn. The Captain's gettin' hot. The Captain's gettin' hot. Ummm. The Captain's gettin' fuckin' hot. *(Aggressive face-fuckin')* The Captain's goin' to shoot a big load of cum in your mouth, Corporal Powell. *You hear me?*

POWELL: *(Choking sounds)*

O'MALLEY: You *want a big load of cum?* The Captain's cum?

POWELL: *Yessir...*

O'MALLEY: *Talk to* me. Want a big load of cum, Captain's cum?

POWELL: Yes, Captain.

O'MALLEY: *Suck that big dick....* Ahhh, a fuckin' good cocksucker. Uhmmm, the Captain's getting hotter. The Captain's getting hotter. The Captain's getting real hot. Ohhh, the Captain's going to shoot a big load. Ohhh, *Ohhhhh. Ohgawdd. Take that cum, Corporal. Take that cum, Corporal. Take that cum and swallow it.* Swallow that cum, Corporal. Come on, Corporal Powell. Swallow it. Drain it all out of there. Drain that cum out of the Captain's cock. Drain all that cum out of the Captain's big cock.

POWELL: *(Moans, chokes, swallows)*

O'MALLEY: You like that cum???

POWELL: *Ummmmm. (Very low to himself)* His toy's as big as Weiser's.

O'MALLEY: Speak up. I can't hear you.

POWELL: Yessir. I was just remarking, Sir, on the hugeness of it. How it choked me. It's so much bigger than any other cock I've had.

O'MALLEY: The Captain's cock is big?

POWELL: Yessir.

O'MALLEY: You say the Captain's hung?

POWELL: Jesus.

O'MALLEY: Corporal Powell?

POWELL: Yessir.

O'MALLEY: Speak up when I talk to you.

POWELL: It's like a fuckin' donkey, Sir.

O'MALLEY: The Captain's got a donkey dick?

POWELL: Just hanging down. Sir. *(Cum drips a long web of* O'MALLEY's *juice into the close-up of* POWELL's *face)* Jesus. Oh, shit.

O'MALLEY: Lick the end of it. Where the cum is. (O'MALLEY guides POWELL's *head by force)* Right there.

POWELL: Yessir.

O'MALLEY: Get it all out. Okay, that's enough. The Captain is satisfied. For the moment.

POWELL: Yessir.

O'MALLEY: *(Buttoning his uniform)* Okay, we're going to have a little deal, Corporal Powell.

POWELL: Sir, a deal?

O'MALLEY: A deal. From now on you're going to stay out of the latrine. You understand?

POWELL: Yessir.

O'MALLEY: And from now on you're going to suck my cock. Exclusively.

POWELL: *(Slow, with feeling)* Yessir.

O'MALLEY: My cock, and nobody else's cock. Just my cock. Do you understand, Corporal?

POWELL: Yessir!

O'MALLEY: When I call you, I want you available to suck my big fuckin' donkey dick.

POWELL: Yessir.

O'MALLEY: You understand? To chow down on my dick.

POWELL: Yessir, Captain.

O'MALLEY: You be out of line one time, that report comes out of my desk and goes to the Colonel. Understand?

POWELL: Yessir, Captain, I...

O'MALLEY: *What?*

POWELL: Can I still be in the Honor Guard, Sir.

O'MALLEY: You can be in the Honor Guard as long as you keep sucking my fuckin' dick. You understand that, Corporal Powell?

POWELL: Yessir.

O'MALLEY: As long as your mouth works, you're in the Honor Guard. As long as your mouth sucks me exclusively, you stay in the Marine Corps.

POWELL: Yessir.

O'MALLEY: Okay. I'm leaving now.

POWELL: Sir?

O'MALLEY: What?

POWELL: Will you stay for a few minutes? Will you lie down with me, Sir. *(Very low)* Will Captain O'Malley lie down with Corporal Powell, Sir?

O'MALLEY: Lie down with you? You want the Captain to lie down with you?

POWELL: Yessir. *(Pause)* Please Sir, lie down with me, Sir.

O'MALLEY: Take my boots off.

POWELL: Yessir...

O'MALLEY: You know the Captain...used to have...another corporal...Corporal   Schmidt....You   remember...Corporal Schmidt?...the Corporal you replaced?

POWELL: Yessir, I met him once. Big fucker.

O'MALLEY: He was a *very* big fucker. You know what the Corporal used do for the Captain?

O'MALLEY *and* POWELL *lie down together*

POWELL: What, Sir?

O'MALLEY: He sucked the Captain's cock.

POWELL: Your big cock, Sir?

O'MALLEY: Every chance I gave him.

POWELL: Your big...Jesus!

O'MALLEY: Before you were stationed here.

POWELL: I never would've suspected, Sir. That guy Schmidt was huge. He was almost as built as you, Sir.

O'MALLEY: How big is your chest, Corporal?

POWELL: Forty-seven, forty-eight.

O'MALLEY: Forty-seven?

POWELL: Yessir.

O'MALLEY: He was exactly fifty-one inches.

POWELL: Sir, he was huge.

O'MALLEY: He had big, big pecs. Yeah, he had nice tits, too. (O'MALLEY *strokes* POWELL's *pecs*) But you got nicer tits.

POWELL: Me, Sir?

O'MALLEY: You've got nice nipples. The Captain's going to play with your nipples. I'm gettin' hard just thinking about Corporal Schmidt: how I used to play with his chest, how he used to suck my cock. I want you to suck my cock again, Corporal Powell.

POWELL: Yessir.

O'MALLEY: You want it?

POWELL: Yessir.

O'MALLEY: Get on it. Come on. Suck it again. (POWELL *goes down obediently on* O'MALLEY) I think the Captain will cum again. Suck me good. Suck me good. Come on! Corporal Powell, suck me good. Suck me good and hard. Suck that big donkey dick. You like that big donkey dick?

POWELL: *(With his mouthful)* Yessir!

O'MALLEY: OK. Suck it. I'm going to play with your tits. Captain O'Malley is going to play with your tits. Umm, nice, nice tits, nice nipples on that big chest. (POWELL *sucks and groans from heavy tit work*) Nice big nipples. Yeah, nice big nipples. Suck my balls. Lick my balls.

POWELL: Yessir.

O'MALLEY: Take those balls in your mouth. Take those balls. Yeah. Suck those big hairy balls. Big, hanging, hairy balls. Come on, Corporal Powell, suck those big hairy balls. Ummm, scab your tits....Lick those balls. Lick those fuckin' balls. You like these tits being played with?

POWELL: Oww, gawd, yeahhh....Jesus, I never knew that. Fuckin' cock...

O'MALLEY: You like that?

POWELL: Yessir.

O'MALLEY: Hey, c'mon get down on that big dick, get on that dick. I'm gettin' hot again. The Captain's gettin' hot. The Captain wants to shoot another load in your mouth...shoot another load in your fuckin' mouth, Corporal Powell. C'mon, suck that big prick. Suck that fuckin' big prick, Corporal. Suck the Captain's big prick. Ummm. You like that big...

POWELL: Ohhh...(*Sounds of choking*)

O'MALLEY: The Captain's gettin' hot again....The Captain's gettin' hot again....C'mon, suck it, Corporal. Suck that big dick (*trailing off*)...

POWELL: Uhnnnnn, unnnnn (*Choking*)

O'MALLEY: Get that fuckin' cock, ohh, the Captain's gettin' hot. Ahhh, *Goddammm. (Cum shot: heavy load from* CAPTAIN O'MALLEY *shoots all over* CORPORAL POWELL's face) Corporal Powell.

POWELL: Yessir.

O'MALLEY: Captain O'Malley thinks you're getting better each time. (O'MALLEY *starts to regain his composure)* Corporal Powell?

POWELL: Yessir.

O'MALLEY: Do you remember that Corporal Schmidt I was talking about?

POWELL: Yessir.

O'MALLEY: Corporal Schmidt got promoted.

POWELL: Yessir.

O'MALLEY: Because Captain O'Malley promoted him.

POWELL: Why, Sir?

O'MALLEY: Because he was a good cocksucker. He was a good Marine. But he was also a good cocksucker.

POWELL: Sir.

O'MALLEY: Now, you goin' to continue to suck my cock good?

POWELL: Yessir.

O'MALLEY: A good Marine. A good cocksucker.

POWELL: Where did Corporal Schmidt go, Sir?

O'MALLEY: Corporal Schmidt was put in charge of Olympic powerlifting and bodybuilding for the Marine Corps in Washington.

POWELL: What a plum job, Sir.

O'MALLEY: Corporal Schmidt got what he deserved, Corporal Powell.

POWELL: I been working out for a long time, Sir, just trying to get *into* that program.

O'MALLEY: You got a long fuckin' way to go before you measure up to Corporal Schmidt.

POWELL: Yessir.

O'MALLEY: Remember, I told you Corporal Schmidt had a chest fifty-one inches wide.

POWELL: I met him, Sir. I couldn't speak when I first met him. That blond giant.

O'MALLEY: He was a good cocksucker.

POWELL: Just lookin' at him...

O'MALLEY: You know what happened?

POWELL: What, Sir?

O'MALLEY: I found out that Corporal Schmidt was suckin' the bodybuilders off. And Corporal Schmidt was not supposed to be fuckin' with the other Marine bodybuilders.

POWELL: Yessir.

O'MALLEY: He was supposed to suck what?

POWELL: *The Captain's cock, Sir.*

O'MALLEY: The Captain's cock.

POWELL: Yessir.

O'MALLEY: He was cheating on the Captain.

POWELL: Yessir. He shouldn't have done that, Sir.

O'MALLEY: You're so fuckin' right. And Corporal Schmidt paid for it.

POWELL: How, Sir?

O'MALLEY: The Captain got pissed. And, you know, Corporal Schmidt had a very nice butt.

POWELL: *(Low)* Yessir...

O'MALLEY: You know what the Captain did with the Corporal's butt?

Close shot: fear on CORPORAL POWELL's *face*

O'MALLEY: I *asked you a question, Corporal Powell.*

POWELL: I can't imagine, Sir.

O'MALLEY: Corporal Schmidt started taking the Captain's big donkey dick up his butthole.

POWELL: Oh, Jesus! That'd kill him, Sir.

O'MALLEY: It didn't kill him.

POWELL: ...a big man...

O'MALLEY: He learned to love it. Corporal Schmidt got so that he had to have the Captain's cock up his butt.

POWELL: *(Low)* God.

O'MALLEY: Constantly. Had to have the Captain's dick up his ass.

POWELL: I never would have thought, Sir...

O'MALLEY: You'd be surprised how wide open your butthole can become after the Captain's cock gets up in it a couple times. You know what that Corporal Schmidt did?

POWELL: What, Sir?

O'MALLEY: When his fiancee came to the base on her vacation...

POWELL: What'd he do, Sir?

O'MALLEY: He was enjoying the Captain cornholing him so much, that he sent that fuckin' girlfriend of his back to Des Moines, and came directly to the Captain, so the Captain could fuck him again. And that night I fucked his butthole, four fuckin' times. I rammed this big donkey dick up his butthole four fuckin' times that day when he sent his girlfriend back to Des Moines, Iowa...

POWELL: Gawd, Sir.

O'MALLEY: ...because Corporal Schmidt loved the Captain's cock.

POWELL: I can't imagine a big fuckin' man like that bending over. God, that's sickening.

O'MALLEY: Sickening, Corporal Powell?

POWELL: Oh, man, that's a faggot.

O'MALLEY: *(Pissed)* The Captain....Look....A lot of Marines here on the base are gettin' cornholed by their buddies. But when you can have a Captain put it to you, and you know how big this Captain's fuckin' cock is. It's for the Corps. For the fuckin' Marine Corps. Just look at the fuckin' rod. One more look.

POWELL: That fuckin' big rod.

O'MALLEY: You know...

POWELL: Fuckin' big dick, Sir.

O'MALLEY: You know, the bigger the cock, the easier it is to take it up your butthole. You know that?

POWELL: Man, it would split it. You mean it didn't split him, Sir?

O'MALLEY: It did split him.

POWELL: He opened wide open for the Captain, Sir?

O'MALLEY: The first time he bled. A little.

POWELL: God, I can't even imagine something like that.

O'MALLEY: The second time, and the third time, and the sixth time, there was never a problem. Corporal Schmidt loved it. Corporal Schmidt loved gettin' fucked by Captain O'Malley. And you know what the Captain wants to do to you?

POWELL: Nossir.

O'MALLEY: You wanna stay in the Marine Corps?

POWELL: Yessir.

O'MALLEY: You wanna get promoted?

POWELL: Yessir.

O'MALLEY: Then Captain O'Malley thinks he'd better take a look at your butt.

POWELL: Ahhh, Sir, I can't do that, Sir.

O'MALLEY: Corporal. Corporal Powell.

POWELL: *Yessir.*

O'MALLEY: Captain O'Malley wants to see your butt.

POWELL: Yessir.

O'MALLEY: Captain O'Malley wants to see it now. I want you to drop those fuckin' shorts and let me see that butt.

POWELL: Yessir.

O'MALLEY: C'mon. (CAPTAIN O'MALLEY *slaps* CORPORAL POWELL) Let me see that butt.

POWELL: Yessir.

O'MALLEY: Okay. Hit the edge of the sack and bend over. Let's see what we can do with it.

POWELL: Awwwwhh, Sir. Please don't fuck me, Sir.

O'MALLEY: Ummmmm. Captain O'Malley thinks the Corporal has a nice butt. Stick it up here in my face. Let me see the opening here. Spread it!

POWELL: Oh, God.

O'MALLEY: Corporal Powell?

POWELL: *Yessir.*

O'MALLEY: You've got a nice butt. A nice firm butt. A good size, not too big, but just right for Captain O'Malley.

POWELL: Ohhh, God.

O'MALLEY: Just right for the Captain. Just right. *(Close shot:* O'MALLEY *slaps* POWELL's *sweat-streaked ass)* The Captain likes it. The Captain likes that butt. *(More slaps on the ass)* Look at that juicy hole.

POWELL: Please, Sir.

O'MALLEY: Look at that nice juicy hole. Do you know what the Captain's going to do to that hole?

POWELL: What, Sir?

O'MALLEY: The Captain's going to lick it. He's goin' to stick his tongue up in it.

POWELL: Ohhh, Sir.

O'MALLEY: Fuckin...

POWELL: Sir...

Long shot: from high angle across the barracks, the camera sees
CAPTAIN O'MALLEY *kneel to tongue*
the exposed ass of CORPORAL POWELL

O'MALLEY: *(Back to close shot)* Umm. Captain O'Malley likes that hole, sticking up in his face, nice virgin hole, nice virgin Marine hole. Gonna get it wet. Juicy. Then plug it.

POWELL: Ohh, Sir, please...please don't fuck me.

O'MALLEY: I'll fuck you if I feel like it.

POWELL: Oh, nossir.

O'MALLEY: But right now I want to lick it out. Lick it clean.

POWELL: Ohhh, Sir. Nossir.

O'MALLEY: I want to lick your butthole clean, Corporal Powell.
CAPTAIN O'MALLEY rims

POWELL: Nossir, all during high school...oh, yessir...I avoided getting cornholed then...(Low) Oh, yessir. Don't fuck me... Don't fuck me....Don't, Sir. Please, Sir. I Don't, Sir. Please, Sir.

O'MALLEY: Corporal, that's nice. You've got a fuckin' nice butthole...a nice butthole...it's good for my fuckin' big tongue...my fuckin' big tongue likes it. It likes lickin' your butthole. Yeah, Corporal Powell's got a nice butthole. Wooo, Captain O'Malley likes your butthole, Corporal, ummmm. Let's take a look at this big cock hanging underneath. You've got a nice cock, too, Corporal.

POWELL: Thank you, Sir. Ahhh!

O'MALLEY: A nice cock. Maybe we can pull it all the way around.

POWELL: Ahhh!

O'MALLEY: All the way around, stick it straight out, straight out between your legs, like this.

POWELL: Ugggghhh!

O'MALLEY: Sure looks good. How many inches you think this is, Corporal?

POWELL: I don't know, Sir.

O'MALLEY: It looks to me like about nine. Nine fuckin' inches of hard Marine cock.

POWELL: Ohhh, God!

O'MALLEY: In the Captain's hand.

POWELL: God, that's driving me crazy, Sir.

O'MALLEY: Do you like the way the Captain strokes it?

POWELL: *Yessir!*

O'MALLEY: Don't you forget it.

POWELL: Oh Goddamn, Captain O'Malley, I never felt anything...

O'MALLEY: We're gonna use your throat too, because you're gonna take care of the Captain while you're here at this barracks. You understand?

POWELL: Yessir.

O'MALLEY: (O'MALLEY *slaps* POWELL *again*) Fuckin' suck this after it's been used.

POWELL: Yessir.

O'MALLEY: Alright. Now you just lay right there and the Captain's going to grease his big donkey dick up. You hear me? *(Silence)* You hear me, Corporal? (O'MALLEY *threatens with his open hand*)

POWELL: Ohhh, Sir...

O'MALLEY: You're going to take the Captain's dick. You might bleed a little bit.

POWELL: Nossir, nossir...

O'MALLEY: You're going to bleed a little bit, because you're nice and tight. The Captain can tell when he sticks his tongue up there that you're nice and tight. The Captain's gonna get your cherry. The Captain's gonna pop your cherry, Corporal. You hear that, Corporal Powell? You hear me?

POWELL: Yessir.

O'MALLEY: The Captain's gonna get your cherry. You gonna give the Captain your cherry.

POWELL: Ahhh!

O'MALLEY: You gonna give the Captain your cherry?

POWELL: Yessir.

O'MALLEY: You gonna give the Captain your fuckin' cherry?

POWELL: Yessir.

    Close shot: POWELL's *face hit by* O'MALLEY's *palm*

O'MALLEY: If you want to stay in the Marine Corps, right? You wanna stay in the fuckin' Marine Corps? Then you're gonna give me your fuckin' cherry, Corporal. Get me some grease. Get me something that I can stick it in there with. C'mon, move it, man. Move it.

POWELL: Yessir.

O'MALLEY: Ummm. Grease the Captain's cock up, c'mon. Grease the Captain's cock up. Corporal. Grease it up.

POWELL: Covering the Captain's big dick with oil.

O'MALLEY: It feels good on the Captain's donkey dick. Grease that big fucker up!

POWELL: Yessir.

O'MALLEY: That big fucker wants in your butthole.

POWELL: Please don't, sir.

O'MALLEY: It wants to pump your butthole.

POWELL: Please, Sir.

O'MALLEY: The Captain's gonna fuck your butt.

POWELL: Oh, Jesus.

O'MALLEY: The Captain's gonna make you feel so good.

POWELL: Yessir.

O'MALLEY: You're gonna want this cock all the time.

POWELL: Nossir.

O'MALLEY: The Captain's gonna fuck you regularly.

POWELL: For the Corps, Sir.

O'MALLEY: Gonna fuck you regularly.

POWELL: For the Honor Guard, Sir.

O'MALLEY: Now, I want that ass turned over. I want you on your stomach.

POWELL: Yessir.

O'MALLEY: Now, let's put your butt up on a pillow. A nice pillow. So you can get ready for the Captain.

POWELL: Ahhh.

O'MALLEY: The Captain's gonna get big and hard...big and hard. He's gonna get you all greased up in your butthole. Awright? He's gonna put some grease up in your butthole. Right down smack in that crack. That beautiful juicy, juicy tight crack.

POWELL: Shit!

O'MALLEY: That Marine crack. Awright.

POWELL: *(Hesitantly)* Yessir!

O'MALLEY: Okay.

POWELL: Yessir.

O'MALLEY: And you're not going to cry, are you? Marines don't cry.

POWELL: Nossir.

CAPTAIN O'MALLEY slaps
CORPORAL POWELL's ass several times

O'MALLEY: Awright?

POWELL: Yessir.

O'MALLEY: The Captain's gonna fuck you in the butt.

POWELL: Yessir.

O'MALLEY: Okay, now let's get into it. Captain's gonna go sorta slow to start with. Right? The Captain's gonna go sorta slow to start with. Okay...

POWELL: *(Moans softly)*

O'MALLEY: Now, let's just put the fuckin' head in, awright...

POWELL: *(Loud moans)*

O'MALLEY: Stick the fuckin' head in...you feel that head going in? You feel that fuckin' head going in?

POWELL: *(Moans)*

O'MALLEY: Bite your hand. Now bite your hand. The Captain tells you to bite your hand. Bite your hand. *(More slaps and moans)* C'mon, Corporal Powell, you can take it. You're a man. You're a big man, a fuckin' Marine. You can take a big cock. You can take a cock. C'mon, you can take a cock up your butthole. Open that butthole up for the Captain. C'mon, Corporal Powell. Captain O'Malley wants to fuck you.

POWELL: *(Groans, moans, agony, grit, and guts)*

O'MALLEY: That's right. Keep shitting. We'll just push it back up in there. We'll push that ass back up in there. We'll open you up wide. Fuck you deep. Hard. Because you're the Corporal.

POWELL: Yessir.

O'MALLEY: The Corporal in charge of taking care of Captain O'Malley.

Two-shot holds, featuring faces of CAPTAIN O'MALLEY *and* CORPORAL POWELL *as the* CAPTAIN *continues to fuck the* CORPORAL *to mutual orgasm. To show time passing, Dissolve both faces slowly down under a montage of* MARINES *on maneuvers, in close-order drill, in combat practice with pugil sticks, in motivational discipline, in heavy USMC brig confinement, sweating in the shimmering heat of the obstacle course scaling ropes, crawling through mud at a* DI's *feet, showering, shaving, spit-shining boots, cleaning rifles, at mail-call, at mess. Montage dissolves into close-up face of* CORPORAL POWELL *alone, jerking off in the half-lighted wardroom. Night. Hall lights come on over transom. A rectangle of light falls across* POWELL's *face, torso, and dick.*

POWELL: *(Alone)* Oh, God! Lights just went off. Must be about nine o'clock. Time the Captain usually gets here. I've had a real rough time today. Jesus. I'm gonna let him just ram me, man, I'm gonna open up...oh, God, three months of it so far...Jesus, I wish it'd been about six by now...what've I ever...God, I wish I knew about this before, man, feels good, massaging my guts, the way he pushes and shoves, just lets himself go and just wrecks me, man. Today I'm not even gonna fight back. I'm not even gonna hold my muscles tense or anything to keep him from pushing my insides out. I'm gonna just let him have his way, and just push and shove...God, I'm gettin' so fuckin' hard thinking of the Captain coming, Captain...*(Loud knocks at door)* Wow, shit, and I'm not even stripped. Who is it? *(More knocks)*

O'MALLEY: Captain O'Malley. *(Door opens)*

POWELL: Yessir.

O'MALLEY: You okay tonight, fucker?

POWELL: Fine, Sir.

O'MALLEY: You ready for the Captain's donkey dick?

POWELL: Yessir.

O'MALLEY: How come you're not stripped? Three fuckin' months I been fuckin' you.

POWELL: Yessir.

O'MALLEY: And every time I've been here, you've been ready for me. You're not ready for me. Why aren't you ready for me?

POWELL: I'm sorry, Sir.

O'MALLEY: You're not ready for me. Why aren't you ready for me?

POWELL: I was getting my head ready, Sir.

O'MALLEY: Your *head?* Captain O'Malley wants your *ass* ready when he wants to fuck you. You understand?

POWELL: Yessir.

O'MALLEY: You're up for promotion. Do you understand?

POWELL: Yessir. I know, Sir.

O'MALLEY: You're up for promotion, fuckin' promotion. You keep this shit up, you're gonna get in trouble. You understand me, Corporal Powell?

POWELL: Yessir, I appreciate what you've done, Sir. I appreciate it a lot for what you've done, Sir.

O'MALLEY: You better fuckin' appreciate what I've done. I been fuckin' you good for three months.

POWELL: Yessir.

O'MALLEY: You need to get fucked by Captain O'Malley, don't you? You like this big Marine dick.

POWELL: Yessir.

O'MALLEY: You like this big Captain's raw dick.

POWELL: Oh, Jesus, Sir.

O'MALLEY: Where's Captain O'Malley gonna put this dick tonight?

POWELL: Up my cornhole, Sir.

O'MALLEY: I'm gonna fuck your cornhole?

POWELL: Yessir.

O'MALLEY: Awright, turn your ass over. Let Captain O'Malley see your fuckin' cornhole. Let me see that fuckin' cornhole. I want you to grease the Captain up.

POWELL: Yessir.

O'MALLEY: Grease the Captain up. Grease the Captain's big fuckin' dick. Big fuckin' Marine cock. That twelve-inch fuckin' Marine cock. The one you want so bad. You want that fuckin' Marine cock, don't you?

POWELL: *(Low with passion)* Yessir.

O'MALLEY: *Speak to me when I talk to you!*

POWELL: *Yessir!*

O'MALLEY: Yessir *what?*

POWELL: I want your...I want your donkey dick, Sir.

O'MALLEY: Where do you want my donkey dick, Corporal Powell?

POWELL: Up my asshole, Sir. Up my asshole, Sir.

O'MALLEY: Way up in your asshole?

POWELL: Yessir.

O'MALLEY: I'm gonna pound your fuckin' butthole.

POWELL: Yessir.

O'MALLEY: Put that big twelve-inch Marine cock up there.

POWELL: *Yessir!*

O'MALLEY: *Awright.*

POWELL: Oh, God.

O'MALLEY: And I want that fuckin' ass up on that pillow.

POWELL: Yessir.

O'MALLEY: Put that fuckin' ass up on that pillow. Let me see it. Spread those fuckin' Marine cheeks.

POWELL: *Yessir.*

O'MALLEY: Captain O'Malley wants to get up in there.

POWELL: Yessir.

O'MALLEY: Captain O'Malley had a rough day. He wants to fuck you good.

POWELL: Awww.

O'MALLEY: He wants to fuck you good today. You hear me,

Corporal Powell?

POWELL: *Yessir.*

O'MALLEY: I'm spittin'. I'm spittin'. Captain O'Malley is spit-shinin' his fuckin' big, fuckin' big Marine cock, spit-shinin' his fuckin' big donkey dick, spit-shinin' his big dick for Corporal Powell's hot sweet ass.

POWELL: *Goddamn.*

O'MALLEY: Take that big fuckin' cock every time...

POWELL: Every time. It's like the first...Jesus...

O'MALLEY: We're gonna stick that big fuckin' cock up your butthole...

POWELL: Oh God, Oh God, Oh God...

O'MALLEY: Oh *God! Let me hear that.* Talk to Captain O'Malley. You talk to Captain O'Malley

POWELL: Jesus, Oh God. *(Moans)*

O'MALLEY: I'm shoving that fuckin' dick in you. Fuckin' you upside down. I'm gonna open you up tonight. Open that fuckin' butthole up. You feel that big fuckin' cock up there? That twelve-inch cock...

POWELL: Yessir, yessir, *(Moans) God, God...Sir!*

O'MALLEY: Captain O'Malley's in you now, Corporal.

POWELL: Ohhh, it feels good, Sir.

O'MALLEY: Captain O'Malley's in you now, Corporal.

POWELL: Awww, Jesus...

O'MALLEY: Feel that big fuckin' prick up in you?

POWELL: Yessir.

O'MALLEY: I'm fuckin' your fuckin' butt, Corporal. I'm deep-fuckin' you, Corporal Powell.

POWELL: I've gotten to love it, Sir.

O'MALLEY: You better love it. You're gonna love it.

POWELL: It still hurts. Oh Jesus. It still hurts after...*(Moans)*

O'MALLEY: Right. Captain O'Malley knows how to handle your fuckin' butt.

POWELL: Ahhhooohhh.

O'MALLEY: Captain O'Malley knows how to handle you, Corporal Powell.

POWELL: *(Moans)*

O'MALLEY: The Captain's gonna keep fuckin' the Corporal's

butt. Captain is fuckin' the Corporal's butt.

POWELL: Oh, yeah.

O'MALLEY: Ummm, the Corporal's butt.

POWELL: Ohhh, shove it, Sir, shove it!

O'MALLEY: Captain's shoving it now, shoving it up in your butt.

POWELL: Shove it. Shove it, Captain O'Malley. Shove it. God-damn. This is your cornhole. Ah, Sir!

O'MALLEY: Tell me fucker. Tell me who you are.

POWELL: I'm the Corporal, Sir. I'm the Corporal in charge of taking care of Captain O'Malley. Hahhh!

O'MALLEY: Captain's got him a little Corporal.

POWELL: Yessir.

O'MALLEY: Corporal ain't so little, though.

POWELL: *(Loud moans)*

O'MALLEY: Corporal ain't so tight no more, is he?

POWELL: *Aaooowww. Nossir!*

O'MALLEY: The Corporal's been opened up by the Captain.

POWELL: The other men *(Moans)* kid me, Sir. They call me... call me, the Captain's *hole.*

O'MALLEY: You are the Captain's hole!

POWELL: *Yessir.*

O'MALLEY: The Captain's wide open hole, now.

POWELL: Oh, Jesus!

O'MALLEY: You're the Captain's wide open hole. C'mon, keep those legs up. C'mon, let me see that cock sticking up from you.

CAPTAIN O'MALLEY gives
CORPORAL POWELL *a heavy butt slapping*

POWELL: Yessir.

O'MALLEY: Higher. Higher.

POWELL: Is it as good as Corporal Schmidt? Is it as good as Corporal Schmidt?

O'MALLEY: Fuckin' better than Corporal Schmidt.

POWELL: Deeper.

O'MALLEY: You give me all, Corporal. You give the Captain all he wants. You take care of the Captain...

POWELL: *(Moans)* Oh Goddd. Oh, more!

O'MALLEY: ...good care of the Captain's dick. You take fuckin' good care of the Captain's dick.

POWELL: Oh, yeahhh.

O'MALLEY: Captain likes fuckin' your cornhole. Captain wants to play with those tits.

POWELL: Goddd.

O'MALLEY: Let the Captain play with those fuckin' tits.

POWELL: Oh, Jesus!

O'MALLEY: I'm gonna bite those fuckin' tits. Let me bite those fuckin' tits. C'mon.

POWELL: Oh, God. *(Moans)* Too much! You taught me too fuckin' much, Captain. You taught me what those fuckin' nipples are for. I love it. Oh God. Jesus. Now when I work out, Sir, I think of pumping my pecs up for you.

O'MALLEY: You keep building those fuckin' pecs up for the Captain. You keep building those fuckin' pecs up for the Captain. The Captain likes those fuckin' big pecs.

POWELL: *(Low)* Thank you, Sir. *(Louder)* Thank you, Sir!

O'MALLEY: The Captain likes your fuckin' big pecs. I like to chew on those big hard nipples.

POWELL: Jesus.

O'MALLEY: And fuck your big fuckin'...

POWELL: Oh, Sir...

O'MALLEY: And shove his big, big donkey dick up in your fuckin' cornhole and ram your...

POWELL: I swear you're getting bigger, Sir.

O'MALLEY: And ram you, and ram you, Corporal. Ram the Corporal. Fuckin' ram the fuckin' Corporal with his big cock...

POWELL: Oh shove it. In!

O'MALLEY: You feel that big cock, Corporal?

POWELL: Oh yeah! Take my asshole, Sir.

O'MALLEY: Ram the walls with that big cock...that big fuckin' cunt.

POWELL: Please, Sir, don't call it that, Sir...

O'MALLEY: Fuck you with that big fuckin' Marine cock...in that Marine cunt...

POWELL: *Nossir.* Please, Sir. Don't call it that, Sir. I'm a man, Sir.

O'MALLEY: You're a Marine fuckin' cunt...You're the Marine

fuckin' cunt that the Captain needs...

POWELL: Please, Sir. Not that, Sir...

O'MALLEY: The Captain's gonna fuck your cunt. The Captain's fuckin' you.

POWELL: *(Moans)* Please, Sir. Don't call it that, Sir.

O'MALLEY *slaps* POWELL's *ass*

O'MALLEY: I'll call it that. I'll knock the shit out of you.

POWELL: Oh, God.

O'MALLEY: You'll be what I want you to be. You hear me, Corporal Powell?

POWELL: Yessir.

O'MALLEY: You'll be what the Captain wants you to be.

POWELL: Yessir.

O'MALLEY: Fuckin' Marine cunt. The Captain's sticking his big, big fat dong up your Marine cunt.

POWELL: Oh Jesus. Oh Jesus.

O'MALLEY: Nice and slippery and juicy. Captain's pluggin' a nice big juicy butt.

POWELL: Oh God, yessir.

O'MALLEY: I'm just gonna pump that butt.

POWELL: Oh God.

O'MALLEY: Give me that fuckin' hole.

O'MALLEY *rough fucks* POWELL
whose face registers an ecstasy of agony

POWELL: Feels good, Sir. Oh, God.

O'MALLEY: The Captain's gettin' hot. Captain's gettin' fuckin' hot. He's got your big ass-lips wrapped around his cock.

POWELL: Ohhhaww.

O'MALLEY: Got your big butt lips wrapped around his fuckin' big twelve-inch prick. The Captain's gettin' hot. The Captain's gettin' fuckin' hot.

POWELL: Sir!

O'MALLEY: Pounding your fuckin'. *Fuck.* Captain's *fuckin'.*
Close-up. Camera moves in for the kill, holding right on POW-
ELL *writhing under* O'MALLEY *until both Marines reach*
orgasm

POWELL: Jesus.

O'MALLEY: Oh God.

Two-shot: CORPORAL POWELL *lays back*
into the big embrace of CAPTAIN O'MALLEY

O'MALLEY: The Captain put a load in you, Corporal. The Captain put fuckin' load of cum up you. Ummm. A fuckin' load of cum up your butthole.

POWELL: *(Low)* Ohhh, I've gotten used to that cock in the last three months, man.

O'MALLEY: Ummm. Speak up. I can't hear you.

POWELL: Sir, I was just talking to myself, Sir.

O'MALLEY: What did you say, Corporal?

POWELL: Sir, I was just saying, how nice and used to that cock I was gettin', Sir.

O'Malley slaps POWELL's *ass teasingly*

O'MALLEY: You like the Captain's cock?

POWELL: Yessir. I look forward to it at the end of the day, Sir.

O'MALLEY: You're gonna keep looking forward to it, because the Captain's gonna keep fuckin' you, Corporal. You hear me, Corporal Powell?

POWELL: Yessir.

O'MALLEY: Captain O'Malley likes your butthole. And he's gonna keep fuckin' it as long as he wants to. 'Cause you're stuck at this base until I want to get rid of you.

POWELL: Yessir. It's worth all of the...all of the kidding I go through.

O'MALLEY: They can kid you all they want. They don't know nothin'. They don't know nothin'. I'm a Captain.

POWELL: Jesus.

O'MALLEY: I think it's time the Captain fucked you again. I think I'm gonna go twice tonight.

POWELL: Sir.

O'MALLEY: What?

POWELL: Nothin, Sir.

O'MALLEY: The Captain is gonna fuck you twice.

POWELL: Ohhh.

O'MALLEY: The Captain's gonna fuck your butt twice. It's good and tight...

POWELL: Ahhh.

O'MALLEY: You got the Captain turned on, Corporal. You got

the Captain...Stick those legs up in the air.

POWELL: Oh, God.

O'MALLEY: C'mon, get those legs up there....Stick that ass up in the air. C'mon Corporal, give me what I need.

POWELL: Oh, Sir.

O'MALLEY: Give me what I need, and I'll give you what you need.

POWELL: Whennnnnn. Yessir.

O'MALLEY: What do you need, Corporal? What do you need Corporal?

POWELL: I need, I need...

O'MALLEY: *(Slap)* Speak to me when I talk to you.

POWELL: Yessir. I need your cock up in me, Sir.

O'MALLEY: You're gettin' it twice tonight.

POWELL: Oh, God.

O'MALLEY: You're gettin' it twice tonight, Corporal.

POWELL: Oh, God, I'm hurtin' now....Jesus...only once, once a night, sir...

O'MALLEY: Captain O'Malley wants you to stand up. Stand up. C'mon, get up, Corporal. Corporal, c'mon. Let's move it.

POWELL: Yessir.

O'MALLEY: Stick that big, beautiful Marine butt up in the air, 'cause the Captain's gonna ram you.

POWELL: Ahhh.

O'MALLEY: The Captain's gonna ram you from above. Feel that big dick slippin' in you?

POWELL: (Pained) Yessir.

O'MALLEY: All the way in, all the way in your big butt. Owww. Captain likes that.

POWELL: God.

O'MALLEY: He likes that big, beautiful Marine ass sticking up in the air, saying, "Fuck me in the butt."

POWELL: Yessir.

O'MALLEY: "Fuck me in the butt."

POWELL: Yes, Captain. That's what it's saying.

O'MALLEY: Yeah, that's what the Corporal is saying, isn't it?

POWELL: Yessir. That's it, Sir. *Fuck me in the butt!*

O'MALLEY: The Captain knows. *(Slaps on the ass)* He loves that beautiful bottom. Look at those beautiful fuckin' Marine buns.

POWELL: Oh, Jesus. Fuck. Fuck.

O'MALLEY: The Captain's cornholing you, buddy. He's sticking that big fuckin' cock up in your butthole. Ummm, Captain likes fuckin' you, Corporal.

POWELL: Ahhh, thank you, Sir.

O'MALLEY: Umm, Captain likes fuckin' you. That's why he's fuckin' you twice tonight.

POWELL: Captain, I'm privileged, Sir.

O'MALLEY: You are privileged and don't you forget it.

POWELL: Yessir.

O'MALLEY: You've got a twelve-inch dick up your ass. A twelve-inch big, juicy, slippery cock. Ohhh, yeah, ridin' that Marine ass.

POWELL: Oh, yessir, yessir.

O'MALLEY: Just pumpin' it, just pumpin' it. Gettin' it big and hard big and rock hard. 'Cause it's gonna shoot another big load up in your butthole.

POWELL: Ohh, Sir, *Sir!*

O'MALLEY: Tell the Captain what you want, Corporal. Tell the Captain what you need, Corporal.

POWELL: Would you shoot on my face, Sir?

O'MALLEY: Shoot on your face?

POWELL: Yes, Sir!

O'MALLEY: You can handle the Captain's cum?

POWELL: Yessir.

O'MALLEY: Think you can handle all that hot cum from out of his big twelve-inch cock?

POWELL: Ahh, yessir. I think so, Sir.

O'MALLEY: What are you going to do with it when it comes out?

POWELL: Try and get as much in my mouth as I can. Ahhh, yeah.

O'MALLEY: We'll let the Corporal...we'll let the Corporal take it for awhile in the butt.

POWELL: Owwwahhh.

O'MALLEY: We'll let the Corporal take it wrapped around the Captain's cock. It looks so pretty going in the Corporal's ass.

That big twelve-inch prick.

POWELL: Owwwahhh.

O'MALLEY: Pounding up against you, Corporal. That's the way you want that fuckin' dick, isn't it?

POWELL: *Yessir!*

O'MALLEY: Captain's fuckin' his Corporal.

POWELL: The Captain's fuckin' his Corporal.

O'MALLEY: A Marine Captain's cock. That's what I am.

POWELL: Ahhowwwahhh.

O'MALLEY: And you're nothin but a fuckin' Corporal. You're nothin' but a fuckin' Corporal. The Captain's fuckin' his Corporal. The Captain is fuckin' his Corporal. The Captain is fuckin' his Corporal, isn't he? He is fuckin' his Corporal. He is ridin' that big ass...

POWELL: Ahhh, yessir, ohhh, yessir.

O'MALLEY. He's ridin' that big Marine ass. Yeah, *(Slaps)* ridin' that big Marine ass.

POWELL: Awww, God.

> *Medium shot of heavy fuckin' as* CAPTAIN O'MALLEY
> *plugs* CORPORAL POWELL

O'MALLEY: Ahhh, yeah. *Yeah.* Captain's fuckin' his Corporal. His Corporal wants to get fucked.

POWELL: Oh, please, Sir.

O'MALLEY: Corporal's crazy about the Captain. Can't forget the Captain's Marine cock.

POWELL: Ahhhowww, ahh, Sir.

O'MALLEY: And don't you forget it. *(Fucking)* Okay, turn over.

POWELL: God.

O'MALLEY: Turn over.

POWELL: I'm fuckin' used man. *(Low)* Ahhh.

O'MALLEY: The Captain is going to continue to use you.

POWELL: Yessir.

O'MALLEY: Because the Corporal likes being used.

POWELL: Yessir.

O'MALLEY: The Corporal likes being used by the Captain.

POWELL: Yessir. The Corporal needs to be used by the Captain.

O'MALLEY: 'Cause the Captain has what the Corporal wants. He has a twelve-inch big fat donkey-dick Marine cock.

POWELL: Ahhh, Sir...

O'MALLEY: The only one that can satisfy the Corporal. Isn't it?

POWELL: Yessir. Ahh, God.

O'MALLEY: Watch the Captain stroking that big cock. I want you to watch while I'm beating that big twelve-inch cock. 'Cause the Captain's going to beat it off right in your face. Right in the Corporal's face. He's gonna shoot the biggest load right in the Corporal's fuckin' face.

POWELL: Ahhh, yessir.

O'MALLEY: Lick the Captain's balls, Corporal.

POWELL: Yessir!

O'MALLEY: You lick the Captain's balls. Just suck those big Marine balls. Suck those fuckin' Marine balls. (Close *shot of* O'MALLEY's *big nuts lowering into* POWELL's *straining mouth*) Yeah. Yeah. Captain likes that. Captain likes it when you suck those balls. Captain's got himself a Corporal, Captain's got himself a Corporal to take care of him. His Corporal's taking damn good care of his cock. Captain likes it. Captain likes it when the Corporal licks his balls, big hairy balls. The Captain's got big balls.

CAPTAIN O'Malley slaps
CORPORAL POWELL's face several times

POWELL: Ahhh.

O'MALLEY: How hairy are they?

POWELL: Very hairy, Sir. Very hairy, Sir. Oh, God.

O'MALLEY: Captain's got a hairy dick too. Hairy dick, and hairy body. Corporal hasn't got any hair, does he?

POWELL: Nossir.

O'MALLEY: You like hairy bodies. You like the Captain's hairy body?

POWELL: Yessir! Please, please, Sir...

O'MALLEY: *Please, Sir,* what?

POWELL: Please, Sir. Cum all over me, Sir.

O'MALLEY: Cum all over you?

POWELL: Yessir! please, Sir.

O'MALLEY: Captain's gonna shoot a big load on your face.

POWELL: *Yessir!*

O'MALLEY: Big load all over your fuckin' face, Corporal.

POWELL: All over me.

O'MALLEY: I'm gonna rub it in your face.

POWELL: *Yessir!*

O'MALLEY: I'm gonna rub the Captain's cum all over your face.

POWELL: Ahhh, Jeez...Sir.

O'MALLEY: All over your face. Your fuckin' face.

POWELL: Jeez, Sir, Jeez, Sir.

O'MALLEY: Uhhh. Here it comes!

POWELL: Oh my God. Sir. God. Sir. My God.

O'MALLEY: Captain's cock is so fuckin' big, it's hard to stroke it. It's hard to stroke the Captain's big cock.

POWELL: Ahhh, please. Sir....Please, Sir....Please, Sir...

O'MALLEY: Ummmmm. The Captain wants to shoot his big load all over you, Corporal.

POWELL: Give me a little in both holes, Sir.

O'MALLEY: Give you a little in both holes?

POWELL: Yessir.

O'MALLEY: Give you a little what, Corporal, in both holes?

POWELL: The Captain's cum, Sir.

O'MALLEY: Both holes?

POWELL: *Yessir!*

O'MALLEY: Deep inside both holes.

POWELL: Some in this hole, too, Sir?

O'MALLEY: The Captain will put it both places. The Captain will put that cum both places.

POWELL: Yessir, and it'll meet in the middle.

O'MALLEY: Both holes.

POWELL: Yessir. It'll mix inside, Sir.

O'MALLEY: The Captain's so fuckin hot.

POWELL: Please, Sir.

O'MALLEY: The Captain's gettin' fuckin' hot.

POWELL: Please, Sir.

O'MALLEY: Fuckin' hot.

POWELL: Yessir, God, fuckin' sweat's drippin' down on the Corporal.

O'MALLEY: Stick your tongue out so you can take the Captain's cum that's coming out of his big dick.

POWELL: Ahhhhgggghhhh! Yessir. Please, Sir.

O'MALLEY: You keep that fuckin' mouth open. You keep that fuckin' mouth open...

POWELL: Ahhhh.

O'MALLEY: Captain's gonna shoot a big load all over your fuckin' face...all over your fuckin' face. I'm gonna shoot a big load all over your fuckin' face, Corporal. It's gettin' close...Big fuckin' load from the Captain's cock...I'm gonna shoot all over your fuckin' face.

POWELL: Oh please, Sir. My God! Yessir. *(With feeling) Yessir!*

O'MALLEY: Your legs are quivering, Corporal.

POWELL: Ahhhggghhh...I want, Sir....Please, Sir. Hurry and cum, Sir. Please, I'm ready.

O'MALLEY: Awright! Shoot that load. Shoot your fuckin' load.

POWELL: Yessir!

O'MALLEY: C'mon Corporal, shoot your fuckin' load. Shoot your fuckin' load. Captain's close. Captain's close...Oh, look at that cum coming out!

POWELL: Ahhhhhrrrghhh, Yes, ahh, yessir.

O'MALLEY: Look at that fuckin' cum. Ah, Corporal, cum's coming out. *(High cries of orgasm)* Ohhhhaaaahhhgggh, there it comes. All over your fuckin' face, it's all over your fuckin' face, Corporal. It's in your fuckin' eyes.

POWELL: I can't see. It's in my eyes.

O'MALLEY: Ow, your fuckin' mouth, your fuckin' chest, ahhh!

POWELL: I can't see....It's burning my eyes...

O'MALLEY: The Captain shot a load. In your hair, Corporal.

POWELL: Yessir.

O'MALLEY: You got cum all in your hair.

POWELL: Yessir. Ahhh.

O'MALLEY: The Captain wants to wipe your eyes, Corporal. *(Post-orgasmic moans interspersed with dialogue)* The Captain wants to hold you, Corporal.

POWELL: Yessir.

O'MALLEY: The Captain wants you to hold him.

POWELL: Yessir. Ahhh. Captain. Ah, Captain. Just lay on top of me, Sir.

O'MALLEY: Big fuckin' Corporal to hold his Captain.

POWELL: Oh, yessir.

O'MALLEY: Ummm.

POWELL: Ahh, Goddamn, you're sweating, Sir. I can feel water all over you.

O'MALLEY: The Captain is drained. The Corporal drained his Captain.

POWELL: Jesus, Sir.

O'MALLEY: Totally drained. You drained all the cum out of me.

POWELL: Yessir. Oh God. Layin' on top of me, Sir. This is really fine. Oh God. I needed that, Sir. I had a rough day too, Sir.

O'MALLEY: You needed it?

POWELL: Yeah, I needed to be pounded. Yessir.

O'MALLEY: Corporal, you just got pounded. You just got pounded and showered on. You got one of the biggest fuckin' loads of cum you've ever had.

POWELL: Jesus.

O'MALLEY: Biggest fuckin load...

POWELL: *Yessir!*

O'MALLEY: I want you to lick it out, the rest of it out of the Captain's cock.

POWELL: Yessir.

O'MALLEY: Lick the rest of the cum out of the Captain's cock.

POWELL: Yessir.

O'MALLEY: Lick the rest of it out of the Captain's cock. Get down on it and lick it.

POWELL: Yessir. Does the Captain have to piss, *Sir?*

Close shot: CAPTAIN O'MALLEY's *face grinning.*

Medium shot: slow motion. CAPTAIN O'MALLEY's *semi-hard dick pisses heavy* and *golden down on* CORPORAL POWELL.

POWELL *drinks fast. Gulping.*

POWELL: OH, CAPTAIN! My Captain!

O'MALLEY *rubs his tight hairy belly.*

The piss splashes in *slow motion, catching the light.*

Both men are laughing.

**How the Corporal came
to be in charge
of taking care
of Captain O'Malley...**

USMC Slap Captain

Quantico. Interrogation Room. 3 AM. USMC Slapcaptain:
Fleet champion kickboxer, clad in fatigue pants, military-issue
teeshirt, heavy combat boots. Rubbing his hands, callused from
martial arts: numchuks, pugil sticks, boduka. High on his left
bicep, a tattoo: red cobra, fanged, coiled, ready to strike in color-
ful relief against his dark hairy skin. His head shaved short in a
white-sidewall military burr. His neck: thick, powerful, cruelly
muscled. Long athletic arms: strong, hairy, muscular, threaded
with veins. His shoulders: solid as a baseball slugger. His hard-
palmed hands: meaty, thick, brutal as a boxer's.

"Shoulders back!" He barks at the young Lance Corporal.
"Stomach in. Eyes straight ahead. Don't look at me, boy, unless
you're gonna ask me for a date. Get your back straight. Head
back." He slams his right fist into his open left palm. "Take your
eyes off me, mister. Maybe you're thinkin' you want to get in my
pants?"

"No, sir!"

A .22 pistol jammed in the waistband of his fatigues. Con-
vincing. His breath, moving close in: thick spit-spray, sweet from
his nightly Tampa Nugget cigar. "You want the back of my hand,
boy!"

"No, sir!"

"Then set your ass down, puke!"

The Lance Corporal sits on the heavy wooden chair bolted
to the concrete floor. Padded asylum restraints snap around his
ankles.

Handcuffs lock his wrists together behind his back. Behind the chair. His head swerves to resist the black-cloth blindfold.

The Slapcaptain's hard palm openhands him up against the side of his head. He feels the hot burning imprint of the slap across his face. Then the blindfold is knotted, secured. He can see slightly out from underneath: thick fingers make metal-toothed electrical clamps chow down on his nipples. He moans at the sharp pain. The Slapcaptain openhands him again. Slaps his face. Hard. Right. Then left. Then right again. Harder. His ears ring.

The Slapcaptain chains the clamps together. His finger crooks and catches the dangling chain at its center, raising the clamps horizontally, pulling them outward.

"You wanna kiss me, boy? Hey, boy, kiss me. Kiss me, boy." It's an order, but the Slapcaptain's voice is reassuring. The Lance Corporal tilts his cropped blond head up in the direction of the Slapcaptain's dark voice. He is not certain how he is supposed to kiss a man, even for the Corps; not certain how he can kiss a man he cannot see.

He leans his whole torso forward, pulled by his tits, raising his blindfolded face up to this man, offering his lips.

But it's not a kiss the Slapcaptain wants.

A fast slapshot.

The Lance Corporal's face rebounds ninety degrees to the right. Then is backhanded to the left. His cheecks burn. Redden. The intense ringing in his head clouds out the Slapcaptain's voice. His head turns tentatively, as ordered, back to the front.

Under his blindfold he sees the Slapcaptain's thick gorilla fingers unbutton the green fatigue fly. His rough palm lifts out an extra-large USMC jockstrap pouching his big hairy balls, overlaid with thick long uncut cock. The Slapcaptain gropes his sweat-stained jock-cup with his left hand. His thick-muscled right arm swings out from his massive shoulder. The Lance Corporal, nose and mouth upraised, sniffs the wet drip of the Slapcaptain's hairy pits.

A pause. Shorter than his breath. Then starts the cadenced tattoo of openhanded slaps: left, right, left, right. *Ten*. His head slaplashed, hard. *Twenty*. Back and forth. *Thirty*. His face: a boxer's fastbag. *Forty*. Saliva in his mouth turning to blood. *Fifty*. Through the ringing in his ears, words, alternating with the

stinging slaps, come through. *Sixty.* What is the Captain saying?
Seventy.

Again. Another volley of openhanded slugs. The big uncut
dick swinging free and mean and hard. The hot spit from the
Slapcaptain's moustached mouth wetting his cheeks, escalating
the stinging of the hard slaps.

He wants the Captain's dick. He wants the Captain's moustache, lips and mouth and tongue. He wants to swallow his heavy
spit. He leans forward. Again, the unseen hand slaps his face.
Hard. Left to right. Again, the ringing overrides the voice he can
hear but cannot distinguish.

"Slap Happy"   Centerfold, *Drummer* 148

His blindfolded head flushes warm up from his neck, to his
cheeks to his temples. He sucks and swallows the warm salt-blood
taste in his mouth. The slaps bruise his inner cheeks against his
gritted teeth.

He cocks his head. Hardened for the Corps. Angles his face
toward the heat and dripping sweat off the Slapcaptain's wet
fatigues. Anticipating. Unquestioning. Waiting. Wanting. He
sees the thick dick and balls swinging out of the piss-wet jock.
The balls hang low. The dick, uncut, blind, hard, rampant, shows
its rosy pisshole.

He leans forward.

The Slapcaptain's piss sprays in a direct shot into his mouth. He gulps, swallows, thirsty for the hot, bubbling, thick, Marine piss that streams faster than he can drink.

Piss: spilling down on his chest, running down his belly, soaking his dick and balls, dripping down the inside of his naked thighs, pooling up under the wet pucker of his asshole bound into the worn seat of the wooden chair.

Again, he leans forward.

The Slapcaptain's tough hands box his face back and forth. His teeth clench. His eyes squeeze closed under his blindfold. His mouth tastes metallic. He smells the crusty cheese of the Marine dick swinging free near his bleeding nose. Both nostrils trickle blood down his upper lip. The hard slaps whip the trickles to blood-spray. He holds his head steady against the rhythms of the Slapcaptain's hand. The slaps slow. The palms grow sticky with the Corporal's blood. Somehow the slaps increase his hunger for the Slapcaptain's dirty cock.

The Slapcaptain plants his hand on the back of his neck. "I want me a bloodfuck USMC pussymouth!" He holds the burr-cut head in his hard-knuckled grip. "Now come on, boy!" The Slap-captain pressures the back of the Lance Corporal's neck, pivoting the shaved head, with the bloody blindfolded face, in his hand, positioning the mouth like a bullseye for his crusty cock.

"I figure I got me one of two things. I either got me an ambi-tious young Lance Corporal. Or I got me a .22 pistol to give a tightlipped gyrene a new asshole."

Still cupping and guiding the Lance Corporal's head, pressing it down with all the power in his warrior-hand, the Slapcaptain nuzzles the bloody nose and swollen lips against his big-veined cock. "Clean it up, boy."

The Lance Corporal sticks his tongue through his bruised lips, and works his tongue-tip in, under, and around the inner lip of the thick foreskin, sucking out the clots of cheese, old cum, sweat, piss, and gun-grease. Not needing an order, he pulls back from the hard cock, with the cheesy smegma melting on his tongue, and swallows.

"That's my boy. That's my good boy." But the level, low

voice is cut off by another slap that starts the ear echo ringing. Behind the blindfold, the lights in his head are dazzling. He is being beaten, slapped silly. He is obedient. The Corps is all. In a moment, less than an instant really, he turns his head round again, straightforward, offering his face.

He is ready. Even for the heavy-handed wallop of this palm-and-backhand slap, stinging his cheeks, purpling his temples, blackening his eyes. The Slapcaptain's hands reshaping his boy's face into the tough, hardened, experienced face of a Marine.

The Slapcaptain giving him a Marine's face.

He feels his nose ready to give way, to break, but the Slapcaptain pulls back; pulls his slap-punches; takes instead his big hand, gripping his hard dick like a brutal nightstick. He beats the bruised, tenderized face with his huge dick, wet with blood and cheese and piss.

The handcuffs cut into his wrists. Sweat and blood pour from his face, down his chest, over his clamped and torn tits. The Lance Corporal's mind goes blank behind his battered face: Halls of...Slap!...zuma...Shores...Slap!...Punch...Shores of Trip... Slap...Punch...Punch! The rhythms of the Slapcaptain's fist and dick beating his face. The ringing in his ears. His chin held tight by the Slapcaptain's hand.

"Kiss it. Kiss it real soft, baby."

He opens his mouth. He's learned what *kiss* means.

"Kiss it." The commanding voice becomes almost soft. "Kiss it...sweetly."

As his bruised lips touch the swollen cockhead, its shaft, backed by the Slapcaptain's fullback butt and thighs, rams the rod through his lips, past his bloody teeth, across his tongue, and fucks long and hard deep down his gagging throat, until choking on the spit and blood and pumping cum, he feels the huge cock pulled like a deep root from his throat, still shooting white clots of cum on his face, feeling the large boxer's hands rough-massage the slick seed into his bruises, slapping him lightly, always slapping him, across the cheeks with his angry red cock, pulling on the chains tearing at his tits, feeling the thick bristle of the Captain's moustache and the Captain's hard lips and the Captain's mouth pressing hard in lust and discipline, against his own lips, feeling the pressure of the Captain's tongue sucking the bloody saliva from his beaten mouth, feeling the Captain's fingers squeezing his cheeks, feeling the mix of the Captain's spit, and his own blood, cum-honkered forcibly back down his throat, swallowing, writhing, tit-ripped, restrained, bound.

His man's face, his Marine face, blindfold ripped away, seeing the spit-wet uniform of the sweaty, dark, handsome Slapcaptain, pulling his tits, making his sweat run, his moans deep.

He looks up at the smiling cruel face, the disciplined face taking him deep now into the Corps, initiated now into the inner rank of the Corps. His hard-muscled body, understanding, thrashes up, bound to the ungiving wooden chair, into a painful arch of ecstatic handless cuming.

"That's my boy." The Slapcaptain's hands hold him very tight. The handsome mouth, moustache, and lips, pressing sweet, hard agony against his own. "That's my man."

Humping straight daddies...

Nooner Sex

Downtown. Noon hour. Bookstore. Backroom. Video booths. In walks the Basic Suburban Daddy: good-looking, early thirties, six-one, robust, husky, not fat from his wife's cooking, looking—in his dark blue, suburban-mall, Macy's business suit—like he probably played a little ball in college. His left hand—good thick fingers sporting a wedding ring—strokes his thick moustache. He's been married long enough for the gold band to be a quarter-size too tight. He walks like a young ex-linebacker: heft to hang on to.

He's the size Daddies are supposed to be.

He has the Look Daddies are supposed to have.

NOONER HUNTER

He's a handsome young father whose wife—his noon- hour hunt says—no longer burns so bright as his new desires for mansex. But he's a good man: a grown-up, responsible Daddy who's no doubt a good husband and father. He has an all-American authority of integrity in his young paternal face. He has, suggestively, the together face of a cop in a business suit: the kind of ambiguous Look so straight you figure he's either plainclothes vice or he's new and experimenting. You read his moves, his innocent, almost nervous cruise, the way he dodges, with expert natural instinct, from a hungry queen and a hungrier troll, and you figure him for the kind of midmanagement corporate achiever whose success affords him the comfortable split-level life.

When you fuck with him, it's not like balling with gay guys (no matter how masculine) who live gay lifestyles. This straight Daddy wouldn't know *lifestyle* from *shit*. *A* man like this Daddy just has his *life*. None of this means that Genuine Straight is any better than Genuine Homosexual, just that to gay men used to gay men's sex styles, Straight Daddies are refreshingly different. And even though some of his suburban life may be less than his young-groom ideas planned it to be before inflation, for him the wife and kids and orthodontia are far from some clichéd claustrophobic nightmare illustrated by some weird Sears catalog. When you fuck with him you put your arms around the firm, hard bulk of all that was ever Daddygood and Daddyhot in the Basic American Dream.

BUSINESS-SUIT DADDYFUCK

You follow him into a video booth. Just enough light to enjoy his handsome, groomed face and his Very-Married Look. He's horny. A bit nervous. His suit feels good against your suit. His body solid through the layers of suit jacket and vest and dress shirt and teeshirt. He wraps his husky arms around you, like he's finally doing the right thing for the right reasons, and pulls you to him. Tie to tie. Double manhug with this daddy. Fucking Papa Bear hug.

His dick feels hard against yours through his suit pants and jockey shorts. He lowers his face to yours. Brushes your face with his thick moustache. He almost kisses as his moustache meshes into yours. His movements are light, are very heterosexual stand-up fuck moves, so used is he to other-gender bodies.

You feel that delicate difference when a man used to stud-fucking women changes over to men.

It takes him a while before his head learns that the man-to-man body-moves are different, franker, heavier, more direct, more reciprocal, more mirrored.

FEELING DADDY UP (& VICE VERSA)

He's exciting because he's different. A straightfucker. You play to his nervous excitement. Stand-up fuck-dancing. Swaying to the ancient music of men. You let him lead so not to frighten his confidence. His dick is hard against yours. He's strong. A big hugger. Chest to chest. Slow-pumping his hips backed with athletic butt. Big muscular thighs alternating with your thighs. Squeezing down on your legs. His hand reaches down to feel you up with an innocence no man has felt you with since you first started coming out. You feel him back through his suit and shorts. His dick through his clothes is mysterious, hard, and his balls are tight.

Neither of you even tries to pull the other one's equipment out.

Chris Duffy, Mr. America   Video: *Sunset Bull*

The excitement, the difference to be investigated here with this Straight Daddy is how hot he is while he's so scared. He has to do what he's doing. He has to feel and hug and bury his warm face in your neck. You, maybe, have some crazy karmic duty to gently aid him. So you hold him, hard and horny, because he is a Straight Daddy doing all the stuff Straight Daddies have to do in these hard American times with no real understanding from their wives and kids and friends.

And deep down you're glad you're the kind of man you are

who can hold on to a man like this and let him feel some comfort and fun and solace physically tendered to him the way he needs male support: physical stroking, loving from the only other kind of person who really understands that Daddies need Daddies too.

So dick to dick, holding on to each other in the comforting half-light, you can't help but cuming in your own pants when you feel him with a deep quiet moan clinch into you, hip-pumping your dicks together, creaming his shorts, getting his thick load off, fully clothed, dicks totally untouched, but full-felt body contact through all the wool of his suit and the cotton of his jockeys.

BACKROOMS: NECESSITY FOR MEN
ON THE CUSP OF MANSEX

It's a rare kind of mansex found usually only during those noon hours when a Straight Daddy has some short time no wife or family or boss can ask him to account for in places like bookstores ambiguous enough to seem macho-straight with their bookracks and video booths filled with T&A, the while, he's hoping, sometimes against hope, to find masculine men who can handle helping out a man initiating himself into the hot beauties of mansex. So you go out into the noonday sun, with the scent of him on your face, and you smile, even though your own shorts are wet and sticky, and you figure there's maybe really only one sin in life: when one of the Straight Young Daddies of America invites you into his intimacy, and you do not come.

Hot Dago Cop!
What a man wants is
what makes him shoot...

Officer Mike:
San Francisco's Finest

Officer Mike Leonardi graduated from the San Francisco Police
Academy righteously proud of himself. He had earned his badge.
He had earned his uniform. He had earned prestigious "motor"
patrol: the black leather kneehigh boots, the blue wool riding
breeches, the heavy leather jacket over the blue shirt that felt rough
and good against the white cotton of the teeshirt he wore over
his hairy chest and shoulders. He liked the weight of the mesh
body armor with its Velcro straps that he pulled tight around his
muscular torso. The added bulk suited his broad shoulders. With
his helmet framing his moustached face, he was a Blue Knight
cruising his motorcycle along the Market Street mainstem.

Mike was born to policework. His dad had been a cop in
Omaha. When his old man was away from the house, Mike had
moved in on his dad's closet. He pulled on the uniform, cinching
the belts in tight to hold the XL-size close against his teenage
body. One day his dad caught him, busted him, threw him up
against the bedroom wall, spread him, frisked him, then cuffed
his hands behind his back. "You're under arrest, son," his dad said.
Mike hoped he'd not notice his hardon in the uniform straight-
legs. But his fathered dutch-rubbed his knuckles across Mike's
crewcut, lightly cuffed his strong chin, and told his son, "You're
okay, Mike. Your old man's proud of you." After that, his dad put
him in Police Athletic League activities. In PAL he learned how
to care for and fire a service revolver.

Now the uniform was his. By birth he was seed and son of a

cop. By right he had earned it. He had double reason to be hardon into it: his big feet and calves wrapped in the high boots; his legs and butt tight in the heavy wool breeches; his hard-muscled chest, shoulders, and arms cinched into the new leather jacket. He enjoyed those first months as the stiff new leather jacket broke in and took the shape of his body. He liked the feel of his tight black gloves when his hands took control of his cycle. He knew instinctively how to kick his leg off his bike, moseying on down to a chagrined motorist, adjusting his utility belt around his waist, freeing his jacket for fast access to the revolver on his hip.

Mike knew he was a good cop. He had a genuine hardon for police work.

Off duty, his thick strong dick rose hard at the feel and smell and sight of himself creaking and sweating in the hot uniform. He liked to practice his moves alone in front of a single huge mirror with one tracklight canspot angling down over his body. These were his private mirror-fuck nights. Zipping, buckling, snapping his uniform. Lifting his hardening cock and big sweaty balls carefully out from his breeches. Appreciating the long juicy hang of his thick meat. Measuring his warm cock against the cold steel of his revolver until his rod was bigger than his gun. His balls rose and fell, rolling over each other, live and moving in his hand. The heat of his uniform under the spotlight raised a light down of sweat on his skin. Rivulets ran from his dark-haired armpits wetting rings into his white cotton teeshirt. He liked the smell of his night sweat mixed with the cycle-exhaust smells left over from his duty.

The hairy crack of his Italian butt itched for the feel of another man's unshaven jaw burrowing between his cheeks. As much as he liked straddling his bike, he liked sitting on a good man's face. He passionately enjoyed a strong healthy tongue probing into the sweat-tangle of soft hair furzing around the juicy pucker of his manhole.

Officer Mike Leonardi was a gold-badge river a man could float away on.

Mike had a special way about him. He reverenced himself honestly; he got off on his look without any vanity. He knew what he was, and he was proud of it by the inch and by the pound. He liked the way other men, from cadets at the Academy to the boys on Castro, studied him. He liked the way some men, older by a few years, checked him out, somehow the same way his father had taken his potential measure that afternoon in the bedroom: they ran their experienced eyes over him like some young stud animal.

He had chosen a profession that made him publicly the man of authority he had always been privately.

And privately, Officer Mike Leonardi was something else. The right night. The right man. And he was ready to give masculine gay men a cop-worship trip to remember. He had understood from his rookie days the kind of stiff-prick salute men gave him. Some of his buddies on the force were confused by the flagrant worship they got on the streets of San Francisco. But not Mike: he had the manly grace to handle even an outrageous compliment. Years before, with his dad's cop pals, he had studied what he wanted to be like when he grew up. Back then he had worshiped from afar the essence of manhood in other worthy men. In the PAL leagues, he had grown husky and big for his age. He had memorized from boyhood the kind of men with the regulation-clipped and groomed, big-muscled and bigger-dicked Look that made his uncut cock slip out of its juice-slick teenage foreskin.

PAL wrestling had taught Mike to be no one-way man. He gave out as good a rough-n-tumble energy as he got. Mike knew how to offer to men the very stuff he found rich and rare among men: heavy dick, ripe crotch, good muscle, sweet pits, big wide span of raw-boned foot. All backed by fullback butt built for thrusting his tense tool the special way a man gets it up to get it on and pump it to another man.

Men found it easy to honor Mike in straight bars and to worship him in private bedrooms. He was naturally a strong center, careful never to diminish any man. He put no man down. He made no man feel small. He saw no need to make a man bottom-out in order to get down to the uplift worship of the Great God Cock. He was so at ease with himself, and so disciplined with his partners, that men found Mike solved the main problem of men needing men to worship: too many barguys, biblically fearing the commandment about not having strange gods before them, refused to be glorious sexual gods to the men who, seeing God in them, understand totally the proper worship of deity is man himself.

Mike let men worship him, rubbing his muscular body, studying his face close-up, chewing lightly on his thick black moustache, rebreathing the breath from his mouth, swallowing his slow spit, tonguing up inside his powerful nostrils, sniffing their way through his curly black hair, licking his thick pecs and rockhard nipples, sucking his feet, eating his asshole, lapping up his hairy balls, deep-throating his olive-skinned cock.

More often than not, Mike led his worshipers beyond his own body into honoring the ideal of manhood they found lodged in him. While they played on his body, pleasuring him with their lust, he talked a hypnotic ritual rap that lifted them out of time and space into timeless, spaceless transcendence where they found themselves a surprisingly integral part of the platonist manhood they idealized.

"You're quite a man," a leatherman daddy, hot in his forties, said.

Mike put one police-gloved hand around the man's cock and balls, and the other behind the man's neck, pulling him close face-to-face. "It takes one to know one."

Mike learned his empathy from older men who had liked the dark, athletic look of the son of one of Omaha's finest. He had been primo among that special breed of big boys who grow up hanging around grown men, holding his own, moseying along as they kicked bullshit back and forth, starring in the PAL leagues, spending summers on highway construction crews. He worked shirtless, sweaty, an olive-skinned tanned adolescent already upholstered with dark hair on his chest and belly and shoulders. He liked the work; it muscled him up for football in the fall. He passed straight through his adolescence with an untouchable masculine grace that drove other men to rib him about the silent waters that fuck deep. His Look was a gift acknowledged around Omaha. Boys his age wanted to be like him. Fathers wanted their sons to measure up. No one talked about it, but everyone knew, Mike was dicking a banker's daughter up on the hill. She had always been a friend; but she was not his preference. Yet he could fuck her because she worshiped the ground he walked on. He never bragged about his exploits. He always came on noncompetitive. For that, less secure, less gifted men, liked him.

Mike was the greatest young guy in Omaha. He was, right down to it, a man's man. What Mike knew, and Omaha didn't, was that a man's man, when defined all the way to its essence, is a far cry from a ladies' man. That was his secret. As much as he liked to bury his face in pussy, and always would keep coming back to it in the SFPD, he knew he needed more the sexual fraternity of other athletic and authoritative men. That frank insight at an early age was his ticket out of Omaha.

"What Wraps around a Motorcycle"

Mike was the finest of the New Breed of Homomasculine Men.

He was smart enough to be friends with his own body. He knew what he needed to keep himself centered. Playing alone nights in front of his mirror, he ran his thick hands, with throttle-callused palms, over his shirtless pecs under his fur-lined leather jacket. He stroked his belly, crossed from shoulder to waist with his fetish addition of a Sam Browne belt that had been his dad's.

He kicked back and stroked himself. He greased his hand to slick his big cock up longer and thicker, self-hypno-ing a Zenlike positive imaging that over the years had added inches to his powerful cock. He knew a man controls his own body, psychs mind over matter, by meditatively pumping his meat as much as by pumping iron. What a man wants is what makes him cum. If he's focused on what image he wants to shoot off for, he can extend himself precisely the way he wants. A man's Look, a man's physique, and a man's dick are all products created out of his own view of himself. Mike played with mirror-fucking; but, in truth, looked into no mirrors more than reflections of himself in his own eyes and in the eyes of other men.

The jut of his big Italian-American chin and the slick shine of his long, mushroom-head dick had caught his first attention as a growing boy, and held his interest as a grown man. His private meditations on his own personal manstuff made him all the better an encounter for all the men whose lives he fucked his way through. He was, in fact, so honestly grateful for the gift of his Look, that often in gyms where some discreet gay man could not take his eyes off him, he'd purposely leave behind the gift of his sweaty jock or headband, as if he'd simply forgotten it, so the man could harvest the gear and take it home for his private pleasure. He had that kind of cosmic equity above and beyond the call of duty.

More than skindeep, his Look was the "handsome-that-is-as-handsome-does." He was a good-looking cop and he was a good cop. He was as real a man as he looked to be. He could fuck a man royally and never fuck him over. There was no difference between his appearance and his reality. He was more than the sum total of his parts.

"You are," a kneeling, worshipful man said to him, "Saint Michael the Archangel."

"Nope. Sorry. I'm just plain Mike, the Dago cop with a dirty mind."

Mike liked to do all the things only men can do to each other. Men liked to watch him jerk off standing over them in his uniform. Because he knew how to make love to himself, he knew how to make love to other men. When he climbed into the sack with a man, he knew all the moves that oil the body-to-body slip and sleaze of man-to-man contact. When Mike put out, he really gave. Guys, who usually left beds somehow unfulfilled, crawled out of Mike's on all fours. He was a good-humored fucker. He knew how to leave a man with a taste of hot cum and cold revolver in his mouth.

His uniform was a second skin tailored to a perfect fit. The heavy natural pump of his self-disciplined body bulked its wool and leather contours out full and rounded. A real police cruiser, he tooled tall on his SFPD patrols, stopping men for the fun and the hell of it the way his straight compadres pulled attractive blonde women over for a curbside chat. He knew the double-rush he caused: first the anxious flush of what-the-fuck-did-I-do-wrong, then the relieved rush when men realized this handsome hunk of a motorcop was checking them out with a casual cruise just to say a friendly hello in the name of the Law. Mike had a talent for making a man's day, and, if the cruise clicked, his night. He was as good at public relations as he was at private.

God! Was there a shitload to love in that good-looking Dago cop with his come-and-get-it killer smile!"

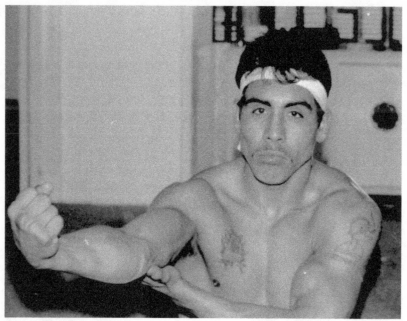

"Fist of José del Norté"   Video: *Illegal Alien Blues*

**A man's lust should exceed
his capacity, or what's a
heaven for?**

Black-White-and-Brown
Doublefuck

Double your pleasure. Double your fun. That's my theme song.
When my butt gets horny, one dick won't do when a man can
have two. Ain't nothing like an interracial doublefuck. Yeah. Figure the gymnastics. How three ethnic guys can climb into the
sack, and two of them can stroke up their hard cocks to full throbbing hardons that, righteously greased, can together slip, slide,
and ram into the third guy's stretch-hole. Feels good up the butt.
Feels supergood to the two studs chute-fucking together. They
get the hot, tight asshole squeezing their two big dicks together.
They get the pleasure of each other's hot cock rubbing wet and
slick against their own meat while they doublefuck their buddy's
butt. Ain't nothing like a big-hung chicano boy, and a huge-hung
gangster black stud, double-pumping their not-gonna-take-No-
for-an-answer equipment up a groaning honky ass.

Hank is all Tex-Mex muscle. Rufe is all Manhattan hustle.

Common sense may tell me that a man's lust should exceed
his physical capacity—or what's a heaven for. But the day I found
that my ofay butt could handle what my head craved—a great
big good old black-and-brown doublefuck, I figured common
sense had never been my strong suit. I wouldn't know how to
stop it if I could. I don't know if it's worth stopping. Some men
do some things; others, others. Doublefucking is what I respond
to. Not necessarily all the time. Because it just ain't that easy to
find. I prefer, sexually, the energy of men. Nothing strikes me
better than to have two energy sticks plugging deep up into my

socket—except maybe three. But I can't figure the gymnastics on how to accommodate that number. And besides, *The Guinness Book* is missing a section on sex.

So for now, I'll settle for one, namely me, divided by two, namely Hank and Rufe.

Hank is long, lean, and lanky, with one of those big-headed long prongs that swings halfway down his slightly bowed legs. A handsome fucker. He shows what he knows he's got. He likes to straddle my chest and drop his dick in close to my face. For study purposes, he says. He sports the Tijuana donkey length needed to perform a doublefuck. And his cowboy body is hard enough to back up the promise of his dick with some special delivery. Hank strokes his meat with the air of authority that comes when a guy realizes he's a sexual Olympic athlete. And real good at all the events. In fact, Hank likes the challenge of offbeat sex. The crazier stuff gets, the longer he stays hard. For a rough-and-ready Tex-Mex redneck, he can fuck like a mink; he can just keep right on fucking and fucking and fucking, until that certain offbeat beatoff something clicks in his head, and the scene turns wild enough for him to go for his fucking nut.

Rufe, who calls himself the biggest hung black stud in town, is just bad enough to make Hank real crazy about slipping his brown pole up against Rufe's black shaft. Something about that spic spit on those two cocks. Something about that honky hawker wetting those two rods. Something about a tight white butthole ready to be used, abused, and double-loaded with two scoops of red hot cum, when it's finally pumped out of those black and brown hoses. Ain't neither man a lazy lover. Or an easy cumer. Both last long in the sack.

What was it Rufe said to Hank the last time they both drove over to stick it to me? "We gonna be fuckin' this WASP-Wishbone all night. You take one leg, bro. And I'll take the other. And when we both get ready to cum, let's make a wish and puuuuullllllll!"

"Yeah, man. Let's donkey the honky."

Rufe paid his dues in Times Square, before he followed his cock to Southern California. He likes the view of LA from my apartment above Sunset. I like the view of his dick hanging in my face. Because I like to see, smell, caress, and lick big hunky nigger dick up to full, potent, fucking size, just so I can memorize for sure the quality of the quantity that's gonna shove its big way toward equal opportunity with a redneck cholo wang right on up my grinning butthole.

Let me be perfectly clear. Just because some of the words I use haven't been spoken lately hardly makes me a bigot. Redneck, nigger, beaner, cocksucker. Fuck. I'm no more perverse than the world-renowned critic Leslie Fiedler saying on C-Span after all the censorship of Huckleberry Finn and the O.J. Simpson debacle that the "n-word" must be reintroduced into the American vocabulary to aid our intellectual discourse and heal racial misunderstandings. *Nigger* was the word used for over two hundred years, by whites and blacks alike, and historically it wasn't derisive, until made so in the mid-20th century. Actually, because of such censorship, just saying some of those "forbidden" words is almost as much an erotic hardon as is actually fucking with a nigger and a redneck cholo. Shit. When Hank and Rufe have me balanced between them, ready for the entry of first one, and then the other, I look up, and I see two hot men made all the hotter by the mix of their ethnic looks, as maybe so I look to them. Any man who denies that interracial fucking doesn't provide at least some turnon has a screw missing—in more ways than one. And a good screw it is too. Especially when it's doublefuck time in the PC Corral!

Hank likes to slow-drip spit in my mouth. He makes me get down and wash out the inside of Rufe's big, uncut meat. Hank's main hardon is forcing me to service nigger dick. He gets up and ready for doublefucking by forcing me to lick and suck on Rufe's big, black rod. Pushing my face down into those tight, wiry pubic hairs. Choking on the beer-can thickness of that big-knobbed cock. Making me sniff and lick and suck and tongue deep up inside that sweet, black butt. Ain't no butts in America built with the pitch and fullness of nigger butt. Rufe's big dick gets hard at the feel of a white trash tongue sucking his checks, cleaning up under his big Mandingo balls, and eating his big slab of dark meat. Altogether, the three of us turn on with the kind of heat that makes the all-American melting pot positively boil. Maybe we can hire us a rice-rocket Jap.

Fully hard, Hank lays back on the bed. His big Tex-Mex dick slick wet. "Get on it," he orders. I look at the size of it. "You heard the man," Rufe says, standing at the bedside, a massive black tower of dick, chest, shoulders, arms. Rufe puts his big black hand, with the hard long nigger nails and the pink palm, on the back of my neck. "Sit on the man's dick," he orders. He half lifts me. Half drops me down on the taco meat. Cock as big as Hank's ought to be enough for any asshole.

But not where these guys are concerned.

Hank pushes up and in with his muscular hips. Inch by fucking inch his knob and shaft disappear. Rufe beats his meat. Long mean strokes. Hank's dick is shoved in for the volume of the fuck. Rufe readies his dick for the hardballing action. Stuffed full of cowboy cock, my ass is spit on, greased, and I'm bent over toward Hank's belly and chest, while Rufe climbs in between Hank's spread legs and aims his big cock straight at my stuffed hole. The feel of the head of his dick against my stretched pucker sparks like black fire. He slaps my cheeks. Once. "Relax, whitey!" Twice. "Open up." Then the head of his dick, slipping in alongside Hank's probe, gains a hold on the ring of my ass. Once the knobhead of that nigger dick roots itself in a butt, hang on. He starts the slow slick slide, shaft to shaft with Hank, up inside my butt, until their cocks are nestled like two, hard hot animals, and their big balls are hanging wet and sweaty and loaded for the cum that some righteous fucking will pump out.

The double entry is the calm before the storm. The double entry is enough to make my dick harden and drip with pre-lube. But the double entry is nothing compared to the doublefuck. Once positioned. Once entered. I'm the ham in their sandwich. With Hank under me twisting my tits and grinning his big gold-toothed, Tex-Mex grin right in my face, and with Rufe behind me, slapping my butt and holding my hips in place, there's no way I can get off Hank's monster cock, and absolutely no way I can get my butthole away from the jabs, rams, and in-and-out, deep slide of Rufe's conquering meat. These boys have got their timing down. They fuck me till they agree they're both ready to cum, and when I'm about to die, they both start jamming the full-length and circumference of their dicks all the way in, wrapping their arms around me and toward each other, until I'm practically crushed, suffocated, between their big heaving bodies, with only enough play left between my cock and Hank's belly to rub my dick till I shoot, with my asshole stuffed with two cocks still throbbing with the last of their red-hot cum.

Common sense may tell me all kinds of stuff about a man's lust, but nothing speaks louder to me than a good old doublefuck in black and white and brown. It's all too human. Amen.

Sonny Butts   Video: *When Sonny Turns Daddy*

Homme fatale...

Cruising the Merchant Marines

Cole Ridge can put his rubber seaboots up on my bed anytime his ship's in port. Ain't a man alive that I'd go overboard for the way I went hook, line, and sinker for a merchant marine as handsome, hung, and horny as Ridge. Merchant marines are a prime commodity down on what's left of the San Francisco waterfront. I know. I've paid my dues hanging around the Seaman's Hall, the Scandinavian Mission, and the Ancient Mariner Bar and Grill down by the infamous old Embarcadero YMCA.

I spotted Cole Ridge first in the basement men's room of the Sheraton Palace Hotel. He was a hulk. Big. Broad shoulders in a flannel shirt. Sleeves rolled up his hairy forearms. A couple good-looking tattoos. Thick hands. Big fingers. A gold ring he never bothered to take off after he bailed himself out of a sinking marriage maybe five years before. Hair pouring up out of the unbuttoned neck. Barrel-chested. He looked too big for the Palace. And right big enough for me. He had the tea room toilet-brigade of Palace queens in an uproar. Those cocksuckers hadn't ever seen a man as genuine as Cole Ridge. They were maneuvering every *homme fatale* number in their tea-room repertoire trying to get Ridge's attention.

Ridge was above all the coy come-ons. He stood at the mirror slick-combing his thick hair as deliberately as a USN bodybuilder flexing a double-biceps shot. He didn't read any obnoxious attitude so much as very seductive aptitude. His full pack of crotch rode way above sink level. I spied his basket bulging with what looked to be an eel-size, thick dick tucked down and over the juicy top of a pair of forward-slung, heavy balls. I figured a big, booming, deep-six voice would spout basso out of his noble nuts.

He caught me sizing him up in the mirror. His good-looking face held steady. Eye-to-eye. Squared off. He took one last stroke through his wet hair, and two final runs of the comb through his thick moustache. His jut of chin was a three-day romp of dark, sexy stubble.

Sure as Horatio was a Hornblower, I figured on the spot that I was gonna get me a chunk of that Big Mackerel and make him feel good in the long slow dick-sucking, pit-licking, ass-rimming process. What the fuck did I care for the hungry eyes and hungrier mouths Clarabowing all around us like a school of lovelorn guppies. I decided to sail directly on up to that steaming cruiser and make us more than two ships that pass in the night. A man needn't read semaphore to know when a merchant marine is ready for some bountiful social mutiny. Like a deep-throating man going down on him smack-dab in the middle of the marble-and-tile, piss-elegant pissoir in the basement of the Sheraton Palace Hotel!

I knelt, felt, rubbed my mouth against the manpack in his faded denims. His big fingers, nails crescented with ship grease, popped open his buttons and flipped out a dick that would have made Moby jealous. Seablue veins twined around his hardening shaft. I sniffed his thick-skinned uncut dick, lightly licking the sea-salt-piss-taste off its big mushroom knob. A pearl of lube juiced up the slit in its rosy tip.

His dick hoisted anchor out of his soft sargasso of hair. Its long low profile filling, changing, engorging until his dick stood mast-straight, tall, and thick. My face moved in under his throbbing cock. I looked up the full length of his big body at his unshaven, angular chin and jaw. Ridge looked down at me. The corner of his mouth rose into a pleased sneer of white teeth that said as much as his quick sly wink. We knew we were partners in crime together. Ridge liked the anxious audience watching us. From deep down by the seafood of his cock and big balls, I could see a circle of men forming, pulling their dicks out, stroking in silent admiration at the heft and haul of Cole Ridge's big equipment.

Games at sea were Ridge's specialty. Later I lay back many times with him in our rack over in China Basin where at night we could hear the far off foghorns kind of reminding me that Ridge would always be coming and going. A month in the City. Three, four, six months at sea. He liked to tell me about sex on the high seas: the boiler-room engineers; the cribs the crew set up with blankets among the cargo in the hold; hard fucking in rough seas; the pecking order of rapes and beatings when young merchant marines, hot out of high school, wanted to see the world, and instead, forced flat on their backs, with dick in their butts, got to see lots of ship-shape ceilings until their teeth rattled.

Cole admitted, late at night, our dicks in our greased hands, that more than once he had helped turn a shipboard gangfuck around. He meant, I think, in all his modesty, that when a young ship's apprentice was crying or cursing out his fuckers, he changed his tune when Cole took his turn between his legs and drove prow first into the kid's port.

Maybe it was Cole's insistent masculine look and his firm, persuasive style that made that young seafood stop resisting, start understanding, and fast accepting what well-driven dick men like Cole use to plow into them. I liked to suck on his dick thinking of all the guys at sea that he had, by the force of his persuasive fuck, seduced into taking a man like a man.

Ridge had that grace. Even men, who never questioned their taste for women, took a look at the command presence of Ridge's essenced masculinity and realized that there were certain comforts a man could only get from another man. For all the release that women could be, men provide men a refuge where women can never tread. Ridge seemed to cause the straightest of men to weigh anchor and sail away into the bright sea of that part of their uncharted sexuality. Ridge made their docking a celebration of manhood. He was a sailor in no danger of falling from grace with the sea.

The surrounding circle-jerk of men beating their pud in the toilet of the Sheraton Palace stroked their meat hard as Ridge reared up. He threw his enormous head back. His big body arched like a sperm whale fluming up from deep waters. His dick exploded in my throat, in my mouth, on my face. His thick, white, gelatinous cum ran from my nose. I swallowed the depth charge of his load. I ate a thousand nights of hardon sex among shadow groups of sailors gathered on starlit decks with soft tropical sea breezes cool on their salty bodies; of men sacked up together in white canvas hammocks with cocks buried deep up butts, fucking to the rhythms of the freighter's ocean-roll; of men who choose to be alone, for months at a crack, with other men who go down to the sea in ships.

Cole bunks with me now when he hitches over to San Francisco from the Port of Oakland. When he ships out, I feel connected to every man he has in every port.

Tricks of the (Rough) Trade...

Show Me the Money!
Hustler Bars

Gay sex is FREE. So a hustler bar is a strange place for a gay man, because a hustler bar is not "gay." There are hustlers. There are johns. Neither leads a particularly urban-gay lifestyle. Rough Trade Tricks are essentially straight. Johns are essentially out of the gay circuit, often young, and not necessarily "rich." Neither cares much for the gay bars of Weho, Castro, or Soho. The johns prefer lower-class "straight" males who don't fuck up sex with sentiment. The hustlers prefer, not necessarily men, but money. Sex is an easy means to cold, hard cash in trade for hot, hard cock.

In a gay bar, the reciprocity is sex for sex. In a hustler bar, it's sex for money. So there I sat, in Los Angeles, in a hustler bar, on a stool near the juke box. I had to remember that the johns, many of whom were more attractive to me than were some of the hustlers, aren't looking for mutual gay sex. They're looking for a "straight" guy who will ball them the way sex used to be before sex was a lifestyle. The mutual satisfaction is a combo of money, power, and sex. Some guys have a need for money and some guys have a need-to-pay. Probably everything that goes down in life has to do with our toilet training. Or something.

So there, in LA, I stood/leaned/sat/paced/leaned/smiled/ watched/cruised with fifty bucks hot in my jeans, begging to pay for it, so I could cross the line and know what the fuck it felt like to buy my way into a specific section of "street-smart, low-life, talk-show trash" that without cash no gay man has any access to. Rough Trade Tricks are usually born in trailer parks in the American south, raised in foster homes, tattooed in juvenile facilities, saddled with one or two young sons by one or two 15-year-old bitches, and educated in prison where the one important lesson they learn is that gay men are an easy mark.

I felt confident as a kid in a candy store. Actually, a john never needs fear rejection, because all he has to do is flash more money at the young and the dangerous. The lower classes are eternally attractive to the middle and upper classes. (Ask Pasolini, the martyred Patron Saint of Rough Trade!) Even heterosexually, every class knows what it's for. No matter what sex trip johns want—S&M, rough trade, suck/fuck, water sports, dirty feet, you name it—anything goes in a hustler bar where the level of play is the kind of primal sex once found in rest stops, YMCAs, bus stations, and carnival midways with mechanics, sailors, hitchhikers, and gypsy men with dirty fingernails who'll do anything for a buck. The natural-born rough-trade hustlers, in their wonderful anonymity and danger and wild taste, should not be confused with the slick urban-gay hustlers who advertise through the "Models Classifieds" in gay papers where the "muscle sex" or "dominance sex" is highly stylized Kabuki ritual. Gay hustlers are high concept. Rough trade is just plain basic fundamental what-it-is.

It's Friday evening becoming Friday night on a full- moon weekend in LA, and the two camps of hustlers and johns sport with each other like friendly Montagues and Capulets. If, in America, money can rent you what you want, then a hustler bar is almost as close as a man can get to sex-with-satisfaction practically guaranteed. Hustlers, in fact, invariably "can guarantee you, man, we'll have a good time."

Twenty-five bucks, average, gets a john a hustler for the first time: no frills, just some laid-back trade getting his dick sucked until the john cums. A return bout costs less. Prices vary depending on the time of night, the night of the week, the proportion of johns to hustlers, and the specifics of the sex trip that the john wants out of the hustler. Frequently, there's cab fare or a tip of about ten bucks tacked on when the "boy" has done his best at turning out a good performance. The essence of hustling, after all, is show biz. And a taxi to a hustler is a status symbol equal to a limo.

A tattooed, well-built, blond, goateed hustler with a buzz cut eyes my table and heads to the jukebox. He plays "I Don't Want to Walk Without You." I stand up and move in near to him, a quarter in my sweaty hand, and scan the selections for a musical reply. My choice: "Hit Me with Your Best Shot." We listen to the music, eyeing each other. *Who is the matador? Who is the bull?* He's more wary that I am. "You wanna beer," I say. "Yeah," he says, "Bud."

At the bar service station, a john leans over to me. "That one," he says pointing at the blond goatee leaning his butt against the jukebox, "will do it for twenty bucks. He's raunchy. Likes to get blown and have his ass eaten. He's quiet. Believe me, I know. He's a bit player in B-movies. Action-adventure flicks. I've licked all those tattoos on his arms. I sucked on him for maybe an hour and jerked myself off till he pushed me back, sat on my face, and twisted my tits till I came. Yeah. Twenty bucks. He's marked you."

I buy two Buds. I bring them back to the hunky hustler who looks like a street-version cross between all of the Butthole Surfers and the terrific Henry Rollins. His eyes are electric skyblue. With the cold beers in my hand, I never felt more like a straight guy off at a convention in a strange town buying a drink for some B-Girl. I can tell I'm having a Frasier-and-Niles kind of moral dilemma. I have no trouble with sex separate from money. But, migod, when sex combines with money, I think of the stereotype that johns ought to be old and ugly and degenerate. Well, I'm not yet old or ugly. But the degeneracy of paying for sex squats awkwardly on my head this night in this hustler bar. I laugh to myself that my bourgeois conscience is much ado about nothing. Actually, I find I really have an almost politically correct "attitude" about going through with this pay-for-play trip even with this guy nobody would believe would have sex with a man unless he actually was paid!

I remember the words my buddy, Old Reliable, who lives to love hustlers, said to me earlier in the evening: "Hustlers are actors. You're the producer. You got the money. You're also the director. Hustlers are Minimalist Artists. They'll do as little performance art as they can, unless you direct them. *Pose! Flex! Beat your meat! Let me suck your pits/dick/ass! Sit on my face! Spit on my face! Shit on my face!* The price can go up. Don't come off cheap. Offer $40 for openers. If you hit it off, if you want more than to suck him off as trade while he kicks back and smokes, if you want him to rough you up a little bit, add ten bucks. You want him to pose for some Polaroids, add another fifteen. You want to shoot some video footage, add thirty. You want him to sleep over, add ten. You want him to cuddle, add five, and breakfast. And tip him by giving him some of your clean socks."

Hiring a hustler is like ordering ala carte. You get exactly what you want. (And that makes hustlers basically "safe sex," because you control the fluid exchange.)

"This is Hollywood," Old Reliable said. "It's a circus. But at least it's the Big Top. All the movie stars and TV people hire hustlers. Judy Garland loved rough trade boys. Rock Hudson loved pay-for-play tricks. Stars pay for performances because they themselves are paid for performances. Hollywood is where America brings its dreams. You can hire your fantasy. The world's great performances aren't on screen. Great performances take place in the sack."

I hand Blue-Eyes-with-Buzz-Cut his Budweiser. I want to proposition him. I want to do it. But I can't. He's so shy or sly, he's not helping. Why do I have to pull the quiet type? I came out tonight prepared with cold cash to be nasty, to go slumming, to fucking buy sex! How un-American to become suddenly a reluctant consumer.

I feel the power is in my pocket: the cash. I think: *Show him the money!*

God! Blue-Eyes-with-Buzz-Cut is hot as a street in Venice Beach! The kind of sweaty macho based on the kind of clean you can maintain when you're living out of a knapsack and brushing your teeth at an IHOP. He's my speed. In a post-Judas minute, I'd take him straight to the bar-room toilet, flop him back against a urinal, and, *do him*—if only coins weren't changing hands.

Then good old lust, like cavalry riding over the ridge in the last reel, develops its own logic. I stare into his incredible eyes. "Hustling," I rationalize, "is the world's oldest profession. Moral-religious trips can't reject thousands of years of sex-theater history." I laugh at my puritanical head, but take very seriously my hardening dick that has no conscience. He takes a swig of beer and peers hard at me. Inexplicably, I blurt out: "I want to exploit you."

"Cool," he says.

Nervous as a virgin-bidder at a white-slave auction, I say: "Ya wanna mess around for fifty bucks?"

Fifty? Why did I say *fifty*? My subconscious is worried whether or not he'll like me. I forget rough trade doesn't give a fuck about me.

His blue eyes pierce into my face. "You ain't a cop, are you?"

Flattered—*god, I'm such a kveen!*—I say, "No."

His face lights up. He actually says, "Show me the money." Hustlers are able to work out deals with a john in a heartbeat. "Let's go," he says, and we stroll out together, with the bar full of johns and hustlers watching our cool-as-shit exit.

Before all, for a hustler, $ = sex.

After all, for a john, sex = $.

That night, Blue-Eyes-with-Buzz-Cut was what he has long been: a terrific piece of ass. That night, I became, at least for once, what I had long had an attitude about: a john. Mmm, I mean, a patron of the arts.

It was more than okay. It was hot! It was a perfect relationship. Pleasurable. Easy cum. Easy go. No hassles. No personal baggage about his old lady pregnant in some Motel 86 on Sunset Boulevard. No listening to some gay guy dysfunctioning about his 12-step program. Hey! That night of my initiation into LA hustler bars proved, I guess, there's no business like show business. Plus if you ain't getting what you want, go rent!

Mike Welder   Video: *Uncut Muscle Mechanic*

Manimals...

Young Deputy
K-9 Cop

Dogmaster you've seen him. Built like a Pit Bull. Big. Squared off heavy muscle. Vet. Professional trainer. Special Services Kennel for the County Deputies' K-9 Patrol. Man in Authority moving under thick pelt of full body fur. Nights, alone with his Dane and Doberman attack dogs, he clips back his fast-growing body fur, naked and hard, in his private quarters behind his own kennel—where a young County deputy waits: stripped naked from his uniform, caged, choke-chained, slow-stroking himself in the last hour before his obedience training begins.

In his quarters: the hum of the grooming clippers in the Dogmaster's big paw-hand shears his own soft fur down to a mean, disciplined, even bristle. The low growl of his two big dogs dozing at his feet. Hungry for fresh meat. The Dogmaster judges the sounds of barking from the kennel in the deep night. He grooms his fur on the back of his strong hands, around his square wrists.

He curries back the pelt on his powerful forearms that read by day like muscular hairy hams, hanging from the khaki Vet shirt he wears attending to the big dogs brought by men proud of their prize studs. His broad mastiff shoulders: hairy. His animal coat of fur thick on his big barreled chest. In the County: rumors of his Special Service Kennel. Knowing smiles. Then silence. Unbroken. In the County: anything is possible.

The roll of his abs: defined in dark washboard cuts by fur. Growth patterns not masking the pedigree of his power, but defining it. Men from the County proud to bring their dogs to him for stud. His pecs and belly soft-bristled, outlined by the natural lay of his hair.

His dogdik: thick, long, mean, bulbous, red, and ready.

His legs: squat, hard, powerful for serious studwork.

His Dane rolls over in his doze, his big balls rolling against the inside of his back haunch. The Dogmaster turns at his tight waist. He looks down at the dog who expectantly opens one eye. He turns back into the mirror. His own butt: round, ripe, muscular; the sweaty crack furred, dark, deep with promises he keeps. The animal spoor about him. The way he enlists a man to help mount his own stud over another man's dog in heat; the two of them together, intent on the perfect mounting. He clips his body hair the same careful length as his close-cropped beard. Its thick growth rises high up his checks, runs down his muscular throat, meets the rising curl of hair from his chest.

Tonight's a special grooming.

His big arms raise up. His armpits run wet with sweat. One paw palms the length of hair on his head, low on his brow, bristling down the animal back of his neck. His other hand running the clippers into an even length across his own head.

Tonight's Special Weekend Duty. Fucking Ultimate Obedience Training. New Young Deputy. Uniform Strip. K-9 Patrol.

The Dogmaster, erect, enormous, clippers in hand. Smoothing his own body. His dogdik drooling. Rich head crowning uncut hairy shaft. His two stud dogs, eyeballing his moves, waiting his command. His attack dogs, Dane and Dobe, hungry, growling low, waiting, killer instincts set on edge by their Master's hulking presence, held at bay by the cold eye of his Command Presence.

The Dobe's pink tongue flicks across his black lips. White teeth bared. Hindquarters quivering. Dick spritzing. The Dane growls in anticipation, starts up, anxious, nosing his way toward the iron door leading to the kennel, excited by the smell of fear a dog recognizes sweating out of a husky man's choke-chained body.

"Stay!" The Dogmaster's voice resonates deep from his big balls, echoes in the hard-tiled room. The two dogs freeze in total obedience. The big dogs are measure of the man. His own animal body: Marine-trained. Former DI. Respectfully nicknamed behind his powerful back at Camp Pendleton and Camp LeJeune: DOG DIK. Disciplined trainer of men and dogs for combat.

Trainer of young USMC Grunts forced by dare, high stakes, and his command, to fight nearly naked with specially trained attack dogs, in the last days of Nam, in the backwash of the DMZ, when men placed hard bets on any good brawl for blood.

Now: known as the best K-9 trainer in the County. The Dane moves in close to his Master: fur-to-fur, haunch-against-thigh. The Dobe sniffs hungrily at the kennel door.

In the County bars, the deputies laugh and wink and say, *shit,* they wish he'd work tighter with them. Independent man. Animal loner. Sharp white teeth flashing easy grin through mat of beard rising up to deep-squint of piercing eye. The deputies, quiet in their silent fraternity, treat his Special Services K-9 training as something better left unspoken.

In the dark fursweat kennel, the young deputy, naked, caged, heavy leather collar and choke-chain around his neck, smelling dogpiss ripe and fresh in the territorial corners, delivered handcuffed for stud, pulled from a prowl car, stripped from his uniform by other tough deputies, hosed down, readied for clipping and shaving and grooming, ordered to endure Special Services K-9 Training, waiting for the opening of the heavy metal door.

Around him, big dogs, caged separately, pad in expectant anticipation, streaming long wet piss-squirts, sniffing, nose-to-butthole, butthole-to-nose. Quick lick of long tongue through the cyclone mesh fence. Lick of dog-tongue to low-swinging dog-balls and fresh puckerhole. Natural animal instinct.

Hairy young deputy, recruited hunk, long-chained from collar to ring in kennel floor, waits the first night of his obedience training. Naked and warm in the animal heat of the kennel. Stripped of uniform, gun, gear, boots, by senior deputies. New to the County. Fresh from the service. Twists nervously the gold ring on his left hand. Special Weekend Duty never meant pissing in his own cage. His dick hard. Scared shitless. Dogs howling. The hum, the steady hum, of the Dogmaster's clippers on the other side of the kennel door. The whine of the Dobe. The low growls of the Dane. He figures he better be ready. He figures maybe now his Reality-Run may be in for a shakedown he never expected.

He remembers some of the deputies' talk. Overheard them. Until they noticed. Until they slammed their locker doors loudly. Until they shut up. Now: clarity coming through his eavesdrop. Clarity coming to him. This is the County. In the semi-dark he figures how it might be: groomed, the Dogmaster, opening his kennel cage, come to shear his hairy body, train him, force-sniffing his nose to commanding butthole, licking of bulbous big red dick. Enormous. Powerful Dogman. Heavy paws holding him in position. The dogmaster's long spit into the crack of his ass. Wild barking from other cages. The Dobe and the Dane pacing, watching, eager. The Dogmaster's snarling mount. The head sliding out of the heavy uncut skin. Insistent. *Dogslickwet.* Fucked in. Deep. Heavy fullness. Plowing. Holding. Pumping. Held firm in place by the Dogmaster's big paws. Only the commanding look from the hairy Dogmaster's eye holding the Dobe and Dane at bay. Only the whim of the Dogmaster not throwing open the locks on the separate cages of the pack of huge trained male fighting dogs.

Only minutes now. The hum of the Dogmaster's clippers stopping. The whine on the other side of the door. The sound of the Dogmaster's hand unlocking the deadbolt. The deep-throated barking rising to full howl and salute, cage to cage, in the dark kennel. Only moonlight breaking through the high, barred industrial windows. The sound of the iron door opening. The blinding light from the Dogmaster's bright, hard-tiled quarters. The Dobe and the Dane bounding into the kennel around the heavy legs of the Dogmaster. His big, hairy body planted squarely in dark outline against the light, shimmering in bristling halo, around the full measure, bulk and height and well-hung heft, of the Dogmaster who waits one long moment in the Special Services Kennel door for the night vision that is his alone, to carry him down the long growling corridor to the deputy's cage, where every move, driven by his crossbred, massive Dog Dik, unbelievably, beyond the captive deputy's imagination, brings out the latent beast in the caged, choke-chained, naked, exultant manimal!

Tom Howard   Video: *Party Animal Raw*

**1978. A night at the baths.
A night at the Slot.**

Fisting the Selfsucker

When a guy blows himself, he blows me away. I mean, how many guys have a double-jointed back? How many guys can even sniff their own headcheese, much less wrap their own lips around their own dicks for the Ultimate Self-Sensuality: Blowing Yourself.

I know several men who regularly go down on themselves. They fold up like army cots; they teasingly tongue the tip of their dicks; then they swallow themselves. Selfsucking makes sense. Think of the gall of some guy presuming to go out and make love to another guy when he's never really bothered to make good sensual love to himself. Since sex, like charity, begins at home, most of us get our sense of sensuality together by jerking ourselves off. That feels awful good. But imagine the pleasure you'd get as an—awkward clinical term—*auto-fellationist.*

Think how circularly perfect you'd feel as a *selfsucker.*

When your lips suck down to the root of your own cock and your own cock is buried deep down your own throat, you've got a rhythmic Humjob played to the tune of "Nobody Does It Better."

SCORING SOUTH-OF-MARKET

At San Francisco's Slot Hotel, 979 Folsom Street, about as low as you can sleaze South of Market, the Cocks' Army of men runs the full scale of 10. Some guys are photogenic muscle gods. Some guys are so "ugly" by Hollywood standards that they're beautiful in an off-beat way. Some guys are just so bad-in-body and low-in-energy that they keep the lights out in their private rooms. These "Troll Holes" are a must to avoid.

But the others. Ah! The others.

At The Slot you need two scales of ten: one for "Looks" and one for "Action." *A Chorus Line's* "Dance: 10! Looks: 3! is right on. For instance, a guy who scores a 10 for Looks may, on the dual scale, rate only a 3 for Action. His looks have made him lazy in bed. So he totals in at only 13 out of a possible 2 x 10 = 20. (Nobody ever gets a 20, because who's perfect?) On the other hand, another guy may be only a 7-Looks, but because he knows he ain't Robert Redford, he really gets it together in the sack and scores an off-the-wall 10-Action for his hot moves. This totals him in at a very interesting 17.

Ain't hardly a game in town where 17 doesn't beat 13 by a mile.

And that's how I met one of the three men I know who specialize in sucking themselves off.

COCKSUCKING

Cock. Suck. The words form in your mouth so self-contained: all tongue and teeth action. Your lips don't even need to move. *Cock. Suck. Cocksucker.* Men who suck cock are a dedicated breed of specialists. They see no failure of manly dignity when falling on their knees in front of another man's full crotch to suck his cock. So it is with men who suck their own cocks. They have the healthy view that their self-contained sexual gymnastics is a pleasant variation on the general celebration of masculinity.

Don't for a minute think that selfsucking is a diversion cornered by gay men. Straight guys, nimble of body and liberated of head, blow themselves with no more thought of their self-play being homosexual than they think that handjobbing themselves is gay. As Shakespeare said, "There are more men blowing themselves, Horatio, than you can shake a stick at."

BENDING OVER FRONTWARDS

This season at The Slot, a buddy and I cruised past Room 326: first door at the top of the stairs. A hot hunk of beef was laid back on the bed made into a four-poster with heavy 4 x 4 beams. He looked built, sick, and twisted—in short: wonderful. He had the body. He had the face. His eyes had the slick look of love. (He scored a solid 9-Looks.) Strangers in the night, we exchanged glances. All systems signaled GO. My buddy and I entered and closed the door.

Long encounters are sometimes best told briefly: I reached into the man's can of Crisco, fingered his butt gently, and as he relaxed, my fist took a long, easy ride into his ass. He was a handball expert ready for a good serve. He moaned. He smiled. His abdominals tightened down to a rippled washboard. His butt, full of careful fist, rose up in the air. He was pulling his hips toward his face. His cock, hard and veined, aimed straight arrow at the target of his bull's-eye mouth. His tongue flicked out to catch the sweet clear lube juicing from his piss-slit.

"You lie back," he said to me. "Keep your fist right where it is."

I rolled back flat on the bed as he rose up, straddling my chest. One of his wool-stockinged feet was on the bed; the other, he planted firmly on the floor. His hard cock stood at attention 18 inches over my face. My elbow, now bent at a right angle, rose straight up to where my hand disappeared into his sweet butt.

To my buddy, the guy said, "Open the door."

A gang of men gathered. Almost instantly. From the hall they watched our hard *pas de deux:* him standing; me laid back, handballing up into his ass arched over my chest. The bigger the crowd got, the bigger his dick got.

I had a genuine exhibitionist, literally, on my hand.

Then, one of those moments, that will for sure flash by as I someday lie dying, clicked into unforgettable focus.

The crowd was big enough. My fist was in full-bore, classical clench inside his first ass chamber. His cock vaulted up past his navel. Everything about the scene was in perfect balance.

He looked at the men in the hall. He looked down at me with *Here-Goes* written all over his face. He was aiming to score a perfect Olympic 10-Action.

"Do it," I said.

With grace no gymnast ever knew, he bent from the waist. His swooping body stayed hard and firm. As he folded down, his cock passed tightly through the canyon between his muscular pecs. His mouth was opening. His tongue flicked with anticipation. His face, as he bent toward his own cock, came down closer to my face. Intense.

Then contact: lockdown.

His tongue touched the tip of his dick. His lips sealed around the head of his cock. Then one final easy push and his mouth swallowed the whole shaft of his prick.

He started the age-old pump: mouth-to-cock resuscitation. His cock slipped wet and shiny in and out of his mouth. His butt sucked up more of my upward thrusting fist as his hips straddling my chest worked the body english he needed to blow himself to smithereens.

Migod! My view, 18 inches away from this beautiful man's face slurping up his own dick while my fist helped support his straddle stance, was a perfect "click."

He began to suck faster, deeper, longer strokes. Swallowing himself. And then, sucking himself almost to cuming, he straightened up, threw his shoulders back, raised his arms like a bodybuilder winning a physique contest, and roared the animal cry of a man torqued with total pleasure.

As he bucked on my fist, his now untouched cock shot by itself: great white globs of cum slopping hot on my chest and face and mouth. With each diminishing orgasmic throe, I inched my fist free and clear.

The crowd didn't know whether to applaud, shit, or go blind.

"Please," he said to my buddy, "close the door."

Alone, all three of us laid back together. My friend was impressed by the passionate gymnastics of it all. "That scene," he said, "was really primal."

"Primal?" the selfsucker said. "Primal? Huh! It was positively Neanderthal."

And you're a positive 18, I thought, on a double-scored possible 20.

PARADISE

San Francisco, in my book, is the place where, when you go there, you get to be your true self. The Slot, when you go there looking for Dance: 10/Looks: 10, is the place most likely to see or help a dedicated selfsucker doing himself, because he knows in such a special City that nobody does it like he does it when he does it to himself.

And "Nobody Does It Better" is the name o' dat tune!

Poster, "The Slot Hotel, San Francisco," by Chuck Arnett, 1976, featuring his fisting symbol as tattoo; collected by author, 1976.

Photograph of Poster   Video: *Domino Video Gallery*

"This story is about me."
—Robert Mapplethorpe

Caro Ricardo

Ricardo Rosenbloom arrived unlikely in my life. Everyone else I ever met needed money, time, encouragement. Ricardo was an adult. His "take" on my life was real and realistic. He pleased me: he was a grownup, superbly accomplished, and appealing to me who had for one-more-time declared my Finishing School for Wayward Boys recently and permanently closed. I had had enough of gayboys who wanted to write but never wrote, who wanted to shoot photographs but spent their cash on coke not cameras, who wanted to sing but never sang.

So here was Ricardo perched brilliantly at the start of a great career. His photography had shot beyond the Manhattan novelty of a new talent in SoHo. The right people sat in Ricardo's studio. The right runs of photographs, dispensed in limited editions, found their way into the right galleries, the right magazines, the right addresses. *Vogue* phoned to ask him to shoot whomever he thought hottest for its pages. We mused over Faye and Fonda, Gere and Travolta. We laughed about names with faces to be shot before they faded. We discovered we had virtually the same values. We shared a taste for money and celebrity. We liked the people behind both. Our talk unraveled in shops on Greenwich where we absently browsed antiques. Ricardo was an offhand collector. He wrote impulsive, enormous, and canny checks for small bronze sculptures of the goat-footed devil.

"Nineteenth-century British," he said hoisting his shopping bag. We walked like two improbable Bag Ladies up Christopher Street to Sheridan Square. Ricardo carried the bronzes in one smaller bag filled with black magic candles and sex magazines. I toted one larger bag, heavy with new, black, rubber hip boots from Stompers. We were ripped and happy with my brief visit with him in New York.

Suddenly he stopped our progress and reached first into his bag and then mine until convinced he had in fact lost in the last restaurant the current *Rolling Stone* with the review of punk-rocker Conni Cosmique's new album "The Luxury of Mental Illness." Conni was Ricardo's friend, his former roommate, and the subject of his current video, *Conni Cosmique and the Comettes.* Stoned on MDA, Conni had let Ricardo search her considerable soul with his RCA-007 color camera. He wanted me to view the tape, but all our lingering in Village cafes somehow left no time to see the raw footage. He seemed a little hurt that we couldn't share his work in progress. One of those moments passed between us when one can't do what the other wishes. "Too bad Conni's not in town," he said, vaguely implying I'd regret it forever.

I figured if Ricardo liked Conni, lived with her when he was fresh out of Pratt, surviving by clerking books at Brentano's and pilfering loose change, then she must be all right. Conni ended Ricardo's clerking career. One night at the cash register another light-fingered clerk was nearly caught in a bad scene. Ricardo was shaken by the wild shouting and accusations of his friend's close call. "So," Conni had said, "quit. We can manage."

"I'm not into celebrities," Ricardo told a *New York Times* reviewer asking about Princess Di, Tennessee Williams, Sam Shepard, Jack Nicholson. "Liza with a zero," Ricardo interjected. About the sundry rich and volatile who sat for portraits through his Hasselblad, he smirked, "I'm into people." Nothing wrong for a Puerto Rican-Jewish kid, reared as a child of divorce in Brooklyn, to prefer his people in a certain charmed circle. Ricardo first made it into Manhattan when he was sixteen.

"Did you ever go to Max's Kansas City?" he asked. "Did you ever *have* to go to Max's Kansas City?" We conversed in taxis and cafes. "I went there every night for a year. I had to. The people I needed to meet went there. I met them. They introduced me to their friends."

Ricardo toyed with the rich and famous as much as they amused themselves with him. One evening at a gallery opening, a wealthy and handsome patron walked up to Ricardo and said, "I'm looking for someone to spoil." Ricardo said, "You've found him." For the next four years they gave each other what they needed. At supper in a corner table at Paper Moon, the patron smiled at me and reached across the table, greeting Ricardo on his return with me from San Francisco, and dropping into his hand a brilliant diamond ring. Nice.

Whenever I pissed in Ricardo's toilet, he looked down, insouciant, from the framed portrait Scavullo shot in 1981. Francesco caught him, hands jammed into his leather jeans, cigaret hanging from his mouth, torn teeshirt tight around his drug-lean torso, his *Road Warrior* hair tousled satyr-like. Once, much later, he wrote me a letter confessing that his main enjoyment in sex was uncovering the devil in his partner. I should have been more careful with this photographer who worked with light and shadow. Lucifer, the archangelic light bearer, was, at least, an angel flying too close to the ground.

"This is," I told Ricardo, "your first incarnation in three thousand years."

"How so?"

"I intuit it," I said. "I get reincarnational readings off some people."

"I'm one of them?"

"My wonder is why you waited so long between incarnations."

The world and Ricardo were on no uncertain terms with each other. In this incarnation, or in past goat-footed Dionysian lives, Ricardo demanded, managed, and delivered what he wanted. Ricardo will, when his next death-passage is appropriate, take his life with the same hands with which he has created and crafted it. He will neatly, stylishly even, finish it. Ricardo is as close a mirror to my Gemini psyche as I have ever recognized. Fucking with him was very much fucking with his total being. Fucking with him was like fucking with myself.

Ricardo always wore black leather, even to the restaurant

bar Paper Moon, where in the thin March afternoon sun, we brunched and talked and drank coffee and Perrier. People waved to Ricardo in New York, hoping he would nod back, the way people acknowledged me in San Francisco. His shows grew increasingly chic. Galleries across the country wanted to be the first on their block to showcase his talent that stripped the familiar masks from famous faces and transformed them. Ricardo's talent was that he created psychic portraits; he was not one of photography's army of motor driven hacks. His insightful work was selling at a stylish clip.

The faces he chose, he chose judiciously, refusing to photograph anyone unappealing to his eye. Except for princesses. Princesses found great favor with Ricardo. Princesses called him early in the morning while we lay wrapped together, slugabed, his body tucked like a furnace around the curve of my back. "Hi, Princess." He chatted on. His body heat melted me to cold sweats. His leather pockets held small plastic bags into which he dipped his finger, sticking it up my nose and his tongue down my throat.

"When we make love," he said, "I want it to get to where it could go anywhere. I'm not as much into physiques as you are. I like to fuck with minds."

"I like big arms, big pecs, and sensitive tits."

"Nobody can work out and have a mind."

"You liked Arnold."

"Arnold was cute. He sat with all his clothes on and talked. He's nice. He's bright. He's straight. The gay bodybuilders I've been with are so big they're like fucks from outer space. I can't relate to all that mass. It overshadows personality. I don't like impersonal sex."

"That's a contradiction in terms," I said. "If it's sex, it's not impersonal. Sex is always personal. Just because you don't know somebody's last name..."

"Aw, Mickey, you don't actually believe that. There's sex with somebody, and there's sex with someone's body."

"You mean," I said, "that sex is mainly prepositions. Some

people you have sex with. Others, like bodybuilders who don't move very well in bed, you have sex *on*. Some guys are so masochistically bottom, you have sex *over*. And others are so sado-aggressive, you have sex *under*.

"Stop," he said. "Never get a writer stoned."

It was six a.m. in a Westside diner. Ricardo pulled my rubber-booted foot onto the booth next to his leather thigh. We had spent the night sleazing through the Mineshaft orgy palace. We were both at the dawn end of a Saturday-night stone.

"Guess who got turned away at the Mineshaft last night," he said. "Mick Jagger. "

"Why?"

"He showed up with a girl."

"Let's don't go to bed this morning. What can we do on Sunday in New York? My flight isn't until six."

"I want to stop by Jack McNenny's shop to check on flowers." He pushed his corned-beef hash away. He ate very little, pouring instead orange juice into his alabaster body. He was very pale with light rose color in his cheeks and blue veins under his paper-thin skin, and, omigod, in that Sunday morning spring sun, I wanted to love him and wanted him to love me. "I have to drop some flowers off personally. Uptown. You come with me," he said. "It's business, but why not? From this one uptown gallery alone last year, I made over nine thousand dollars. I spend it all collecting things. Not the least of which," he shook my boot, "is you."

"Bullpucky flattery." I changed the subject. "Your performance art show with Conni Cosmique is in June?"

"Conni deserves to be a legend. I photographed her from the start."

His lens had given him frozen images of her. Through his camera he recorded the time lapse dissolves of their friendship. Jesus. I, at thirty-eight, looking like what a thirty-eight-year-old man should look like, sat across from him, at thirty-one, looking like a faunchild. What were the dissolves of our relationship? I was old enough to be connected with the tradition of erotic words. He was young enough to be the essence of photographed rock'n'roll. Our differences fit: words and pictures.

"We need to get more done on our book," he said. "That is if we ever get down to it." He stubbed out his cigaret. "It's got to be commercial and handled through a private source. A publishing house will rip us off."

"My text will be less censored than your sex-and-fetish photographs."

The Greek boy waiting on us asked, "Separate checks?" Then he glanced at Ricardo squeezing my rubber-booted foot in his crotch between his thighs, and then at our hands held across the table. A true Greek, he answered his own question. "One check," he said.

"Your photographs need to be more suggestive than literal. Instead of a handballing shot of penetration..."

"...We need a nice ass shot with a can of Crisco sitting next to a fist rising up in the foreground."

"A sexual still life," I said. "Let the viewer's mind mix the three elements. "

He changed the subject. I wasn't supposed to talk about his work. "Why don't you stay through tomorrow night? Warhol's giving an Academy Awards party at Studio 54."

"My boss expects me back. The printer is returning the blue-line for our next issue tomorrow."

"Come on, stay. That leather rag you write can live without you one more day." He twisted my boot. "Come on, stay."

"Don't, Ricardo." I pulled my boot away.

He held my hand in place on the table top.

"You know," I said, "it embarrasses me that I have to work. At a job-job, I mean. I've never had to work before. Teaching wasn't work. Teaching was a labor of love, around the clock seven days a week, always with papers to grade, living with lofty responsibility, and, shit, it never mattered if everything went down the tubes of those thankless lectures. Did all those words evaporate as soon as I spoke them, or did some of them actually lodge forever in some of my students' heads? I mean, now, working from eight-to-five embarrasses me. Especially in front of you. I'm a writer hired to hack it out for *A Man's Man*. Wouldn't Thoreau be really pissed? You, on the other hand, work so very effortlessly."

The afternoon before, Ricardo had sat me down in his SoHo studio. The sun slanted through his loft windows, across my face, and hurt my eyes.

"You okay?" He unscrewed the legs of his tripod.

"Yeah."

"Come on, Mickey. You're lying."

"How embarrassed do you want me?" Why did the sonuvabitch always have to press the tender nerve. "I don't know why."

But I knew why. Ricardo's eye was true. His camera-eye was truer. I finally understood why Indians feared the soul-revealing, soul-stealing devil lens. We both played at being cynics abroad in the world; maybe he wasn't playing; maybe mine was only attitude; maybe his was real. His sight and insight cut through bullshit. In conversations, we threw snide asides to one another. His honeygreen eyes worked overtime. The first night we made love, his tongue licked repeatedly across my eyeball. That was a probing first. No one had ever so directly fucked my sight. Sitting in his sunny studio, I feared his eye, *malocchio,* his evil eye, his wonderful eye that through the added eye of his lens might see me suddenly different, might see not my appearance but my reality. I had seen others whose faces he had photographed. In real life they seemed so much less than the reality he froze into the single frame. I did not want to be diminished. I wanted to be transformed. My fear of his camera was primitive.

Cameras, after all, are the guns of our time. Hadn't Harvey Milk, as it turned out with high irony, owned a Castro camera shop? Yet I wanted Ricardo to see through his Hasselblad what he wanted to see of me. I feared him seeing me harboring resistance to his art. My right eyebrow in photographs too often rises up in arch opposition to the process that tries to capture a whole person in a single frame.

Yet I wanted to give the devil his due. I wanted him to have his way with my face. With me. I wanted to give way to him because I can never give way to anyone. I cannot submit to a man I cannot respect. I wanted to give Ricardo the surrender he wanted from me. I wanted to give Ricardo the sweet, sweet surrender I needed to give somebody just once in a lifetime. I feared he might slip in the shooting. I feared he might somehow fail to transform me, because of my resistance, reluctance, recalcitrance, because of my arched eyebrow, into the portrait he desired.

In fact, he shot me effortlessly and quickly. He sealed the roll of film and handed it to his assistant working in the darkroom at the rear of his loft.

"The contact proofs will be ready tomorrow," He said. He hugged me.

I made us instant coffee in the kitchen while he rolled joints in the living room. "Something's burning," I called. "Have you lit something?"

He came out to me in the small, jumbled kitchen. Under a silkscreened icon of Jackie Kennedy veiled in multiple-image mourning, an ashtray broke from smoulder to blaze on the table littered with Con Edison receipts and letters from galleries. Ricardo brushed the small fire to the floor and stomped the flames with his black point-toed cowboy boots. Minor disasters stalked us: insane Saturday night kamikaze rides up the Avenue of the Americas; a young gayman shot in the shin by a mugger in the lobby of a Charlton Street apartment building; a naked man falling out of a piss-filled bathtub to the concrete floor of the Mineshaft. Ricardo laughed. "You're paranoid," he said.

"Signs and omens are everywhere."

"I read that homosexuality can cause paranoia."

"Homosexuals have real reason to be paranoid."

He lowered his eyes. His mouth grew thin, tighter. Ricardo resented resistance. Ricardo loved congenial compliance.

I made a thousand excuses that night trying not to go to bed with him. He was pissed, but in control. He deflected my bedless hints. I wanted to enjoy some neutral time together. He needed time to work his seduction. He suggested supper at Duff's on Christopher Street. We lingered long. He plied beautifully subtle ways to untangle my none-too-ambivalent attitude. He led me the way a good dancer seduces his partner into bending to full dip. Ricardo, for some reason, wanted me, as me, with him, not in anyway forever, just particularly for that night of the afternoon he had shot me.

"This is my farewell tour to New York," I said. "I'm joining a monastery. This is it for sex. I'm tired of life in the fast lane. I'm getting born again."

"Mickey, come on. Yeah. Sure."

"I mean it, Ricardo. I'm tired of fistfuckers and dirty people. I'm tired of everybody always being sick with hepatitis and amoebiasis and clap and crabs and you name it. Our lives are a constant search for new ways to be disgusting."

"Look at your eyes."

"What do you mean?"

"You're dirty, Mickey. I knew you were into hard sex. You have a face that could have been drawn by Rex. I could tell you were dirty by your eyes when I met you."

"What about my eyes?"

"You've got dark circles."

"I won't in two weeks. I'm not kidding. I'm heading back to California, I'm doing my own version of being born again. I don't want my face to look like a collapsed cake baked at too high an altitude."

"Dark circles are what I look for. Interesting people have dark circles."

"Ricardo Rosenbloom's famous raccoon-effect."

"So you'll never have sex again. You'll just think about it. Just write about it for that monthly rag you work for. Just jerk off thinking about it."

"Hard sex leads to hard times. None of us ever thought that Gay Liberation would end up in an Intensive Care Unit."

"You need hard sex."

"I'll settle for soft."

"You shouldn't spread yourself around so much."

"I've always wanted to see everything that was going on. As a writer I have to. I never meant to turn into the Wife of Bath."

"You should do it with one person. With me. Not with every man at the Mineshaft. You should have come home with me the nights you've been here."

"I couldn't."

"Come on, Mickey. What do you mean, you couldn't?"

"I mean, I could, but I didn't want to."

"Didn't want to what?"

"Didn't want to have hard sex, which is what we always have. I really only wanted to see what was going on. I never spread myself around. I didn't want to get dirty. Not even when I got dirty. There's been a madness on us all for some time."

"There's no madness. What is, is. And the fact is, Mickey, deep down in your secret soul you're dirty, nasty, filthy."

The green glass lampshades in Duff's lit pools of light over separate tables. The waiter offered to fill our coffee cups yet another time. Ricardo waved him off. I waved him on. He stopped. Ricardo and I reversed waves. We laughed.

"Let's just pay the check, " Ricardo said.

We spread our cash across the brown table under the green light and pulled on our leather jackets.

"Born again?" he asked.

"Born again," I said.

What a half-breed! He smiled his best Puerto Rican smile, and nodded that all-knowing, seductive Jewish look he transmitted so easily with his eyes. He held out his tongue, peered narrowly at me, and shook his head *yes*. "You're dirty, Mickey."

At the door, the cold spring night chilled straight through our leather jackets. Ricardo headed out onto the crowded midnight sidewalk. A couple hundred guys cruised up and down Christopher from Ty's bar to Boots and Saddles. I always walked faster than anybody I ever dated, but Ricardo always walked faster than I.

Knowing full well we were headed toward disaster, I followed his fast pace up to Sheridan Square. The showdown was coming right on cue. His arm almost raised to hail a taxi. I blocked his view of the oncoming traffic. It was midnight on March 31. A little after.

"Well, Red Ryder," I said. "Where we goin'?"

He looked at me. His pale skin flushed with the cold.

"I have to go home," I said. "I have a lot of work tomorrow."

Into his eyes came that look I've see so often in other men's eyes when finally I, so much a conciliatory Gemini, reverse, and tell them, somehow for the first time, I have a will of my own.

"I'm a very disciplined person," I said, "too disciplined with Catholic guilt, and since I've known you, I've traded writing for fucking. I've preferred to spend time with you."

He eyed me, impatient as a coiled serpent, listening.

"Since we've met, I've taken the luxury, yeah, the luxury, of spending time with you. My drug intake has gone up a hundred percent. You tell me you want to use fewer drugs and have a wider range of sex." I pulled my collar tighter around my neck. "I can't range any further into the kind of sex you want unless we take more drugs. And I won't. I can't. I refuse. Look at you, these last weeks you've produced minimally. I'm not producing at all. We've fallen into the bad habits of those gayboys I hate to see wasting their time cruising each other on the corner of 18th and Castro."

"Maybe we both need this interlude, this time-out together," he said.

"For what? To develop our next creative stages? To write the book we'll never write?"

"You live it up to write it down."

"Yeah. Sure. This is what's left of Thursday. Monday, when I'm back in San Francisco and you're here, I'll have to write up a report of what I did and publish it in the next issue."

"Listen, Mickey, if you want to do anything, you can. You do."

"If we go back to your place, we'll have sex. We'll be up late. We'll wake up late. We'll have sex again. I won't do what

I must do to survive. Fuck it, man, I'm supposed to be here on business."

We stood a long time in absolute silence, stoned on grass, in a myriad of lights and traffic. Finally, Ricardo, staring into mid-distance, said, "It's stupid."

"Everything is."

"It's stupid." He wasn't even holding one of his usual Marlboros to punctuate his gesture. "I'm not in love with you."

Oh God. The subject is up. He brought the unspoken up. Oh Jesus.

"But when two intelligent people make excellent love, if they don't do it when they can, it's stupid."

"If we did it tonight, it wouldn't be good."

"You should have rested up last night."

"I only came once. I cum more than that everyday. Cuming isn't the point. I'm on vacation. You're not. I'm embarrassed. I work at a silly-ass job-job . I don't want to work. This year my vacation is only six days. So I should have stayed in last night?"

"It's all stupid."

We grew cold standing on the curb. Hidden dumps of frozen snow stood unmelted in dirty alleys around the corner. He tried to be so reasonable.

People milled around us. Bits of conversation froze like cartoon balloons in the air: "Nobody cares about the other guy, ya know?" New York was on the eve of another transit strike. A man, pissed off in general, and not expecting us to answer, sort of asked the crowd waiting to cross with the light: "Can anybody tell me how to get to Greenwich Street, or should I just go fuck myself?"

"Let's get a taxi," Ricardo said.

"For which way?"

"I'll drop you off."

"Don't commit yourself to a direction," I said. "Maybe you ought to go out too."

Ricardo waved a taxi over and climbed in. I followed. We sat far apart.

"Charlton and Sixth." I said.

We rode silently. No hands on each others' knees now. Where was that curious dyke photographer? Earlier that day she had wanted to shoot us together when she discovered us sitting in Stompers Gallery and Boot Shop. She was doing a book on gay couples and she liked the way our arms and legs twined so well around each other.

She was right. Our bodies were a perfect fit.

Ricardo held his honey-green gaze straight ahead.

The cab turned the corner. I fished out five bucks and held the money folded in my hand. When the cab stopped, I pushed the bills between Ricardo's clenched fist and his leather-chapped thigh. I turned full face to him, and the perfect rhythm of my words spilled out: "What you said you're not, I think I partly am." I meant "in love." I climbed out, closed the door, and walked off without looking back.

New York, New York. Alone again. Naturally. And I wasn't even looking to be in love. Maybe I didn't want him. Maybe more than him, I wanted the idea of him. The ideal of him. I was cold walking back to the 2 Charlton Street apartment where I was crashing near Jack McNenny's flower shop. Unlike Lot's wife, I didn't, wouldn't, couldn't look back. Exits, by then, I knew how to make, by heart. No one's ever left me; I've always left them. Sort of.

Ricardo Rosenbloom was excellent stuff.

Two mornings later, on the Sunday after Easter, lying again with Ricardo in his loft, I felt his arm wrap around my neck.

"What I said the other night," he whispered, "I didn't mean."

I kissed his long artist's fingers. I said nothing. No need to.

Later that morning Ricardo was to meet me for brunch before my flight. Instead, as I finished packing, he phoned from Paper Moon. His interview with *The Times* was running over. Somehow our relationship perversely thrived on such ellipses. Again, we were to have no dramatic farewell scene. Two months before, when he had come to my Victorian flat in San Francisco on magazine business, and stayed six weeks to make love, I had bought a fast-lane ticket and accompanied him back to New York rather than say goodbye. We gained another ten days. But now, this Sunday, no final kiss before jetting back.

"I wanted to get really crazy. I wanted to go so far with you," he said over the phone.

"I didn't know we had a deadline."

Were our ships in convoy for two months never to connect again? If so, then what-was must remain always so dear to my heart and my head. We rarely dared say "love." We had no need. Life is a series of beautiful gestures: a look, a lick, a touch, a word, sex verging on love—each and all enough.

We were parting again.

I stood at the phone near my backpack. He stood in a booth at Paper Moon with clever people waiting to spoil him more.

"Thank you, Mickey," he said.

"Thank you, Ricardo. Caro Ricardo."

A taxi took me through heavy Sunday traffic to the East Side Airline Terminal. On the radio the BeeGee's were insistent on "Stayin' Alive." A Carey Airporter Bus drove so slowly through the bumper-to-bumper cars to JFK that once it was halfway into the airport drive, I jumped the bus, begged and bribed a taxi driver to get me through the jam to the United Terminal. He balked, refused, until an airport taxi manager forced him to take my fare. He drove so reluctantly, I exited the taxi in heavy-stalled traffic, and ran two hundred yards in a headwind, juggling my backpack, a book from Ricardo, and a large photograph of Conni Cosmique drymounted on posterboard. The wind and exhaust blowing through the dirty brown grass caught the photo like a ship's sail. I pulled Conni like a lover to my chest.

"No luggage to check?" the ticket agent asked. "Go to the head of the security line or you'll miss your flight."

I ran, heart pounding, through the terminal, newspaper wrapping shredding off Conni's huge photograph, past curious travelers killing time, past phone booths where I had planned to page Ricardo at Paper Moon, down the ramp, into the plane, into my seat.

"I want, I need, I love, yes, love, with incredible respect, this man Ricardo Rosenbloom," I wrote at 25,000 feet in my journal, "even though we may never really for long times be in the same city or country. He travels to castles with princesses, after all. By day, I job-job. By night, I write."

"I'll send you a print of your photograph," he had said from Paper Moon. "It's quite good actually."

I wanted to see. I almost couldn't wait, I wanted to say, to see what vision this sophisticated photographer had found in me. I liked, as Ricardo would say, all the "takes" he had on reality. I wanted to see his "take" on me. I had to see if I looked dirty: not from the inside out—that I had always known—but from the outside in. I had to know if I had a gay face: the haunted, hunted, distorted kind. I had to find out if my face had become like the Fellini faces in the bars and the baths: a dead give-away of whatever it was that made us all different from other men.

Through the torn newspaper wrap, Ricardo's shot of Conni Cosmique's enormous face stared at me with one inquiring eye.

Two months in a life is not much. Two months in a year is considerable. Maybe we were too hot not to cool down. My affairettes usually run the wash-tumble-and-hang-it-up cycle. Whose don't? But this time something special passed between us. Revelation. Reflection. Lust. Darkness and light. Good and evil. Maybe even love. That's the value of even impersonal ships passing in the night: reassurance that in the night sea-swells other lights, rising and falling, loom closer out of the distance, and for a brief passage, a single man, borne back against the current, is not forever alone.

Donnie Russo   Video: *5 Guys in a Whorehouse*

Silver-Screen Blues 1980

B-Movie on
Castro Street

Lover Trouble," O'Riley said. "Just like Bette Davis." O'Riley was Luke's best friend. Luke ignored him. Luke couldn't even remember where he had slept the night before. Whose bed had he kicked back the sheets from that morning? He was on the run. This was the chase sequence from a B-movie. Suicide wasn't the answer. Homicide was. Why should he kill himself when he could kill his lover? No court in San Francisco would convict him for killing the handsome, two-timing sonuvabitch.

But, he told O'Riley, murder-suicide was too gay. His lover had become too gay. Everything in San Francisco had become too gay. Castro was a cast of thousands trapped on the backlot of a weird movie studio that kept shooting the same film loop over and over. Luke resisted the casting. Everybody was looking like everybody else. Originality was so rare you could get stud fees for it.

In the mirror opposite the table where Luke and O'Riley sat, Luke studied what was left of his face. He was looking closing-time-tired at eight o'clock at night. Rub on the Noxema. What comes after Oil of Olay? Surgery of Olay. Lover trouble puts lines in your face. Especially when you love the guy with your heart as much your dick. What the fuck had they done to themselves anyway? Faggots are supposed to be their own best creation.

His lover Chuck had said to him, "Our relationship is noble and manly and good." Chuck had looked directly in close-up into Luke's face the way Luke now looked directly into his own eyes in the mirror. Then Chuck had said, "Trust me."

That had been Luke's first mistake.

He sat in the bay of his friend O'Riley's front room. The third-floor apartment faced the huge neon marquee of the Castro Theatre directly across the street. The rosy light glowed so warm and bright that O'Riley rarely turned on a lamp until the marquee went dark after the start of the last feature.

"*Trust*," O'Riley prodded. "You drifted off on *trust*."

"Betrayal." Luke toyed with nasty word associations the way he played with the antique silver spoon next to his empty coffee mug. "I should never have trusted any man living in San Francisco."

Sounds of bumper-to-bumper cars, pickups, and bikes rose with a mix of bar-music from the street below.

"San Francisco isn't a city," Luke said. "It's a hunting ground. First you have to be good-looking. Second you have to be hot. Third you have to be kinky. That's the Castro Breaks."

O'Riley was the Mary Worth of listeners. His Mr. Coffee gurgled on his spit-waxed sideboard bought downstairs at The Gilded Age. A Warhol print of Marilyn hung in a chrome frame on the soft mauve wall. "You trusted the wrong guy," he said.

Luke twisted the spoon once used by stars in the studio commissary before the MGM auction. He was intent. Intense. "Do you know what it's like to look into eyes like Chuck's and see yourself reflected in each deep blue pupil? A lover's eyes are a doublefuck."

"I thought you disliked the term *lovers*," O'Riley said.

"We both hate the label."

"But you are lovers."

"No." Luke was definite. He set the spoon down precisely on the wooden table. "No." He hesitated. "Yes. Okay, lovers. Jeez. Is that the only way to express it? Why not best friends, partners, fuckbuddies? Anything but *lovers*! *Lovers* is weighted with expectations."

"You're sounding like lovers."

"We're friends. Friends expect honesty, trust, a little affection."

"You get a lot of sex out of him." O'Riley needled. "A lot!"

"I love him but we're not 'in love' with each other. He says he loves me."

"I don't care what you call it! Lover trouble is so Hollywood. There's more desperate movie queens on Castro..."

"I'll kill the iron-pumping sonuvabitch! With my bare hands! I haven't pumped my own tits up on those fucking Nautilus machines for two years for nothing!" Luke heaved heavily as he spoke, his pumped-up pecs rising and falling.

Luke's lover Chuck was a bodybuilder. Tall, dark, handsome. A looker. A real show-stopper. In the first days of their relationship, Luke had adjusted fast to the fact that his new friend was everybody's type. "I hardly have any friends." Chuck had confided. "They all want to be fans." He had said it with no vanity. And Luke loved him for it. He had seen cars at 18th and Castro rear-end each other. He had seen guys fall up the steps at Paperback Traffic. He had watched the crowd in the Norse Cove grow quiet as he and Chuck walked in to order jack-omelettes with a side of cottage cheese. Luke had never heard of omelettes. He couldn't remember anybody back in the Midwest eating omelettes for brunch. Straight people ate eggs for breakfast.

"Nobody knows the cause of homosexuality," Luke said to O'Riley. "I think it's caused by omelettes and brunch."

O'Riley poured the coffee into the mugs. Perfectly. Like a scene from one of those old Warner Brothers seven-hanky weepers. "Your problem," O'Riley said, "is that you never really moved to San Francisco. You moved to Castro." Then, acknowledging the keys hanging on Luke's belt, left side, he added, "Excuse me. And to Folsom." He stirred his coffee with the spoon Luke had tossed aside. "Do those keys mean something or are they just junk jewelry?"

"Funny. But not very." Luke took a hit of the steaming coffee.

"*Left* means...*Top?*" O'Riley drew out the sentence for sarcastic effect.

"*Left* means *negotiable.*"

"How gay!"

"You got it. Gay! Chuck came from a dirt farm in Oklahoma. He had a great career in Kansas City as an attorney. His very attraction was that he was an unspoiled authentic male. No pretensions. His straightforward preference for men never spilled over into fag behavior." Luke warmed to the thought of those first days when Chuck had visited San Francisco. "Before he moved here, he used to describe Castro as the place where you could, unfortunately, see men doing to themselves things you hoped you'd never see men do to themselves. He used to insist that homosexuals don't have to be gay."

O'Riley hid his chuckle behind his coffee mug muttering something about protesting a bit too something or other. "I know," he said. "I hear all these reactionary types saying they prefer to be called queers, faggots, cocksuckers."

"Sounds to me like they're into what those sleazy *Drummer* ads call VA."

"Excuse me. I was a nun in my last existence. What's VA?" O'Riley asked.

"VA. Verbal Abuse. A sexual humiliation trip."

"Oh. You mean like the Governor of Nevada calling us *queers* when he doesn't want to rent state property for the Gay Rodeo?"

"Chuck coined the term *homomasculine.* He says manhood is more than sex. He says homosexuality focuses too much on the genitals. He says homomasculine men shouldn't ape heterosexual coupling. He says we should live in an open fraternity."

"Your Mr. America sounds like the Oracle of Delphi. Only piled higher."

"Some guys are lucky," Luke said. "Natural stars. As smart as they are good-looking. Good genes. Good grooming."

"Good drugs," O'Riley countered. "Some guys pump up their bubbletits with steroids. Just like your little Chuckie—I've seen him pop those little blue pills. This season they're the in-drug on Castro. With enough steroids, cottage-cheese omelettes, and workouts at the gym, a guy can pump himself up like a bloated dog in the noonday sun. Don't you try and tell me that all of Chuck's unnaturally natural beauty is genetic and athletic."

"You're sounding envious." Luke spread a small smile on wry.

"I've looked in your refrigerator. I can read. I saw the package of anabolic steroids. Nandolone Decanoate. And the needles. How long has he been shooting himself up? Since before he won those physique contests, I'll bet."

"So what?' Luke resisted out of habit any attacks on Chuck.

"I guess," O'Riley said, "there's a little bit of Faust in all of us."

"In San Francisco you don't deal with people, you deal with the drugs they're on. What's the difference if it's coke, Quaaludes, or steroids?"

"Every faggot wants to be Judy-Judy-Judy. Uppers in the morning. Downers at night and fucked senseless by rough trade till dawn."

"Shut your mouth! Judy was a good woman." Luke was firm.

"You want tea and sympathy?"

"I'm here for nothing more than to watch the rosy glow of the Castro Theatre marquee be kind to your face. If wrinkles hurt, you'd be screaming."

"How'd you like a mouth full of bloody Chicklets? Some fags deserve bashing." O'Riley enjoyed tripping Luke's circuits.

"How can you stand living right on Castro? Your address is a cliché." Luke said. "Your zip code is as much a sign of your sexual deviancy as all this designer crap you bought on sale at Work Wonders. Shit! Work Wonders! That ought to be the name of a gym." Luke was pissed. "Designer apartments. Designer muscles."

"So what's wrong with gay guys pumping a little natural muscle on their bodies? Even if half of them ride their Nautilus machines sidesaddle. Makes them look like healthy cadets from some military academy. I live on Castro because I figure with so many All-American boys on the hoof, there must be a prep school somewhere in the neighborhood. How else can you account for it? Just like a college town. The Norse Cove is the dining room of the city's largest Animal House."

"You're a bitch."

"You're a bastard."

"Do you have the strange feeling we're doing the Hepburn-Finney dialogue from the final scene of *Two for the Road*?" To O'Riley, life was a movie to be edited in the living of it. In this at least, he was in total accord with Luke—and the Castro Street millions.

Luke couldn't let the conversation stray too far from Chuck. "I have the strange feeling I've been seduced and abandoned by my fuckbuddy partner who has betrayed homomasculine fraternity and has gone gay, Gay, GAY!"

"Would a guy with muscles do that?"

"When he moved here directly into my apartment, he was pure, unspoiled, a golden god..."

"And now he's a muscleclone whose only visible means of support is the window ledge on the front of Donuts and Things.

"You have a way with words," Luke said. "I'm not sure I like it."

"Come off it. I've watched that little group of tittypumpers you and he hang out with leaning in the sun for fucking hours in front of those jelly-filled donuts. Don't you get tired drinking all that coffee from those yellow wax cups? And why are you the only one who keeps your shirt on? You may not have all the muscle, but they certainly treat you like one of the boys."

"Fuck you."

"Isn't that what you've always wanted to be? One of the boys?" O'Riley unscrewed an imaginary pill bottle. "Have a steroid. Take two. They're small. Try a handful. Be one of the boys! Stand in front of that fucking donut shop and watch your livers turn to green pudding and drain out onto the sidewalk. One of a dozen side-effects. No wonder Chuckie's favorite movie *is High Anxiety.*"

"He says he likes it because it's so unusual to see a group of

Jewish actors having fun."

"I told you he's a fascist. Homomasculine fraternity, my ass! He's a sexual fascist! He even wears that muscle-cut teeshirt that says 'Only The Strong Shall Survive.'"

"Don't get politically correct on me. I'll throw up." Luke rubbed his stomach.

"Those little muscle pumpers won't fuck with anybody who isn't better built, or who isn't better looking and hot or who doesn't work out at the same gym. Maybe that's what your Arnold Chauvinegger calls fraternity. That's not brotherly. That's sexual fascism. I'm down on what's happened to my neighborhood."

"I'm sorry we all helped it happen. Mecca became a ghetto. The ghetto stratified. Lots of guys are leaving the City."

"I don't know what those muscle freaks see in you. Either you've got the biggest dick in San Francisco, or Chuck's the biggest bottom in town." O'Riley grinned. "I know you do love to use your whips and chains and tit clamps." He mock-rubbed his tongue around his lips. "How big *is* your dick?"

"Twelve inches."

"Only if I let you fuck me twice." O'Riley grinned.

"We've never fucked."

"We never will fuck. That's why we'll always be good friends. That's why you'll still be sitting at my table drinking my coffee ten years from now. Long after Chuckie's dead and gone from steroid rot. But I suppose you'll still be at home alone, stoned, running all those videotapes you shot of him posing in body-beautiful contests and of him jerking off his big cock in your bedroom."

"He *is* hung. Not all bodybuilders are compensating."

"Spare me. You know I've never been susceptible to his charms."

"I don't care about how he looks or how he's hung or how great he's built or how good we are together in bed. He can get old and sick and skinny and impotent...

"With steroids, he will."

"...I'll still love him."

"Hum me 'Hearts and Flowers.'" O'Riley made a small violin: forefinger over thumb.

"Hey! I need somebody. So why not the best somebody?"

"Everybody needs somebody...or settles for somebody."

"I think, I mean, I thought..."

"Funny how verb tenses changes when an affair is breaking up."

"I think I need him. I know I want him. Not exclusively. Not all the time. We have threeways. We both fuck on the side."

"So what exactly is the problem?" O'Riley wanted a bull's eye.

"He's spoiling himself, turning gay, prick-teasing guys who honestly like him when he has no intention of following through and fucking with them."

"That's turning *very* gay." O'Riley was no fool. His sex life was a knockout. He got exactly what he wanted from young street hustlers he rented by the hour from the Tenderloin and off Market Street. "I have little patience for anybody who isn't getting what he wants. And even less for somebody who is getting maybe what he deserves."

"What's that mean?"

"I know you've taken steroids too."

"For four fucking weeks, big deal! The anxiety they cause made me stop."

"Why were you so stupid to take them?" O'Riley's disgust was not feigned.

"I wanted to keep up. I wanted to be able to keep on keeping on with him."

"So where do you get off thinking you're so much purer than him?"

"Fuck off. I'm not. Everything I say about him is just as revealing about me. Whose life is it anyway? Mine. Besides, it takes two," Luke said.

"Really? I always think of Castro somehow as half of Noah's Ark. You know: one of every kind!"

"Maybe it's not him. Maybe it's just my life we're talking

about. Maybe I've stayed too long at the fair." Luke's thoughts sometimes ran like Streisand lyrics about somebody done somebody wrong.

"Aren't we all just playing the lead in our own little movies." O'Riley liked to score points. "Chuck's only a supporting character, after all. Not your co-star." He absently fingered several snapshots of his street boys lying on some books stacked neatly at the edge of the table. They were basically heterosexuals. With their own brand of bullshit. They stayed straight even when they laid their ass on the line for a john. They made plain and simple distinctions. Nothing complicated. O'Riley, at thirty-two, had long before lost his taste for Byzantine gayboy games.

"I need somebody kind of special." Luke said. "Chuck has some body, but maybe he no longer has his soul. Maybe he sold it for all that physical beauty. Steroids screw up the personality. Maybe his own good looks have betrayed his soul the way I feel he's betrayed the one main thing I gave him in love. The only thing one man can ultimately really honor another with: trust."

"You expect me to believe that you love that stereotype for more than his face? He may not be my type but I know what a heartbreaker he is on the street."

Sometimes Luke felt like he was Dirk Bogarde pining on the beach over Tadzio in the last reel of *Death in Venice*. "Listen. I had to work around the fact he was supergorgeous in order to get at his real self."

"Just like he had to work around the fact that you're not supergorgeous to get at your real soul," O'Riley said.

"I tell him the truth. Nobody else ever tells him the truth. They tell him what they think he wants to hear on the outside chance that they'll get in his pants. Chuck has the most-kissed ass on Castro."

"He loves you for your mind. Right? You may not look more than average but you've got a great personality. Right?"

"I thought it could work both ways," Luke said.

"Chuckie likes big strong 18-inch arms." O'Riley could rub in salt with the best.

"He'll never find bigger arms than mine to embrace him."

"So he's built like a brick shithouse and you've got that wonderful skinny euphemism: a swimmer's body. What do you two do in bed anyway? Everybody at the Norse Cove is taking bets."

"I know. Him into muscles. Me into leather." Luke grinned.

"How do you two put it together? Exactly? For two years all I've gotten from you is vague generalities about long hot nights of sex, drugs, and rock 'n' roll. I know you're both animals."

"We do what Oscar winners do when they get home from the Dorothy Chandler Pavilion—we fuck. With the physique trophies in the bed. Or at least that's what we did the night he won his first contest."

"Cute." O'Riley rolled his eyes.

"He calls me 'Coach.'"

"I'm beginning to sense who's on top."

"Can you imagine what it's like to lay a first-place bodybuilder the night he's won four trophies? Can you imagine what it's like to lift up a pair of legs that have just won Best Legs in California and fuck his ass?"

"I think I can imagine it." O'Riley said and hit his coffee deliberately. "That's the problem. That's why you've got Lover Trouble. That's why you can't sleep. That's why he's out prick teasing without putting out on his big macho come-hither look."

"I don't get it."

"You're running around with a muscle-ninny who can't believe—and won't admit—he likes a brainy, sex-talkative type like you who knows how to play his head like a banjo...and fuck his ass!"

"He keeps whispering to me late at night that next to jerking off, I'm the best sex he's ever had," Luke said.

"So to you he'll admit it. But his build and his face require a certain cool attitude. I'll bet he can't admit he's a queer cocksucker."

"He'd never say those words."

"That's the trouble with that whole twisted little group of bodybuilders who pose at being carpenters and painters and construction workers. They can't stand the fact, the *fact,* man, that they're gay. Not homomasculine. Not homomuscular. Not homodiddlyshit." O'Riley looked hard into Luke's face.

"I think they have a harder time than the rest of us."

"Don't cry for me, San Francisco." O'Riley pushed his chair back in disgust.

"Seriously. Deep down they think *straight is* better." Luke was making an earnest plea for them. "They see their bodies, their clothes, their work so close to being straight that they're crazed to pass for straight. They even talk about 'passing.'" Luke had sort of bought the bodybuilder script.

"Like a butch bunch of good niggers!" O'Riley shot back. "Shit! Give me a good honest clone or queen any day. And still they need honest, gay, faggot queers like you to worship them, adore them, keep them. Muscles are just another fetish. Right behind dirty jockstraps and cigars."

"I like big guys. I like muscle. I like the jock look," Luke insisted.

"Bodybuilders are a crock. They're all hustlers. Economic, emotional, you name it. They need transfusions of energy. They have to replace all the energy they put out in the gym." O'Riley sucked air through his teeth. "Hustlers. I know from hustlers. My life is young street trash. Believe me. Chuck is a hustler."

"No," Luke said almost too emphatically. "That's not true. He hates hustlers. He wrote an anonymous letter to *Iron Man* magazine exposing his feelings about the muscle-hustling scene. Guys do their posing routines straddling various doctors' chests. The doctor jerks off. They collect their modeling fees in oral and injectable steroids. Chuck refused to do that. He hates muscle-hustlers."

"Did he share your rent for the last two years?"

Luke hesitated a moment too long.

"See. He's *not* a hustler *only* if you play semantics. And, God, how you two like to play semantics. Call him a mercenary. That's a fashionable word these days. El Salvador, Angola, all that *Soldier of Fortune* magazine crap."

"Don't," Luke said.

"Why not? You need some truth. Is this a war movie? Are we all supposed to be nice to bodybuilders because their gym class leaves at dawn?"

"Shut up," Luke said.

"Castro may be the Western Front but unlike you we won't all be quiet. Not when a select little fascist group starts hustling, cannibalizing, exploiting, vampirizing the rest of us just because they've got big pecs and biceps. Bodies may be what a lot of guys think man-to-man sex is all about. But any guy who's been around the block knows it's more than just standup sex in a backroom. And I don't see anything wrong with that either. Sometimes when you're fed up and worn out with interpersonal relationships, nothing feels better than an honest impersonal sex encounter. Frankly, that's what you need. Some no-obligation, no-expectation fun-for-the moment sex."

"Ain't you just the Oracle of Delphi yourself."

"I know what works for me. Period. Right now you don't know what works for you. That's all I'm saying. Have a tenth-rate nervous breakdown over the sonuvabitch if you must. Moviequeens love mad scenes. Enter innocent as Juliet. Exit mad as Ophelia."

"I love him."

"Isn't that from *West Side Story?*" O'Riley was a thesaurus of lyrics.

"What?"

"'I love him. I'm his...'" O'Riley sang. Off-key.

"Yeah. I suppose. 'And everything he is. I am too.'"

"Don't you just wish!" O Riley laughed.

"Cunt!"

"So what are you going to do while Mr. Gorgeous prick-teases his way through the Castro letting only the favored ones feel up his baseball-sized biceps?"

"I told him he can have anything he wants." Luke said.

"That's what I always tell my hustlers too."

"I mean it."

"We always mean it—until after we cum." O'Riley leaned in close to the table.

"So what am I going to do? Commit suicide or commit murder?"

"Just wait. Wait it out. Wait till he finds that he's never going to find a jerk or a john who loves him more than you do. More, by the way, than he deserves. And hope while you're waiting that the steroids don't kill him with cancer before he realizes what he's got in you."

"And what should I do while I wait?"

"Beat off. Sleep around. Become a masochist. I don't know." O'Riley drained the last of his coffee. "Maybe just be there when he comes crashing down." He stopped. "He will come crashing down, this high-flying adored of yours. We all come crashing down. You, me, him, Evita. Sooner or later we all regret our high-wire acts, swinging nights from the chandeliers, without a net." O'Riley reached across the table and held Luke's hand. "Don't spin your wheels too long. Don't waste your energy. Remember *Carousel* when Shirley Jones sang, 'What's the use of wondrin' if the ending will be sad.'"

"I'm not wondering. I've tried to be the gentleman he always wanted us both to be. I'm not masochistic enough, maybe not at all, certainly not enough to do this self-effacing bit. I've got a lot of anger. A lot of anger. A whole lot of anger I don't know what to do with. We've never even had a fight. We've never in two years yelled at each other. Now I have all this anger," Luke said.

"Then one afternoon when he's out preening in the sun with the boys," O'Riley began, "you head on in to the Star Pharmacy and buy a couple bottles of something really scuzzy like *Jade East* cologne and walk up to him and slosh it all over him. If he's gotten as gay as you say, and truly as tacky in public as I've seen, with all those other voluptuous muscle showgirls, he'll love it."

Luke grinned at the scenario. "He's so proud of his big biceps," he said. "I'd rather take out a contract and have both his arms broken. Make him into the Venus de Milo of Castro. I'd like to see what his vanity-pump looks like after six weeks in a pair of casts!"

"I love these anti-masculine *Nine-to-Five* fantasies," O'Riley said. "Just like Fonda and Tomlin and Parton ganging up on a defenseless man."

"He told me he feels so empty. He told me how much he really dislikes all those other muscle guys. He says they don't have the symmetry, the face, the look. He plays up to them because he likes the way they all play up to him."

"Mutual ass-kissers. Real vanity. Narcissus drowning in steroids."

"I hate him. I love him. I want to sleep with him tonight," Luke said. "Omigod. Passion. I have such passion."

"This is a small town. Word travels fast. I've heard he owes money."

"There's more gossip than truth on Castro. Everybody owes money to somebody. These are hard times."

"I suppose it's not hustling when you just borrow," O'Riley said softly.

"Don't be cynical about him. Please. Don't believe all the street talk. Chuck's not evil. He's not a hustler. In his heart, he's a gentle man. It's just..." Luke's voice trailed off.

"Just what?"

"Just that moving to the City has turned his head a little."

"And he's turned a few heads."

"So why's he punishing me?" Luke hurt way deep down. More than he ever thought he could hurt. "Because I told him the truth?"

"Kings used to kill the messenger who brought them the truth."

"He asked me. He honest-to-God asked me why he was so unhappy here in San Francisco. I made a mistake. I told him what I thought. That maybe even he can't have everything he wants the way he wants. Everything he owns is at my house. His clothes. His trophies. How can a man so strong be so fragile? He's on the run. It's like he won't..."

"...can't..."

"...face me." Luke was stymied. "Why's he so embarrassed? Why is he making me feel so embarrassed?"

"Because you are a famous couple. Visible. Because you know about him. He never suspected anyone would ever get to know him the way you penetrated his defenses." O'Riley spoke deliberately. "You know the private truth. He's paranoid that your information will become ammunition."

"I told him I was a safe person. I told him for two years that he could hide out in me whenever he wanted." Luke raised his eyes to the soft glow of the ceiling. "I'd never hurt him. Not anymore than you hurt a hysterical person when you slap him." His lower face pulled taut. Lines formed. He held back on the cry being pinched out by the hurt. "Omigod. I love him."

"For two years, he took, right? He took. You gave."

"He gave too. Some things. But now he's hiding. He won't let me give. Not anything."

"That's a reverse hustle. That's a sting!"

Luke had not intended any of this to go this way. He had not known exactly when his life had turned into a grade-B movie. He had read somewhere that in an hour of film you actually watch twenty-seven minutes of total darkness. Your eye chooses to watch the light of the fast-illuminated single frames flashing one after the other through the projector and onto the screen. If the film slows down, like in old-time movies, the screen seems to flicker. Luke was afraid. He was beginning to see life that way. He was beginning to see the darkness between the frames. There was really no such thing as a moving picture. Just a barrage of fast stills. The film could slow down. He could see the darkness. The celluloid could break.

"I have nothing to say about human sexual relationships." O'Riley said.

"Except," Luke could feel the flicker, "they don't work."

"Of course not. They're illusions. They pretend to work. Relationships are at best a truce." O'Riley pushed himself back from the table. The glow of the Castro marquee haloed his strawberry-blond hair. "My father told me that for forty years he woke up in the morning and looked my mother straight in the eye everyday and said in a very calm voice: 'Now don't start anything and there won't be anything.'"

"That's cynical."

"That's finite truth. It sums up the whole big deal of human relationships. He just wanted a truce."

"I hate it all." Luke couldn't finish his coffee. It would keep him awake, and he didn't know where he would sleep that night.

Across Castro, an usher in a brown leather jacket was up on a ladder changing the theater marquee. His hands shifted the last letters of a Woody Allen title around to spell out *Casablanca*.

"Did you see the Allen film?" O'Riley asked.

"Chuck says he's too New York, too Jewish, too bleak. He doesn't like him."

"No wonder. Allen's good at relationships. Real good—at dissecting them."

Luke couldn't face going back to the apartment to find Chuck gone again. He knew he was going to have to throw him out. Everybody in town wanted Chuck in the sack and he was going to throw him out. It would be a new experience for Chuck, but it gave Luke small satisfaction. He'd be left alone in his apartment, like someone sitting by the side of the road at the scene of an accident.

"At the beginning we're all charming." O'Riley said. "At the end, we're all assholes. Allen has this girl accusing him, 'But you're not like we were at the beginning. You were so charming.' And Allen says, 'I was just doing my mating thing. I was using up all my energies. I couldn't keep doing this. I'd go crazy!'"

"So that's what people do?"

"At the beginning, the movie we're living is no different from the movies we watch. At the beginning, you think you're both so intelligent, so full of life the first few days, weeks, months. Then reality creeps in. You start accusing each other of leaving jockstraps on the floor and dishes in the sink. You call each other idiots. You leave angry notes about who owes exactly what on the phone bill."

If Chuck was gone all night again, Luke figured, why should he sleep alone, just on the outside chance he'd come home. He'd be better off heading down to the Brig to find someone negotiable to cuddle with.

"Maybe I'll join the exodus from San Francisco. Move north to Sonoma County. Get back to what I came out for. Unspoiled men. I think the dream here in Mecca is over."

He said sort-of goodnight to O'Riley and walked down the three flights and out onto Castro. The usher across the street was standing on the sidewalk studying the lettering on the marquee. He was wiping his nose in a red handkerchief he stuffed back into his right pocket.

Luke figured maybe he'd go take in *Casablanca* the next night. "Here's looking at you, kid." And all that bitter sweet farewell stuff.

He walked uphill toward Market Street, away from 18th.

A young guy leaning against the Bank of America said, "Joints?"

Luke wasn't at all sure of what he'd think about tomorrow when today would be yesterday.

Mickey Squires

**Why, when the temple is finished,
must the God depart?**

The Best Dirty-Blond
Contractor in Texas

Last summer, Kick was my general contractor. "They been cal-lin' me Kick since high school." His drawl was West Texas. His build was blond brick shithouse. "One night after practice, the wrestlin' coach hears all this commotion in the showers. So in he comes, voice first, shoutin', 'Hey! What's the problem?'"

Kick stretched out the length of my couch. "There wasn't no problem," he said. "Just the wrestlin' squad horsin' around. You know? Wet towels snappin' at wet butts."

He looked good laid back on the canvas dropcloth. "The coach was a big fucker. Dark. Handsome. I remember him strut-tin' into the shower half-stripped himself. Torn VMI tanktop. Big bulgin' jockstrap. And a pair of sweaty gym socks that had worked their way down his hairy calves."

Southern men take their old sweet time, lingering on every detail. Kick was no different. I handed him a beer. He was smil-ing a big grin at his reminiscence.

"All us guys freeze, see, right where he catches us. The noise dies down to the hiss of the showerheads. The squad's all lath-ered up. Big ol' healthy country boys! Soap runnin' outta our pits, down our bellies, and off our crotches. The coach stops stock still. Big arms crossed on his big pecs. Legs spread. He had a mean streak, and a look-to-kill on his face. He studied us one by one. Tryin' to find the rough-housers."

Kick paused. He looked hot as hell himself in his jockstrap and his heavy, cotton plaid shirt. His sleeves, rolled up tight past his thick forearms, nearly split apart around his baseball biceps. "Anyway, all us wrestlers freeze where he nailed us. Me? I'm caught in the middle of the shower. Buck-ass naked. With him squared off at me directly. He checks out every face. When his eye meets mine, I kind of hit him with my best shot. You know: without changin' my not-so-innocent expression, there I stand, this adolescent jock, sort of challengin' this bodybuilder coach whose brother's a fuckin' Texas Ranger!"

Kick's hands, square and hard from gripping his 28-pounder hammer day after day, lay palm down, with his callouses slowly stroking his peeled-open faded 501 crotch.

"Our eyes lock. Somethin' flashes between us. He drops his eyes, real deliberate and slow, sizin' me up as maybe the ring-leader. Then he catches a load of my dick. Can y'all see it? His big arms unfold even slower. He rests his chalk-covered hands on the waistband of his jockstrap." He imitated the coach's redneck voice: "Jeezus H. Keerist!"

Kick enjoyed telling on himself.

"Then this fuckin' coach, who's got a rep as the biggest stud around town, lifts his eyes off my dick, and looks me straight in the face, like, maybe he's noticin' for the first time some home-grown competition that he's gonna have to either put up with, or put down some."

Kick stretched out his muscular left leg from his butt, then rocked his construction-booted foot slowly back and forth, snapping his ankle with cracks like far-off rifle fire. He slowly savored this part of the story. He dropped his left boot, topped by sweaty gray wool sock, down across his right foot.

"So the coach stands there in the middle of all the steaming water sizin' me up. Not sure whether to buddy me up or punk me down. The whole wrestlin' squad's open-mouthed. Then, 'Son,' he says, 'you shoulda been born a bicycle—hung with a kickstand like that!'"

Kick's square jaw, covered with two-days' growth of dirty-blond bristle, smiled. "So I been called Kick ever since."

I walked toward him, knelt next to him on the couch, and

buried my face on the warm manpack of his crotch. His hot balls hung big under his animal-size dick. He rubbed his hard hand soft across the back of my head, and flexed his butt, pushing his crotch up into my face. He smelled the way only a dirty-blond working man can smell: with the sweet raunch that comes naturally from hard, honest labor.

That summer, Kick was more than my general contractor.

I had hired him first for business, but we hung around each other for pleasure. He was my type. He was everybody's type. He said he felt there was no bullshit between us. We kept life simple. Clear. In my nearly finished house, we slept in the same bed that we fucked in. We played sexual muscle games and fetish fantasies. We had free rein with each other and with any other men we wanted. We lived our days of heaven moving through a fraternity of tradesmen. We checked out the subcontractors Kick hired: beefy masons; tattooed young plumbers; smooth-skinned framing carpenters; muscular roofers, tanned and shirtless, jeans spattered with asphalt.

Kick was no handyman fixing up a remodel. He was a licensed general contractor building my new house. His eyes, the same steel blue as his tempered hammerhead, could size up a situation, or another man, fast. He could shoot the shit with the best; and he was as good as his word. His subs respected him. His construction crews idolized him. The ladies at the County Permit Office swooned for him. Me? I loved him.

"I want to build you a house," he said, "that men look good in."

Kick had taken his southern redneck look and turned his naturally athletic body, through heavy weight training, into handsome muscle-bulk, carved with definition and roped with vascularity. His blond body was hairy. He stored a clippers in the bathroom to trim back, but not fully shave, the pelt on his big pecs and washboard belly. Thick spun gold covered his forearms, the back of his hands, and his fingers. His barbered hair, clipped close on the nape of his neck, and shaved and snipped around his ears, ran the full blond spectrum from dark through dirty-blond to golden.

His jaw grew black-blond bristle fast. He kept his thick moustache clipped closer to classic regulation than a State Trooper. His blond moustache was a golden brush, trimmed straight across the precise line of his disciplined upper lip. Men, even straight men, read his construction-muscle look, and watched his handsome blond face break into a grin wide as Texas. His killer smile narrowed his focused eyes, and sent that blond moustache, that had become his trademark, spreading across the pickets of his perfect white teeth.

To clients and crew, Kick was as ideal a general contractor as he had been, back in high school that next season under that wrestling coach, a perfect senior varsity captain. The dark-haired coach, Kick confessed one night, had wrapped his big arms around Kick's body; and Kick had hugged him back like he had always known the way two men use their big arms to pull their bodies tight together, muscle-to-muscle. The coach had rubbed off on Kick. It showed. Kick had grown up to be the way a man should be. He had achieved the look of a man in authority. He was born with the gift, coached further into it, and he learned how to present it. The Authority of Command Presence. Other men took to it, and because of it, to him, and because of him, to me, and all together for that year we had a hard-balling good time.

Kick and I were Hunters. We both loved men. Masculine men. We checked out the places where men move and talk and smell like men: building supply yards; construction diners; cop bars; truck stops; straight gyms; athletic events: collegiate wrestling and gymnastics, professional powerlifting, and physique competitions. At more than one bodybuilding contest, sitting in the audience with my left hand tucked under my right arm and resting on Kick's massive guns, I knew that his build could have beaten any muscleman on stage. I savored what his big blond uncut muscle-dick tasted like in my mouth. We shared real personal secrets.

We were Fetishists. We got hard zooming in on the way

men's clothes rode their bodies: the collar on a faded flannel shirt, frayed by rubbing against a sun-leathered neck; tanktops, their white ribs stretched to a hole, then a run, tearing over the big full bulge of hard pecs; heavy cotton teeshirts, size-large, whose sleeves fit tight around pumped biceps, and whose massive shoulders stretched the cotton tight across chests, dropping it tentlike, full and loose, down over the tight abs; heavy wool socks and boots and sneakers on hard working calves; gymshorts exposing thick thunder-thighs; tight, bulging jock pouches with flat sweaty bands framing hard Dallas linebacker butt; the squared-off look of a motorcop's helmet chinstrap, his reflective sunglasses, his wool shirt bulked out with Second-Chance body armor, his badge on his chest, his utility belt: cuffs and gun riding over his breeches and knee-high black boots, his thin black-leather gloves turned down from his gold watch band on his thick wrist.

Kick and I were Harvesters. We "found" men's clothes: scouted, hunted, harvested, "borrowed" them, and fucked, jerking off wearing the stuff men had somehow carelessly "lost." The Harvest List was long: a bodybuilder left his posing trunks dangling on a bench in the green room after the Mr. West Texas Contest; a framing carpenter forgot a pair of sweat-smooth leather gloves that tasted of his handsalt; a finishing carpenter left hanging on a nail the pit-soaked sweatshirt he'd stripped off in the heat of the day; a plumber, showering at the house before a date, changed to his sports clothes and forgot his white cotton jockey shorts with a single skidmark where the briefs had ridden up the crack of his sweet male butt.

Kick and I were Hunters and Fetishists and Harvesters. Making love to each other in my nearly completed house, we made love to all men everywhere. Nightly in my bedroom, we both knew our moves to conjure on the clothes we "borrowed."

Pulling on his harvested coconut-oil-stained posing trunks, Kick walked into the tracklight can-spot mounted in the raw-beamed ceiling of my bedroom. His cockring made his kick-stand dick fill the tan nylon briefs like a raging hardon. He moved his massive muscular body through his posing routine with all the grace of a stud put out to show.

Kick radiated Command Presence.

His blond hair and moustache caught the intense pinpoint spot. His arms grew massive, as his fist pumped up his forearm, and his forearm leveraged his biceps to their knotted peak. The triceps and delts on the back of his upper arm popped alive.

We had these evenings, these special evenings, when together we stroked dick and pumped muscle and pushed out the bounds of the finite.

Kick was changing now, taking off on the male energy stored in the muscleman's trunks. I knelt in close to him, feeling the heat of the spotlight mix with the heat of his sweating body. We locked our energies together. He nodded, and I squeezed pure olive oil into my hands and slicked up his hairy bodybuilder physique. Construction work had tanned his blond skin a deep brown in the Texas sun while intensifying the golden fur matting his legs, butt, belly, chest, and arms.

In the mirrors opposite us, I could see him changing, evolving, becoming, transcending.

The line of his jaw bit down as he flexed his shoulders, neck, pecs, lats, arms, and legs. His neck became a vascular, vein-popping column of muscle. Tense. His broad shoulders mounded like symmetrical scoops of bronzed ice cream. His pecs filled: lower and upper. He flexed and rolled them. Striations of muscle appeared through his paper-thin skin.

He nodded for a hit of popper. We shared it.

He moved into a right bicep shot, adding a left. His body quivered with excitement. His arms were his big guns. He dropped his left arm straight on down to a classic fist. He opened and closed his fist, pumping up the power in his forearm: the kind a man likes to sit on. The veins and cuts rose, wrist to elbow, and flowed, almost by his sheer willpower, to his upper arm into a lightening display of vascular muscle. He swung his right arm up, moving his inner right bicep close in toward his face, bending his elbow and dropping his forearm, wrapping his cupped hand around the back of his clipped blond hair. Now full profile, moustache and tongue first, he nosed deep into his armpit, hairy and sweaty and corded with the power of that private spot where arm and shoulder and back and chest muscles all converge and connect.

Our faces met in his muscle 'pit. I ran my nose and my own moustache across his moustache, breathing in his hot panting breath. He held the pose, generously, giving me luxurious time to nose down and tongue his 'pit, and lick and stroke my way closer into the mystery and manifestation of muscle than most men—even musclemen—ever get, because Kick knew all the secrets.

I worshiped muscle. I beat my meat with my right hand. I stroked his oily muscle with my left. We moved, flowed, from pose to pose, playing with the light, with the oil, with the mix of his muscle look and my worshiping look in the mirrors in the half-finished bedroom.

Kick stripped off the posing trunks. I wrung his sweat into my mouth. His huge dick, free of the briefs, sprang to hard life. I handed him the Crisco. He lubed up his hand and greased his throbbing dick with his fingertips. He smiled at me kneeling next to his cock, between his huge legs. I reached for the coke. He pulled open the head of his dirty-blond uncut meat. I dropped a line deep into his piss-slit. He dropped to his knees, opposite me, and tooted me up the same. Snowed in, a hard dick can be jerked for hours, sensitized to all the stroking, but somehow anesthetized from premature cuming.

Reflected in the mirror, we knelt knees to knees, face to face. Kick loved me and I loved him and we both loved muscle. The tracklight spot beamed down on us like energy from another star. He flexed body part after body part, inches from my face. Sweat rained on us. His muscles thickened, glistened, sweated, pumped, and filled: harder, more beautiful, more powerful, more brutal, more animal. His belly defined itself to bulky abs, then split to washboard definition deeper than the fingers I rubbed through the crevasses of his rippled gut. His championship arms had grown big enough to tear the sleeves off teeshirts. His shoulders hunkered down: broad, side to side, and thick, front to back.

He raised up his shoulders and pecs, barreling out his chest, spreading his lats like angel's wings from his waist up into his dripping 'pits. His pecs raised, rolled, locked: hard. He tilted his face up to the spot light. In the mirrors for himself, and from my angle between his spread thighs, Kick's particular face became in the deep-shadowed spot, the Universal Essential Male Face. The general contractor he was disappeared behind the Blond Moustache that was no longer specifically his. He was the Universal Man. The Ultimate Blond Muscleman. From ancient god and warrior to classic athlete to contemporary male in authority.

From that Face, man-to-man, Kick's voice said to me: "It's all yours. It's all ours." We hit the popper, and, slowly, for my eyes only, he shot off pose after pose, with me licking, tonguing, sniffing, fingering, sucking, rimming, tasting, adoring, worshiping all the man-muscle that I always from my boyhood thought was possible, but thought would never happen.

I laid back on the floor. His thighs and hard dick straddled over my belly. My hand ran up across his pecs and out to his arms. My own dick, without the coke line to harden it against cuming, would have shot long before. Instead, I palmed his big balls and licked his muscle sweat from my hand. I ran my fuckfinger back between the tight crack of his ass and touched the tip to the hard bud of his hole. He flexed its circular rim. I felt the squeeze of juice and sweat soak my finger, and licked it clean.

In the heat of passion, in that light, on those nights in that house under construction, Kick was more than Kick.

I stared up at him straddling my belly. I beat my meat, adoring his man's body with my eyes and hand and hard cock. He stared into the mirror, lord of the spotlight, kneeling across an adoring man's body. He had traveled outside himself, posing, flexing, beating his own dick in total worship of Absolute Muscle.

Kick was more than Kick. He was Adam before the Fall.

He raised his right arm, flexed, and finger-combed the short clip of his dirty-blond, Brylcremed hair. He was no longer the general contractor who had arrived on my empty lot, wearing a large white cotton teeshirt that stretched, in crimson letters across his chest, the one word: TEXAS. He was no longer just one of those wild maverick young males who had grown to southern manhood listening to the Allman Brothers in the back seat of a red Mustang convertible.

His personal aura in the spotlight, in the mirror, across my belly, loomed up larger than life. He was heroic. He was the kind of leader soldiers gladly die for; the kind of champion athletes dream of becoming; the kind of lover I'd give the deed to my ranch.

Kick was a dirty-blond Muscle God.

Repeatedly he ran his callused right hand through the track-light halo of his blond hair. He tucked his nose and moustache into his muscle 'pit. With his own man's tongue he licked out the sweat of a god. His left hand took long, hard, powerful strokes on his dick: big dirty-blond dick, the tight big blond lip of uncut skin slapping back easy, exposing the rosey-blond flush so right, so singular to the head of a dirty-blond dick.

I could tell from his familiar rhythms that he was on target to shoot.

My style, each night, was to hold back innumerable chances for orgasm to wait to cum in concert with this transcendent god-manbeast straddling my body. His whole frame convulsed into the crab-pose—the most muscular pose that knocks physique audiences dead as the muscleman gathers, pumps, and hardens every single muscle in his body down to barbaric, fierce intensity. Kick's head, jaw, eyes, all locked into midspace: between the mirrors and his mind's eye, somewhere over my body.

His hand beat his meat intensely.

My hand pumped my dick against his swinging balls.

"All that muscle!" I said. "That fucking incredible muscle! I love your fucking muscle! All that dirty blond hairy animal muscle!"

His teeth grinned and gritted at the starting-trigger of my words. Guttural sounds escaped from his throat. Wild animal cries. He wanted my words. I worshiped his muscle. We worshiped all Muscle. From his cordoned neck, he roared.

Our heavy loads shot out together, primeval, volcanic, hitting his pecs and his arms, spraying my face, running down his abs, splashing my mouth.

Now that Kick has finished my house, we're not together daily. Nor need we be. His specifically picked construction crews are gone to other jobs. My bedroom is complete with his work and his energy. Whatever entity we conjured for the year Kick lived with me among the 2x4s and power tools somehow remains. Sort of like we built this house, and created for it forever a manly spirit, a muscular ghost, that in all the years to come, will, at night, when I'm alone in my bed, overshadow me with a dream of manliness and muscle from which I hope I'll never wake.

Ultimate Warrior,
Colosseum Gladiator

Earthorse

Earthorse shifted his big, blond, muscular body uneasily. He could remember nothing from before the Final War. Not his parents. Not any particular home. Nothing. He had been born, he had been taught, as part of the New Cycle. But there the teaching had shifted, divided, confusingly. Earthorse had been reared to obedience by the Matrix. But early, because of his handsome, wild good looks, other voices had whispered to him, telling him of an Outlaw Life beyond the Matrix.

Earthorse had at first been confused. He knew no certainty beyond the balance of his own brawny body. He attended to the teachings of the Matrix more than he listened to the Outlaw whisperings. He suspected that something lay beyond the Perfect Circle of the Matrix, but he had not meant to veer off the Circle. He was, after all, a superior athlete in the Federation Games. Earthorse had always been eager to please.

Ultimately, he knew, it was his very physical perfection that would cause the Matrix to torture him slowly through the Process of Perfect Harvest. Earthorse was tied in total bondage.

Earthorse understood the New Order of Things. The World Federation had reinstated the death penalty. Not in the old way. Not in the wasteful way of the old revolutions with their guillotines. Not in the cruel and unusual manner of the ancient States of the old North American continent. The Federation had shown him holographic documentaries of the old wasteful barbarities.

The day of his own sentencing, the day the Federation Didax had stared straight down into Earthorse's blue eyes to declare him unfit, perhaps, for anything but Harvest, they had immediately hosed him down, blown him antiseptically dry, and led him stripped into the Experience Therapy Chamber.

The Elite of the Federation Guards tied him naked into a contoured lounge-rack. Its leather surface was warmed from within. They strapped down, in the worthy Name of Didax, Earthorse's ankles, thighs, waist, chest, neck, and forehead. They attached small electrodes to his long thick unclipped dick, to his large furry sack of blond balls damp with sweat, to his nipples rising defenselessly on his large hairy pecs, and to his wet tongue, and to his ears. Earthorse quivered.

The Federation Guards stepped back from the lounge rack. On a signal, they showed him they could raise or lower the lounge in any part. They could rotate his big body, spotlighted under multiple laser beams, on its base. Another signal sounded, and the well-muscled Elite of the Federation Guards checked his bindings once more.

The door to the Experience Therapy Chamber opened automatically. The bare-chested Guards made way for a Federation Medax. He was like the others: perfectly built, and neither kind nor cruel. Efficiently the Medax pulled apart the lower and upper lids of first Earthorse's right eye, into which he dropped a warm solution, and then the left.

Earthorse tensed every muscle in his huge bound body.

At his signal, a brawny guard walked toward the lounge, his big commanding dick swinging down nearly the long length of his hairy thigh. He held a pair of Contagoggle Lenses that with his big fingers he slipped neatly beneath the upper and lower lids of each of Earthorse's eyes. Earthorse realized he could no longer blink. They had taken away from him his ability to look away. The Medax signaled the guards and followed them from the Experience Chamber.

Earthorse, tied into the contoured leather lounge rack, heard the door shush closed. The blue lighting that came from nowhere returned to nowhere. He lay unable to blink, alone in the darkness. He knew they wished to discipline him, even to the point of torture. They wished to edge him to repentance, to re-entry to their Circle.

He had been at the time of his capture, two days before, the most celebrated and handsome stud-athlete in the Federation.

The lounge began to undulate beneath him. He grew warm in the fetal darkness. Comfortable. He heard a faint hiss and smelled an unidentifiable smell from his childhood. The lounge moved slowly, unpredictably, like some live leather beast beneath him. His body began to flow along its hot contours like slow lava inching down a crevasse. In his darkness was no up or down. This was, Earthorse had been told, the Preparation. Before he was to be Harvested, he was to see, the Federation Didax had sternly warned him, the Enormity.

Earthorse had dared to be different.

The Federation knew that he had thought tangentially. The fundamentalist Wastrel implications (and the whole Tribunal had agreed with the Harvesting Judge) were heretically enormous. Earthorse, they accused, had not conserved. He had misappropriated psychic energy from the Federation's single-mindedness. Earthorse, the prosecutor said, had thought "tangentially." They called it that. They said he had strayed from the thinking of the Perfect Circle. He had been surprised. He had never really taken the Outlaw whisperings seriously. What he had been thinking, he had presumed was merely a distraction, a kind of daydreaming, the way he was day tripping now, bound naked and alone, with his eyes held uselessly, uncontrollably open in the darkness.

Holographic Cinema had been his pleasure since childhood. He was excited then as he was relaxed now: almost against his wish. The Holocinema had always automatically altered the viewer's consciousness. The Didax Committee had regularly transported each Youth Compound Cadre to the Holographic Cinema Domes where the Cadets witnessed Cosmic History and learned the myth and thought of the New Conservationist Culture. Earthorse's Compound Cadets had lain about helter-skelter or sat cross-legged watching in every direction inside the Dome. They had sighed almost with a single voice as the battery of lasers, hidden in the circling walls, burned silently into life.

The first two beams intersected and at the point of their intersection a chair was projected. One boy, one of a set of six clonic brothers, had tried to sit on the chair which his eyes and ears convinced him really existed. But he had fallen quickly to the padded floor of the Dome. The other Compound Cadets laughed at him. One big-armed teenage brute even punched his shoulder, but he seemed not to notice. He was dazed by the short circuit between what his senses told him existed and what his experience proved did not.

"The chair," a Voice intercommed softly, "is a hologram. A projection actualized in thin air by the intersection of laser light."

The Cadets lying obediently about sat up. Interested. They were at the time no more than sixteen and seventeen years old. The Didax Matrix had programmed this crop's sexual and asexual breeding fifteen and sixteen years before. The Cadets were perfectly formed with the hard bodies of strong young boys, and they recognized within their Compound the clear superiority in the walk, talk, and looks of the young Earthorse. Something in the slower, moseying way he moved.

"To the chair," the Voice intoned, "is added a table." Two more lasers glowed on. "And on the table, ancient writing instruments: a fountain pen and a bottle of ink . Spread beneath the table is a layer of Old Planet hay ." Another pair of lasers crisscrossed the Dome. "You may, the Matrix suggests, perceive the scent of the new-mown straw." Earthorse inhaled deeply.

"Concentrate," the soft Voice counseled. "Become the smell of the hay." Earthorse stared straight into the golden yellow straw and smiled.

"In our Cinema Sensorium," the Voice easefully continued, "each of your senses will be stimulated to consciousness levels recognizable by your mind. Until this century, the Cosmos was new. Many things lacked names. The Federation Didax makes a simple matter of waking your consciousness."

Laser light interlaced the Dome, knitting the six dimensions into projected reality: height, width, breadth, time, sound, and transcendence. Didax recreated whatever the Cadets called for. They reached for apples and their strong hard fists closed around nothing. "You must become the apple," the Voice said, and across the Dome floor the Cadets rolled and wrestled in hot panting harvest. They stretched their naked bodies to chase a laser of a galloping miniature horse. Their hands stroked nothing.

"The pony is," shouted a Dark Cadet with a beginning of fine black hair across his strong pecs, "a handsome animal."

The holographic film unreeled through the lasers. The pony galloped in circles through the Dome with the Cadets whooping behind him.

"Catch him! Catch him!" the winded Cadet shouted. "Feed him the apple!"

A large boy, it had been himself Earthorse remembered, had made a flying leap to the pony's back. He had wanted to please the darker, hairy, muscular Cadet, but he had only fallen through the projected laser pony and landed in a heap on the Dome floor.

The Dark Cadet had looked down at him. For a moment, their eyes locked, and, feeling a stirring in his young dick, Earthorse focused hard on the hairy built body straddling over him in well-hung heat. Earthorse felt droplets of sweat form on the dirty-blond bristles of his thick young moustache. The Dark Cadet slowly groped his own large balls, smiled, and said in his quiet deep voice: "You've frightened him off." The laser light and direction had changed.

"The pony's hiding in that cave," the third of the six clonic brothers shouted.

The Cadets slowed from their chase and milled about. Lying naked on the floor where he had ignominiously fallen, Earthorse tried staring straight through the laser projection. He wanted to see behind it, through it. But the Dome was filled with nothing else. The floor beneath him began to undulate.

"Come on then," the Dark Cadet said, reaching, offering Earthorse his strong hand. "Get up and follow with us."

"Why?" Earthorse asked, and the floor convulsed beneath him.

"Become one," the Voice said, "with the cave and the darkness."

"Why?" he asked the taller Dark Cadet.

"Be with us," he said. "Circle in with us as Didax has taught. You must not be willing to disbelieve in the Sensorium." Earthorse raised himself from the floor. "I will believe," he said.

The Dark Cadet smiled. His whole body flexed with a triumph of authority.

Earthorse watched him glow in the purple laser light of the cave. He reached for the Cadet's hand. The Cadet held steady. He closed his big hand around Earthorse's own large fist. He was, Earthorse knew from the heat of the Dark Cadet's hard touch, no thin-air laser projection.

As the Cadet pulled Earthorse to his feet, the other Cadets shouted at what they saw. Awed. They stood stock still, crowded together, huddled, in the roaring center of the Sensorium.

THE LASER CAVE WITH ITS DARK HORRORS FADED IN AROUND THE CADETS. NEW LASERS BURNT THICK INTO THE GLOOM. HIGH-PITCHED SCREAMS SURROUNDED THEM. THE ROLLING FLOOR TOPPLED THEM INTO SWEATING, COWERING HEAPS. THE TEMPERATURE IN THE DOME ROSE SHARPLY AND THE AIR GREW STEAMY WITH THE OLD PLANET'S POISONOUS VAPOR. EARTHORSE WAS CERTAIN ABOVE THE SHOUTING HE HEARD AN ANCIENT AUTO HORN HONKED BY THE GHOST OF A LONG-AGO INCINERATED CABBIE.

There was no ancient word or sound or sight that the Federation's Reality Retrieval Synthesizer could not in all authenticity reconstruct on computerized hologramovies. Earthorse crawled on his belly through the naked writhing Cadets. He looked for the Dark Cadet who had towered over him. He found him.

"Believe on all this," the Dark Cadet whispered so close into Earthorse's face that he could smell the fresh warmth of his sweet breath. "Become one with it."

THE CADETS CHOKED, THE AIR HAD BECOME UNBEARABLE. AN ANCIENT SUBWAY TRAIN ROARING THROUGH THE CAVE DEAFENED THEM. IN ITS WINDOWS, MUMMIES OF THE OLD PLANET HUNG WASTED AND DEAD-FACED BY ONE HAND OR THE OTHER FROM METAL POLES. THEIR GREEN FLUORESCENCE SHRANK AWAY TO A RED PINPOINT IN THE CAVE OF SHADOWS. AGAIN THE FLOOR QUAKED AND THE CAVE BURST OPEN TO THE RUSTGRAY BLOOD-SKY.

WHAT HAD HAPPENED TO THE OLD PLANET WAS HAPPENING NOW: BUILDINGS EXPLODED; BODIES ROCKETED THROUGH THE FLAMING AIR; BRIDGES

SWAYED AND COLLAPSED AS RIVERS REVERSED IN
THEIR COURSE; THE CRUST OF THE LAND BURST
APART AT ITS SEAMY FAULTS SPEWING UP THE LAY-
ERED DETRITUS OF A MILLION BURIED CIVILIZA-
TIONS; THE OCEANS SIMMERED WITH ATOMIC
BOILS, MELTING OIL TANKERS AND WARSHIPS AND
IGNITING THE SAILS OF WHITE PLEASURE SLOOPS.
THICK GREEN CLOUDS OF POISON BROKE FROM
BURIED CITY MAINS, ROILING UP TO THE ATMO-
SPHERIC SMOGSHELL WHERE THEY BURST INTO A
FIRESTORM.

The six clonic brothers curled fetally close to each other. The
other Cadets lay frozen in Armageddon terror. One of the clones
rose to all fours, retching into a Sensorium bag. Earthorse and the
Dark Cadet sat cross-legged, face to face, with their arms around
each other's big shoulders, furry chest to furry chest. Absorbing
everything. Their big dicks lying head-to-head down on the floor
between them.

THE SOUND OF THE FIRESTORM CUED UNDER,
THE EVIL PROJECTIONS DISSOLVED INTO A SINGLE
GREEN MUMMYFACE DIALING DESPERATELY FROM
A MELTING PHONE BOOTH.

Then that too faded. The lasers tuned out. The conditioned
air returned to normal. The floor of the Sensorium came to rest.
After a moment's silent debrief, the naked Cadets began laughing,
quietly at first and then wildly, like boys who have braved through
an initiation of terror. The Sensorium Dome echoed with their
laughter. The Dark Cadet laughed too. It was the way his laugh
began as a cruel snarl of upper lip under his black moustache, that
prompted Earthorse to ask: "You were frightened?"

"Frightened?" The Cadet quietly, firmly wrapped the palm of
his hard hot hand around Earthorse's big dick. He continued to
laugh. "Frightened? Of the Old Wastrels?" He gripped his hand
tighter around the lower half of Earthorse's sex muscle.

That was the moment, Earthorse now remembered, that his
Tangent had first sprouted on the outer circumference of the Per-
fect Circle of Didax and the World Federation of the Ultimate
Matrix.

Earthorse reached back. He wrapped his own hand around the dark-rooted dick of the older Cadet. He gripped the big hot shaft hard and felt the dick veins roll under his pressure.

"You're hurting me," the Cadet said. He laughed and squeezed Earthorse equally hard.

"*You're* hurting *me*," Earthorse said.

They both smiled, tightened, and then relaxed their grip. "What is your name." Earthorse did not say it like a question.

"I can become anything," the Dark Cadet said. "What difference in a name?"

"A difference to me," Earthorse said.

"Today," he said, "call me Merar."

The Cinema Sensorium exit swung open and Merar had risen, stretched his full height, soothed his dick back down to some engorged softlike thickness, and walked off to join three other older Cadets from the Federation Compound.

Earthorse had seen Merar twice since then—both times at the Federation Olympic Games; and then, curiously, a third time in a Cinema Sensorium hologramovie of Merar's winning physique performance. Earthorse himself, as part of the same programmed Matrix, had grown strong and golden. He lay awake at night with images of the Dark Cadet pounding in his head and in his dick. Earthorse was the genetically engineered Perfect Circler, so the Federation Coach had written to Didax. The sheer ability of his legs and torso and head had been honed to perfect balance. To the video holograms of his golden physique, powerful and hairy and defined, Didax had himself personally responded the way an emperor long ago responded to his Champions.

Shortly, the official Federation Sculptor had requisitioned Earthorse for the central figure in his heroic triptych commemorating the Rise of the World Federation. The Olympic Vidtex had provided the sculptor with hologramovies of Earthorse in motion; but, the sculptor had insisted, holograms would not suffice. For a painter, maybe. But a sculptor must touch. So Earthorse had been ordered to his studio where he was stripped, oiled, kneaded, and curry-combed from head to toe, each joint and muscle and bristle carefully scrutinized, manipulated, studied. Upon finishing his examination, the sculptor had pronounced

Earthorse: "Magnificent." He in his long flowing robe stood back from Earthorse's naked body as if he had himself sculpted his flesh. "Magnificent!" he repeated.

Earthorse said nothing, but the sculptor took no notice. Earthorse was losing, despite himself, the center of their Circle. The Tangent in his mind grew away from the others' common ellipse in fits and starts of illegal micrometers.

UNSETTLING DREAMS OF THE NIGHT CREPT BACK TO EARTHORSE: TWO HORSEMEN BROKE THE FLAT HORIZON. THEIR HEADS ROSE IN THE DISTANCE AGAINST THE BLUE. THEY ROCKED EASY IN THEIR ANCIENT SADDLES. THEIR HORSES SURGED AGAINST THE REINS. THE MEN WERE WARRIORS, DARK AND BEARDED. THEIR HELMETS CAUGHT THE SUN. THE MEN AND HORSES WERE ARMED WITH FUR AND LEATHER. THEY ROSE PROUDLY AGAINST THE FULL LINE OF THE HORIZON. EARTHORSE SAW BEHIND THEM A TRAIL OF DUST AS THEY MOVED IN THE SLOWMOTION DREAM OPPOSITE HIM. A ROPE STRETCHED TAUT BEHIND THE SECOND HORSEMAN. GRADUALLY HE MADE OUT THE ROPE'S BURDEN: FIRST THE BOUND WRISTS, THEN THE STRETCHED ARMS DISLOCATED FROM THE BLEEDING SHOULDERS OF THE HAIRY MUSCLED MAN WHO WAS NAKED AND DYING BUT NOT DEAD.

SILENT ABOVE THE SAD PROCESSION A GREAT BIRD HUNG MOTIONLESS, FOLLOWING THE HORSEMEN TRAWLING THE WASTREL SIDE OF HUMAN MALE-FLESH. THE BIRD CAUGHT A DRAFT AND CIRCLED TIMELESS ABOVE THE HORSEMEN. THEY RODE EVENLY ONWARD, ACROSS A RIDGE ABOVE A STILL LAKE. WAVY IN THE NOONSUN SHIMMER, THEY DOUBLED IN THE PLACID LAKE REFLECTION. THE DESCENDING HOOVES OF THE UPRIGHT HORSES MET PRECISELY THE RISING HOOVES OF THE INVERTED WATER HORSES. BELOW THEM, AND ABOVE THEM, THE CARRION BIRD CIRCLED NOISELESSLY. IN THE MOUTH OF THE BOUND

MUSCLEMAN, THIN WIRES ROLLED HIS TONGUE INTO A CYLINDER SWELLING PURPLE FROM HIS MOUTH. HIS FINGERS, BALLS, AND DICK HAD BEEN TIGHT-WIRED THE SAME. THE HORSEMEN, PROUD AND STRAIGHT, DRAGGED THE TANGENTIAL MAN, HIS MUSCLE-FLESH SCRAPING RAW, OFF INTO THE NOON BRIGHTNESS.

Earthorse had thought the dream only a memory from his secret nightmares, but a sudden shift of the recumbent lounge rack to which he was bound jerked him back into the Full Circle of the Experience Therapy Chamber. The procession of torture had frightened him in his sleep and now again. He had not noticed when exactly it was that the Sensorium lasers had slowly faded into the dark Experience Therapy Chamber.

He registered no surprise that the Federation cinefiles contained hologramovies of his most private dreams.

His mouth grew dry. He could neither blink nor turn away from the replay unreeling all around his bound body.

"As a Tangential Thinker," the soft Voice floated through the Experience Chamber, "you must try hard to refocus your increasingly short attention span on the Perfect Circle of Federation Consciousness. Without the perfection of the Circle, you are not whole. You are parts. Without rehabilitation into the Circle, your Tangential Parts will be harvested by the Federation for redistribution throughout the Matrix by Didax's order."

Laser light scanned his naked body: patches of red and violet glowed from his head and groin; his immense chest radiated magenta; his powerful legs orange. Earthorse tried to will to blend his rebellious Outlaw energies into the Perfect Blue. His were now the forbidden colors of Tangential Distraction. He strained to project the Ideal Didax Blue of Circular Consciousness. He truly wished to waste not; for without his contribution of energy, the Circle suffered.

He begged to understand. Always he had known the Whole was greater. Yet now Didax, with all the power of the Matrix behind him, would label him an Outlaw Wastrel and mark him for Harvest. Earthorse had obediently by day fit tightly into the Circle of Didax, programmed, to all their close scrutiny, quite properly; but by night the dark mustard dreams he could not control had leaked, tangentially, he guessed, from some atavistic activity of his steaming pituitary. Earthorse had been alarmed, afraid of the cold sweats of his naked sleep giving him away. He was hardly surprised when the Compound Night Monitor had cautioned him suddenly one morning, almost before even he was aware that nocturnally the Dormitory Scanners indicated that his Circular Energy Flow had shortened.

"Help me," Earthorse had said then. "Help me now," he called into the void of the Experience Therapy Chamber.

Somewhere a generator started with a whine. Earthorse recognized it as a recorded sound from a holographic history unit on industrialization. A new lesson. Multiple Transcendence Lasers crisscrossed the Sensorium Chamber.

"The warden and other officials have already assembled," the soft Voice said. "Observe the Wastrels' nervous anticipation. The rest you will experience completely. Totally. With all the old Wastrel feeling. We are here to help you. Aversion to the Wastrel old way of life may aid, even at this late moment, your return to the Federation Energy Circle. Your senses shall become one with the linear Wastrels of the Old Planet."

IN WAS LED THE HOLOGRAPHICALLY RETRIEVED PRISONER. HE WAS STRIPPED, SEARCHED, AND SHOWERED. WETNESS FILLED THE CHAMBER. THE PRISON BARBER SHAVED THE TOP OF HIS HEAD LIKE A MONK. THE CONDEMNED MAN PULLED ON HIS OWN BURIAL CLOTHES: A CLEAN KHAKI SHIRT, A SHORT JACKET, KHAKI PANTS WITH THE LEG SLIT TO THE KNEE. HE FELT, FEELS, THE WASHED SOFT-NESS OF THE UNSTARCHED KHAKI.

BEHIND THE ONE-WAY WINDOW STANDS THE EXECUTIONER.

THE GUARDS AND A CHAPLAIN COME IN WITH THE PRISONER. HE IS YOUNG. HE IS HANDSOME. HE FEELS THEIR HARD UGLY HANDS FIRM ON HIS BIG ARMS. THE WARDEN ADDRESSES HIM BY HIS FIRST NAME. HE HAS NOTHING TO SAY.

"THEN," SAYS THE WARDEN, "HAVE A SEAT,

PLEASE."

THE UNIFORMED GUARDS STRAP HIM IN VERY QUICKLY: HIS ARMS, WRISTS, ANKLES AND HIS CHEST. IT IS FAMILIAR. THEY ATTACH ELECTRODES TO HIS HEAD AND LEG. THEY STUFF HIS NOS-TRILS WITH COTTON TO TRAP THE BLOOD. THEY TIGHTEN THE LEATHER MASK OVER HIS FACE. THEY STEP BACK.

THE GENERATOR WHINES AGAIN. AN EXHAUST FAN WHIRLS ABOVE THE CHAIR. A GUARD SIGNALS THE EXECUTIONER. THE SWITCH IS THROWN. THE MUSCULAR, HANDSOME PRISONER LIFTS AND STRAINS AGAINST THE STRAPS. HIS FISTS CLENCH. HIS BLOOD BOILS. HIS HEAD EXPLODES. HIS BODY SLUMPS TO A RELAXED POSITION. THEN THEY DO IT AGAIN.

A DOCTOR OPENS HIS SHIRT AND LISTENS THROUGH AN ANTIQUE STETHOSCOPE. "I DECLARE," HE SAYS, "THIS MAN LEGALLY DEAD."

Redness flushed through Earthorse's whole being. His own fists clenched. Didax and the Matrix had paced him through the program of the other man's old-fashioned Wastrel execution. Yet the Medax and the Elite Federation Guards pretended to be neither kind nor cruel.

"Linearity," the Voice came through many filters, and no lon-ger sounded capable of human passion, "is imperfect. Beyond the line is the Circle."

Earthorse focused intently, but his energy no longer con-verged at all with the program. His laser-scanned flesh was a dis-integrated rainbow of glorious color displeasing to the cool Blue of Didax. "The Circle is vicious!" Earthorse shouted. "It feeds on itself! Beyond the Circle," and he paused as the hot mustard tangents crossed in his head, "is the Spiral!"

The lounge rack shook violently. Earthorse felt he was strapped to the back of a horned-skin, cold-blooded muscle-lizard whose long neck could rise, turn, and devour him in its hot, wet, salivating mouth.

"Alternation!" he shouted.

The Holographic Sensorium faded fast to black. Only the soft disembodied Voice remained: "Alternation merits alteration."

The sentence, Earthorse knew, was now irrevocably pronounced.

Time had taught them the necessary use of everything. Generations before, they had nearly exterminated themselves with Waste. Only slowly have they recovered at all: regrouping out of the Old Wastrel ruins, focusing first the Old Planet's interior energy, then the energy of the Old Planet's one star, and finally the unified energy of the small human circle surviving the end of the terrible plaguing Waste.

It had happened. It was recorded. One day a woman, two years plugged to a dialysis machine, asked the courts, not for much, she said, just one kidney from her incurably insane brother. At first, the court had refused; but the woman was insistent, demanding. She pleaded against the foolish Waste. Her brother needed but one kidney. Other sympathetic survivors of the ongoing Waste picketed, lobbied, pressured the judges. Before the onslaught of the harridan women, the courts that had once protectively declared the brother insane, bowed, and now declared him suitable for Harvest.

The woman became the symbolic center of the New Energy Matrix. The judges of the court, themselves survivors, granted her rights to her brother's body. She excised his kidney, and he smiled dumbly at her on a public video show. She sold next his eyes, right and left, and the hammer and stirrup in each of his ears. She sold his hands which to him, blind and deaf, were useless and wasted. Finally, in one grand auction, she bartered off his remaining kidney, both his lungs, his gonads, and his heart. She was inspired that the New Federation Medaxes had perfected the nonrejectable transplant.

She died, finally, a very rich old woman, by her own hand, peacefully passing in the presence of Didax. In the early days of the Federation, she was venerated as the Mother of Harvests. Her energy, the Matrix pronounced, had given central focus to the Perfect Circle from engineered birth to scientific Harvest.

Thereafter, a caste of Outlaws, mostly rogue males, was segregated aside, hunted down, kept in camps. They were basically arrested Tangentials, who, since they refused to function wholly, were Harvested partly. Only clones were bred for specific parts and were in demand by only the most narcissistic. Earthorse knew he had somehow become one of the criminal Tangentials, shorted out for malfunction, as the Matrix diagnosed—and for excellent Outlaw reason, he now for the first time thought. Outside the Matrix, outside the Perfect Energy Circuit of the Great Blue Didax, lay a different, alternate world!

Earthorse had to laugh. Out loud. Even bound immobile, he laughed. The Enormity indeed! Because he had once been so Elite, his parts would command the bidding of only the wealthiest and most influential Harvesters. He laughed again, unblinking, in the silent and dark Sensorium where, hidden, he knew they were all listening. He laughed louder, for above him on the perfectly circular Dome were appearing the glowing red digital letters of his final computerized sentence.

Earthorse was a Tangential Thinker, far outside Didax's humorless Circle, and he roared at the absurdity: they, who so darkly conserved, condemned him. He read aloud each of his body-parts as its title appeared for sale on the Vidterm screen. He wished only that his wrists were not shackled so he might applaud the prices as the Federation bidding rose higher and higher on his Harvest Futures.

He neared convulsive hilarity as the names, the famous names of the highest bidders locked in next to his auctioned parts. Earthorse had been a Champion Circler at the Federation Olympic Games and his parts, the envy of many, had not been forgotten. Even his testes were sold to an aging intersolar shipping magnate.

Then seizure!

The Federation power began to drain him through the electrodes the Elite Guards had clipped to his dick, balls, nipples, tongue, and ears.

Didax's suffocating Blue filled the room and stung his unblinkable eyes.

The Elite Guards pretended to be neither kind nor cruel. They watched his torture. They were hung and hard. They were what they were: whole and against him, laughing and jibing at the magnificence of his auctioned body parts.

In the Blue Dark of the beginning Harvest, Earthorse spied one Dark Face, more powerful now in its square-jawed manhood than it had been even as a Cadet, handpumping his enormous dark meat, hardened at the sight of the perfect blond muscleman strapped down at the mercy of the Elite Guard.

The Dark Face over the sensuously moving dick seemed to say: "Though you seem to be lost and in the shadow of death, fear not, for my energy is ever with you, and will never leave you to face your perils alone."

The last lock-together of look was wordless. Effortless. Lightening.

Grinding his big body down into the hungry Dark Blue, Earthorse steeled himself and laughed. He laughed loud and long. He laughed as long as he could spit and piss and fart and shit against them.

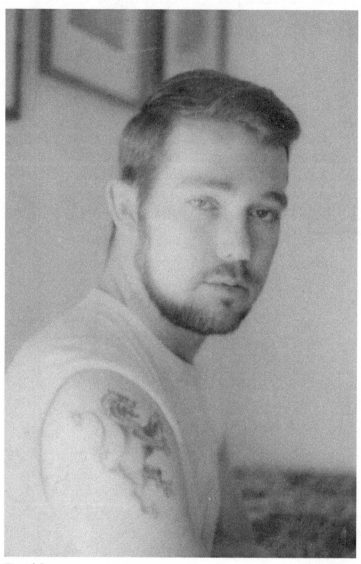

David Sparrow

**I started my quest for Blonds
the day I discovered I wasn't one.
I penetrated Blondness
as far as a non-Blond can go...**

By Blonds Obsessed:
Hollywood 1981

Hollywood. 5 AM. This is what it is. After a hard night under red light doing standup sex at the Meatrack. A soak in a steaming bathtub in a white-tiled room in a once-fashionable 1930's apartment hotel. The superhot water running from the tap. Like blood. Enough of my life lived to know the cumulative thrust of the rest. This is what it is for the duration.

All my lovers gone. Asleep in others' beds. Having their own private dreams which they always had anyway. Soaking alone. Stoned on the remains of a drug cocktail: a little acid; a snort, just one of MDM; finally, a Quaalude. All this brings the cold sweat of clarity. The tub comforts me. Warms me in this last hour before dawn. The last of the night that Ingmar Bergman called *The Hour of the Wolf.*

This is the hotel where Judy Garland used to bring her roughtrade fucks. The Hollywood Freeway runs like an aqueduct cement raceway outside the window. This place. This hour. This isn't the bottom. It's just the bottom line. Drugs and dawn. Coming down and heading toward daylight faces you toward truth. You can't have sex with close to 12,000 men in your life and not know something more about yourself than, say, your parents who only bedded each other.

I pull the white-rubber plug with my toe. The water level slowly lowers around the laidback island of my body. Steam rises from my pecs and belly. Geysers of ancient bodyscape. Images of my obsession form in the steam: blond men, ancient blond warriors, thick blond barbarians, long lineages of fine featured sculpted blonds. My dick, whacked to a night's pulp, starts and throbs once, rolling over on the receding water. Thoughts of blonds give my dick a life of its own.

You either like blonds or you don't. But if you're a gentleman whose preference has a blond preference, you understand the obsessive-compulsive adulation, worship, and symbolism of blond men. Honest, idealized manliness is never half-revealed. When it's there, it's all right there in front of you!

I wrap myself in my friend O'Riley's generous terry towels. He's asleep with one of the stream of beautiful young hustlers who flow day and night through his apartment. Yesterday afternoon I bedded the latest of his boys. A handsome platinum blond fresh from the Navy. An MP stationed at Treasure Island. He was playful in bed. Affectionate. Wild blue eyes. Stunning white teeth. Animal. Predatory. I felt like a dark-complexioned Tarzan in bed with Boy. When this Wild Child was being born, I was marching on Washington, that August of 1963, that last summer of Camelot, cheering-on King having his dream. This young blond is the first man I've fucked with who doesn't remember where he was when Kennedy was shot. He touched my thick black moustache, and then touched his own good blond moustache. "I want mine," he said, "to be as thick as yours." I gave him thirty-five dollars. More than the going rate in Hollywood. Just stuck it in his shoe. So he could go out later that night with his girlfriend.

I traipse off to the living room. Too wired to sleep. Too full of the straight blond from the afternoon. Too full of the blond men I balled with at the Meatrack. Too full of the blond San Francisco cop I had told, only three weeks before, that for a hundred reasons, most of them other blonds, I no longer wanted to be exclusive lovers with him. One blond is never enough. No matter how built, hairy, hung, handsome, and hot. One blond always leads to another.

If outer spacemen ever landed and looked only at my photo

collection to figure what Earthmales looked like, they'd con-
clude they were all blond. I'm willing victim of this passion for
blond men. That's the bottom line I've only lately realized. Out
of the armies that have marched over me, the blonds predomi-
nate. No man should fear to admit the basic truth of his life in
the dawn's early light. In fact, it's quite alright to pare one's life
and taste down to its basic simplicity.

Without myself being a blond, I have penetrated the Blond
Mystique in numbers and quality as far as a non-blond can go.
Oddly, some blonds reflect very little on their blondness, or,
almost perversely don't like other blonds. I must admit I started
my quest for blonds the day I discovered I wasn't, and they were!
My hardon passion, in bed and out, has since brought a certain
understanding of Blondness. Sort of like Bette Midler in *The
Rose*, I live my life for blond men, for all the blonds, platinum
to strawberry, around whom my love and lust have circulated.

The video-recorder clock reads-out 5:06 AM. Outside,
hardly any traffic cruises up the Hollywood Freeway. From the
bedroom down the hall I can hear the relaxed sounds made
by the sleeping blond MP whose scent is still in his white cotton teeshirt left carelessly on the couch. I can only laugh to
myself. I'm wired, awake, and alone in L.A., down from San
Francisco, to scout Southern California blonds. I take a hit from
the teeshirt's sweet blond-sweat pits. Better than popper. Am I
too hungry? Like Sebastian Venable. Tired of dark meat? Try
light. Try blonds. Doesn't everybody have a hungry heart? For
something.

I don't try to understand this passion for blonds. No! This
obsession with blonds. This obsession that puts me in thrall
to blonds. In lusty bondage to blonds. Blonds can hustle me
for anything they want. And they do. Blonds have more fun
only because by almost universal agreement everyone grants
to blonds the Highstuff and Highstyle they naturally assume
without question is owed them. Without any visible means of
support, blonds drive Corvettes and fly off to Puerto Vallarta.
All expenses paid. As if by magic.

Blonds live different lives. Are different people. Are regarded differently, specially, from boyhood on, by non-blonds, and by other blonds. Blonds tell me so. They tell me about being blond. How two blond men, passing in the street, no matter if gay or straight, acknowledge to each other the fraternity of their blondness. A non-blond, until let in on the secret, never really notices the energy-flash blond-to-blond. Blond men dazzle, because they reflect more light than they absorb. Blonds radiate energy. They move through the world with special grace, seeing themselves reflected in other men's eyes.

It is no narcissism for a blond to groom his gift, to maintain the upkeep of his blondness, to get off on his own blond goodlooks. Because the gift of blondness is so fragile, and needs such balanced tending, a blond can go wrong, can fall very fast from grace with the sea, if he is not very careful in his attitude about his gift. Narcissism can be a blond's fatal flaw. His Achilles heel. As long as he tends his gift, and keeps ego-vanity from crediting his own self with what lucky genetics has bestowed on him, he is the kind of Classic Blond who reminds us in these post-hippie and bleached-punk days of the way clean-cut blond men, military or athletic or redneck or suave, once ideally were.

Like Billy Budd, blond men are mythic reminders of what Adam was before the Fall. Like Melville, Whitman, and Tennessee Williams, I'm a sucker for the symbolism of blonds. I ache for the ancient male innocence, integrity, and virtue that blonds somehow remind us has been so, well, if not lost, changed.

The terrycloth towels have cooled in the predawn chill. I'm wrapped now in a large babyblue thermal blanket. The kind of blue that goes with blond. Blonds select clothes with colors coordinated to their degree of blond: platinum, straw, dirty, sleek, greased, towheaded, strawberry. They favor white cotton teeshirts, plaid flannel shirts, jeans faded blue as their eyes, collegiate athletic gear, military uniforms, fresh white jockstraps bulging tight against golden tanned blond skin.

Wrapped in blond-blue, my head speeds, mind races, heart pounds, dick hardens. I may have to jerk off, may have to take care of saluting blondness right now, by myself, in this apartment of beautiful Boulevard hustlers, because the aching possibility lurks to indulge myself in sweet grief and sorrow over all my blonds who have come and gone.

We've all had so many Gentleman Callers. Mine predominately blond: Vikings in past lives; bikers, bodybuilders, surfers, MPs in this.

Specific blonds: who were who they were exactly, personally.

Generic blonds: who represented all the blonds of their general type and look.

Universal blonds: who transcended themselves, and took me, a non-blond, the way Peter took Wendy and Superman took Lois, on a high flight up through the Absolute Essence of the Ultimate Blond Male Look.

Of all the blonds, there was one singular sensation, who for three brief years in the mid-70's was my Universal Blond Lover. He was my type. He was everybody's type. He benefitted from it, and he was lost because of it. With a winning grin, a flash of flinty squint of blue eye, a turn of sculpted head, a curl of lip, a run of finger over his regulation-clipped blond moustache he could transmorph himself from college jock to USMC captain to CHP trooper to every Look that men can have that always looks good but always looks better on a blond.

But he was, I think, in this hour before dawn, too infinitely perfect to last in an imperfectly finite world. Somehow his own blond body turned on him, grew suddenly, uncontrollably cancerous; and he shrank away like a dying golden sunset on the sea of white hospital sheets. ''I'll never leave you but once,'' he said. He was golden, and then he was gone from me.

I can't be sad, not forever, because while we loved, we loved perfectly. And because as a non-blond, I penetrated, through this Ultimate Universal Blond Man, to the very heart of blondness. I can only miss him now and ache for the access this Blond Angel gave me to the worshipable essence of blondness.

Before he passed on, my blond bodybuilder told me about his blond boyhood, about being a blond teenager, about the gift

of genetics that he so carefully manicured and tended. I have
the snapshots of his boyhood: his blondness at age two; at nine,
with the fall of blond hair wet on his forehead as he climbs into
the wooden rowboat, smiling into his father's camera; at eleven,
sitting in a Sunday School suit, all blond seriousness, with a
Bible in his lap; at twenty-two, as a blond Marine PT instructor;
at thirty, blond in an LAPD motorcop's high-booted, breeches
uniform that was his fetish; at thirty-two, in the first of the
five physique contests he entered, under my coaching, like some
bulked, big, beautiful, blond muscle beast. The audiences went
berserk for his blond presence. We drove home, four out of the
five contests, with our 280Z full of *First Place* and *Most Muscular*
trophies. I have the photos and the movies I shot. Now that he's
dead I have the trophies.

As he lay dying, he told me, with the looks slipping from
him in the last weeks of his illness, about his blondness. About
his blond goodlooks. About how it had been. About how he
had handled it. About how he had always been grateful for the
gift. Many nights, he said, when he was home alone with the
tracklight spots and the mirrors, he would jerk off in salute to
blondness. He was honestly, without vanity, turned on to blondness with all the intensity of a blond for blond. Blond goodlooks.
Blond muscles. (Oh, yes! Blond muscles are different from other
muscles, the way thick big blond uncut dick is different from
other dick.) "And when I cum," he said, holding my hand in
his blond hand, "when I'm alone and cuming and looking at all
this blondness, all I can say to God, or whoever, is, 'Thank you!
Thank you! Thank you!'"

Over and over, so many nights, he kept the perspective on
his blondness and said, Thank you. I participated with him. I
had more sex with him than any other man. Not just sex. Blond
Sex. Celebrations of blondness. Rituals of blondness. Palm-
ing the clipped nape of his blond redneck. Sniffing his blond
moustache. Studying the golden fur on his muscular forearms.
Rubbing the thick blond animal pelt of his washboard belly.
Licking his blond armpits and sweet blond asshole. Jerking off

in rhythm with his long strokes on his enormous blond dick. He was Every Blond Man to me. And to others. On Castro, cars rear-ended each other; men fell up stairs; restaurants grew silent when we entered. All because of his groomed, turned-out, stunning blond style.

I'm not sure he really died. Not sure, because his blondness was so essential, I joked with him from the first night we met, that I was on to his secret: he was from another star. He was not from this planet. He was so much the Essential Blond Male, it was as if Extraterrestrials, scanning the Earth to print-out the perfect male form, had drawn his form and face up in blond outline and filled it with the grace of Universal Protoplasm. He was to me a god, and gods never die. They transcend. Perhaps, if he did not die in that hospice in San Francisco, whoever sent him here simply beamed him back up. Sometimes I wonder if he really existed at all. Maybe I just 'checked out' for three years. But I have all his letters, a thousand photographs, three hours of movies, his clothes that still smell blond like him, his uniforms, his physique trophies and posing trunks. And always, sad dreams of him. I also have a small wooden box full of blond hair that I gathered from the barber cloth in his lap. Fine, silky, fragrant. I sometimes want to—how can I admit this—touch it, sniff it, taste it, cum over all that beautiful clipped blondness. My God, can a blond ever know how much a non-blond loves and misses him!

Being blond did not always make him happy. Cannibals for handsome blond meat accosted him, presumed he hustled, grabbed at him, punched at his muscles often out of jealous aggression mixed with lust. Bold photographers stepped right up to him. Flash-units popping. Shy ones shot from the hip. He was strained to be pleasant to them all. He was amused by the attention. He never grew cynical about it. Just truthful. Hardly anyone, he said, and I knew, ever told him the truth; they told him what they thought he wanted to hear in order to please him so they might get him into the sack, because they saw his Ultimate Blond Look would give them the Blond Fix they wanted, needed, lusted for more than anything. Hardly anyone wanted him for himself. Even I had to get around the fact of his attractive blondness, had to discount it, had to pretend it did not exist. In order to love him, and not just his blond goodlooks, I worked my way around his handsome packaging. And loved him even more. He was not just a looker. Handsome is, before and after all, as handsome does.

He was the sun. I was the moon. I was at his side, and I ached for him the way the dark man aches for the blond Tadzio in *Death in Venice*. No one, I know, ever suspects the tension and terror, the anxiety and sadness inside men of great beauty. Some nights I simply had to hold him to comfort him, this big handsome blond whom so many pursued as an object to be possessed, fucked, devoured, and thrown away like a syringe that shoots up an ultimate high.

For his sake, because of his bewildered pain at finding the darker, non-blond side of existence, I'm glad he's dead. He wanted the world to be all blondness and light. Right to the end. I survived him. I have a Black Belt in Existentialism. Yet somehow blondness lives on. Blondness always lives on. Blondness finds its perfect repository, this season in one man, next season in another. It lasts in each as long as he selflessly tends his gift of self. The essence of blondness, ironically, often does blonds in, you see, because the world is not blond. Not any more. The dark future, geneticists predict, holds a new evolving human face and coloring: a honey-brown complexion with almond eyes and high cheekbones and slender nose. There will be no more blonds.

Blonds are the atavistic, ancient, barbarian, pure-Druid past. That's why we hold them so dear. They are the golden sunny symbol of what was once so fair and pure and clean and holy and noble. That's all disappearing now on oily tarmacs of dark-skinned terrorism. Blondness is a gene as recessive as virtue.

We hold blonds and value them because they are an endangered species. There will come a time when there will be no more blond men. My God! No more blond men. That's a world I don't want to live in.

This is the last of the dark night. I sit here waiting for the golden blond dawn. I slip a cassette into the video and watch electronic blonds in slow-motion, A collage-tape of blonds filmed and recorded by my friend O'Riley. Blonds are repositories of manly beauty. The Marines always idealize the Corps in posters of blond men. I grease up my hand.

Blonds are translucent, transcendent. Taurus blonds. Leo blonds. Libra blonds. Showy blonds. Shy blonds. Blonds are sun-gods. Gods of Light. Lucifer was a blond: a blond archangel of light. Jesus, if he exists at all, is a blond, because everyone through the history of art has pictured him as a blond. Everyone knows that God, if he is anything at all, is a blond.

I put my greased hand on my stiffening dick.

So I fold tender young blonds to myself. I hold big chunky balding beefy blonds tight in my arms. *I know that Death will certainly be a Big Blond. I know that Charon ferrying souls across the Styx must certainly be a blond. I ache for the best blond muscleman I ever fed and clothed and housed and fucked and loved, and hope his soul is blond-bright with light forever.*

I will in years to come stare into the eyes of ever younger blonds, hoping to see his blue eyes looking back, reincarnated. Old Souls destined to meet and meet again.

Drugs, no matter what they say, taken rightly are wonderful. Acid in one night can accomplish what otherwise would take a lifetime.

I hit the amyl. I stroke my dick. I conjure blondness on my cock.

Dirty blonds. Sleepy blonds. Greasy Harley Sportster blonds. Redneck blonds. Married blonds. Hustling blonds. Bodybuilder blonds. Young puppy blonds. Mature blond daddies. Blond dick. Sweet clean fresh-washed blond meat. Blind blond cock, uncut, thick with heavy blond cheese. Thick-veined blond dick. Heavy-hung blonds. Broad-shouldered blonds. Big-armed blonds. Tight blond butt.

Sniffing a blond brush of moustache is the ultimate hit of blond manliness. To eat blond ass. To sniff blond pits. To suck the sweat from a blond athlete's cotton gym shorts, the sweat from a blond's teeshirt. To run tongue around the way the tight rib of rolled-up sleeve rides hard against a pair of bulging blond biceps. To lick a blond's furry blond balls. Burying nose in all that golden blond crotch fur. Sucking blond dick. Tonguing blond butthole. Fucking blonds. Fucked by blonds. Face-fucking an ultimate blond face.

Wrestling with blonds. Boxing with hard, tough blonds. Tattooed blonds. Trucker blonds. Farmboy blonds. Cowboy blonds. Swimmer blonds. Southern blonds. Blond down of hair matted across blond undergraduate gymnast calves and thighs and cheeks. Blond feet. Blond bodybuilder legs. Title-winning blond legs. Dropping dick between those blond legs, feeling the blond physique champion flexing for you. Kissing your face. Blond tongue. Blonds with sweet breath. Cigar-smoking blonds. Blond cops. Blond troopers. Disciplined blonds. Tortured blonds. Dominant blonds. Leather blonds. Bearded blonds. Blond bristle on a square blond jaw with three-days' growth of dirty blond stubble. Broad expanse of tanned, hairy, thick blond pecs. Blond voices with southern drawls. Blonds in bondage. Exhibitionist blonds. Troops of blonds. All-American jock blonds. Faded blonds. Straight blonds. Bi-blonds. Homomasculine blonds. Cocksucking blonds. Perversatile, incredible blonds.

To wrap my arms around the "Whole Cosmos Catalog of Blondness" is to reach for the warmth and light and glow of the sun, is to belie for an infinite moment, frozen out of finite time, the impending eclipse of all things bright and blond.

Yesterday afternoon's blond MP was much like the first of the young blond boys from my friend O'Riley who gives me blonds for my birthday and holidays. O'Riley is sophisticated. Civilized. Generous. He feeds my obsession. He gives me blonds. The first gift was a twenty-two-year-old strawberry-blond fireman from Travis Air Force Base: a young husband, the daddy of a two-year-old baby boy. He was my first pay-for-play, and I was shy, at a loss what to do, what to demand. Hustlers, I've since learned, are minimalist artists; what you don't get is due only to your deficiency as a director of the mattress-movie you're shooting. So, dismissing the fact that he'd been paid cash, I focused on his blondness, and fucked him the way blonds should be fucked. I fucked that little blond Air Force dream of a daddy, cupping the nape of his strawberry-blond neck in my clasped hands, tonguing and sniffing his blond breath through the blond moustache on his perfect blond upper lip.

Beware of blonds.

All else notwithstanding, blonds will drive you crazy. You give them your money. You give them your hungry heart, and they look at you curiously—the way only a blond can look at a non-blond. As warm as blonds get, even as hot and overheated as my One Universal Ultimate Blond, there's always that icy cold blond center of solitude. Of privacy. That no one non-blond gains access to. Or can even know. Hitchcock was crazed by the mystique of blonds.

Bette Midler in *The Rose* was obsessed, driven, fucked, killed by blond men. Haunted at the beginning of the film by an icon-poster of the blond James Dean, Rose is gangbanged on the 50-yard line by the southern blond football team. She takes up with a brown-blond chauffeur, and then with a young blond soldier. During her concerts, the young security roadie at the lip of the stage repeatedly parades his protective blondness into her close-ups. His constant, subliminal presence is like some bright guardian angel between Rose and the dark crush of her fans.

Finally it's a paunchy blond leftover from the football team who sells Rose bad dope that kills her while a new generation of football blonds practices in the background. The Rose could die for blonds. And does. In the end, the young blond soldier turns into the Blond Angel of Death who switches out the naked lightbulb in Rose's garage, dimming out the last fading image of James Dean's blond tousled head.

It's 6:11 by the digital video. The dawn light through the windows has finally become brighter than the lamplight. The traffic on the Hollywood Freeway is picking up. Sunday morning. In an hour the young blond MP asleep in the other room will awaken, stretch, and walk naked toward me like a sleepy young god rising from the sea with vine leaves in his blond hair. All across Los Angeles, blonds are waking up with morning hardons, pissing, shaving, showering, pulling on their jeans.

I've cum twice more just jotting these ramblings down about blonds. That's the secret of all my writing: I do it with a hardon. I type for awhile, and then I jerk off. I have to. A writer has to live it up to write it down.

One thing I know for sure: blonds will break your heart and your balls and your bank account if a non-blond lets them. And a non-blond will. I know. I've had the best of blonds, and been had, really had, by the best of them all. He left me because of cancer he caused in himself. With poisonous steroids that make blond muscle bigger and harder. But with terrible side effects. Sometimes a blond will sell his soul, just like a non-blond, to be more of what he is.

I've been admitted as far into blondness as a non-blond can go. And despite that icy cold core, and because of their sunburst heat and light, I'd never for a minute, not even in the deepest, darkest night of the soul, ever deny my passion or my quest after the mystique of blond men.

For all the joy of their blazing brightness, for all their brilliance and mistakes, for all the pain of their icy solitude and reserve, non-blonds must remember in reaching out to blonds that blond men are not gods, but are only angels flying, maybe, too close to the ground.

**Our pecs belong
to the Sundance, Kid!**

Titsports

Mantits are the great underdiscovered underground pleasure of
20th-century foxes. Male tits are to male sex what fine tuning
is to television. Titsports are a hot man's offramp to Alpha Cen-
tauri. Dick and butt are primary erotic zones, as obvious as the
mouth for cocksucking. Male-sexuality, however, is a list as big
as your fist of growing homosensual sophistication.

A nose can learn that a whiff of armpit is headier than a hit
of popper. A tongue can learn that a kiss down the throat can be
quite continental, but rimming is a guy's best trend.

TITS: 2000
Good sex is more than the finesse of fine ass. Good sex is more
than Genital Gymnastics. Good sex is discovery of the geography of the male body's erotic potential. Some guys turn on
naturally wherever they're touched. Other guys, still tainted
with their parents' attitudes about the propriety of missionary
sex, dismiss more adventurous sex as too kinky for them.

Their very giggles, as Freud diagnosed ticklishness, are a
sign of sexual fear. Figure it out: humor, more than not, deballs
an erotic situation. Nothing, for instance, can empty a Back
Room faster than two queens camping it up smack dab in the
middle of all the other guys' heavy-duty manstough.

Some guys' manly sense of play leads them on their own into
games beyond dick. Other guys, ripe for tutoring, have to be led
down the very unprim, rosy path to Big Boy Secrets. That's a real
male initiation rite of passage.

Homomasculine men have moved from their First Coming

Out (genital homosexuality) all the way to their Second Coming into total-body homosensuality.

And tits are the wave of the future.

MANLY CHESTS
"Blow in my ear and I'll follow you anywhere."

Twist a guy's tits and he'll follow you everywhere.

The mystique of the male chest is a natural history of masculinity's strength, bravery, endurance, and heart. A Man Called Horse popularized the Plains Indians' absolutely male rituals more psychologically significant than any ass-paddling by the Tejans fraternity at Texas A&M. The Amerindians, living by the code of what was natural, rather than what was normal, clue in homosensualists, who much prefer to be natural rather than normal, that chests belong to the Sun. (Perhaps, homomasculine men are more primal than their heterocivilized brothers.)

Not for any small reason did Amerindian compatriot of Marlon Brando, Russell Means, the hero of Wounded Knee, dance the Sun Vow Ritual as his affirmative counterpoint to the deballing of the Native American Male. Bodybuilders, many of them homo-muscular only, in their formal posing presentations, always include a generous number of chest manifestations, and always to great applause.

"Chest out! Stomach in!" Dialog delivered daily by every Daddy and DI on this undisciplined planet.

Men have long been measured by their barrel-chests, recently by their defined slabs of vascular pecs, and lately by the gauge and tread of their nipples.

TIT TRIANGULATION
Titwork is sophisticated stough--once a man makes all the connections. Connections are what homosensuality is all about. An athlete knows the cause-and-effect connections of how his physical systems interrelate. A Camp Pendleton Grunt knows that if his USMC jock is too tight his dick gets hard, bent, and attention. Discovery of dick, with its upfront demands, is easy

as reaching from your nose to your hose. A baby boy can do it.

So how does an adult ear become eroticized?

How do a man's tits get hot?

Question: How can a man graduate any one of his body parts up erotically?

Answer: With a little help from his friends, his head, and his hands, he can be tutored into some sensual consciousness raising.

Tits, for those men who have yet to spark contact with those magical male dials, can be educated, if not absolutely wired, into geometry's strongest form: the triangle. Once the brain synapses the connection between a man's two tits and his one dick, the energy patrix on his torso lights up with new, clear power.

BASIC TRAINING
Basic sex is to sophisticated homosensuality what Army Basic Training is to the Sophisticated Training of a bodybuilder. This is no putdown of good old standbys like cocksucking and fucking. Homosensuality tends to savor all the stops along the way before getting to the usual shooting match.

HOW DO YOU SOLVE A PROBLEM
LIKE YOUR ASSHOLE?
Consider asshole. Straight guys protect their butts the way women protect their tuna. Why? Straights, when not patting buns on athletic fields and courts, call each other, "Asshole!" All-Americans shout, "Up your ass!" To foreigners, "Fuck you, asshole!" must sound like the American way to say goodbye.

Myron/Myra Breckenridge drove straight into cowboy Rusty Godowsky's butt just like the Viet Cong fucked every American POW asshole in captivity. A military doctor, who happens to be gay, revealed recently that every POW coming home had VD up the ass. What better way to de-macho the downed American Fryboy than to have some "little gook prick" shoot a load of diseased cum up his butt in bondage. Not too much publicity on that number simply because the media figure that those heroic POWs had enough adjustment simply returning to a runaway American culture.

The homosensual point is that, at least theoretically, these POWs learned something through the use and abuse of their asses: either they hated it, or they hated themselves for liking it. What an ultimate and ironic Straight Macho betrayal: to have one of your own body parts tell your head that something you thought you could never relate to actually feels, well, not so bad, I guess, at all.

Many gay men, growing up with this straight-and-narrow attitude (and that's all it is: attitude) about male ass, have some difficulty learning the pleasure of getting plugged by a dick at the YMCA. What do they think the "A" stands for anyway?

Once, however, a man emigrates from the dark interior of America, he can more freely get plugged in the sweet, dark interior of himself.

Consider this progressive Coming Out: first, using your asshole as the Way In, as well as the Way Out, has to be gotten around. "Well, maybe I'll let you kiss it" becomes "tongue it" becomes "finger it" becomes "fuck it slow" becomes "fuck it hard" becomes "can you add a little dildo in it" becomes "got any bigger dildos" becomes "douche it lightly" becomes a "four-quart enema" becomes "fist it" becomes "double fist it."

That's what happens to the simple joys of maidenhood!

Actually, that rising range is a man's Real Graduation Ceremony as he stakes out progressive ownership of the territory of his own body. Interesting, how the Terror of Penetration graduates up to an Absolute Appetite for Penetration!

TITS AND THE GREASY MECHANIC
Tits get hardons. That's the bottom line: three hardons are better than one.

Tits to the titillated are a hardon difficult to live without once a man has thrilled to the charge those two little fuckers can put out when played properly. Warning: once charged, Tit Men need their tit fix. Nightly.

Titsports are habit-forming.

Since the Mondo-American male knows more about his car than he does about his body, this analog may illustrate the value of teaching a pair of old cogs new tricks.

Tits are to the dick and body what the positive and negative terminals on a Sears Diehard Battery are to a hot car. The right tit and the left tit are the plus and minus battery terminals providing the current necessary to ignite the gas to cause the controlled explosion within the cylinder, thereby driving the piston downward, causing the heart of the engine, the crank-shaft, to turn its torquing power to the transmission through the driveshaft to the axles, thus causing the car to lay rubber from a standing start.

A guy can learn a lot about sex from fucking with a mechanic! (Especially in greasy, sweaty, faded-blue Big Ben coveralls, but that's another trip!)

MASTERS & JOHNSON

Tit response is one of the main differences between straights and gays. Gay men, generally not uptight about their bodies, and mouthier about exactly what they want, are willing to experiment more widely. Masters and Johnson codify what sensualists already know: homomasculine men dare to "go for it," dare to learn the physical connections worth learning, because they realize the multiple of pleasure they'll reap in return for their effort.

As one Tit Man said, "You might as well grab all the gusto. You might as well take possession of your body because as A Chorus Line testifies, "tits and ass won't get you jobs—unless they're yours."

BODYBUILDER PECS

Tits assure Affirmative Action. Oh yeah!

Ever notice a bodybuilder at the tubs? Notice how he holds back? Far from being stuck on himself, he's not even waiting for another bodybuilder necessarily. Chances are he maintains his own space because he's tired of Genital Chauvinists coming up and humping his muscular thighs like Cocker Spaniels. To them, his physique is unique; they cum fast and leave him: used, abused, and bored. They may think they're original, kneeling in adoration, sucking his dick. But Mr. Physique has seen it all before.

Betcha he'll wanna getcha if you try a little man-to-man resuscitation. Forget his dick for the time being. Cup your hand around one of his Big Pecs. After all, he majors in bench presses to pump his chest.

Get inside his sensual focus. Bodybuilders, who know their art, are sophisticated sensually way beyond dickcentricity. A man in heavy touch with working out his major body parts, carefully isolated for a week's split routine, knows something about sensuality that is sexuality plus. Arnold Schwarzenegger said in Pumping Iron that a good workout feels as good as cuming and cuming and cuming. (There's a qualitative difference between the spasm of ejaculation and actual whole-body cuming. Lots of men have spasmed. How many men have really cum?)

Scratch a bodybuilder's pecs and ten-to-one you'll find a Tit Man.

Begin to play "Chopsticks" to Chopin all over his chest. Either use thumb and forefinger of both hands, one pair to each nipple; or, if you've a handspan wider than an octave, you can with one hand play both his tits and use your other hand for further man-ipulation.

Very often, men who chose to express their masculinity through the medium of muscle are heavy-duty sensualists. Too often, musclemen are sensually under-read.

TWO SINGULAR SENSATIONS
Man-to-man chest action, whether it's Tits-for-Two Mutuality, or whether it's a Sadist topping a Bottom's tits, ought to be an Olympic sport. You can, however, and should call "FOUL!" if, when you start rollerballing your partner's tits, his eyes go glassy, and his tongue lolls out, and he takes off to a passive galaxy.

Titwork is so hypnotically explosive it makes some guys hit bottom faster than the Hindenburg.

Ain't nothing worse than a sex partner who gets so laid back by your well-orchestrated trip that he forgets you exist. You might as well be a dildo and he might as well call Dial-a-Clamp. Passivity of the partner too often comes with the territory of Titmania. Remind him that he also has hands, and you also have tits, and a four-handed duet is often more fun than a piano solo.

Masters and Johnson ought to further their study: for the man who has done every S&M thing, and wants MORE, why is it that Eine Kleine Tit Musik dropkicks him into a capacity, if not a voracity, especially in a heavy S&M scene, to take more? Is it that mantits, tuned and torture-tested, triangulate to the testicles in a transcendent power grid?

TITPAIN: A NEW DEFINITION

One very proper San Francisco man is so celebratorily into mutual tit play that he carries to the wonderfully infamous South of the Slot Hotel whatever tit toys, beyond hands, that a man's mind can conjure. He is a Saint of Tit Torture. Clothes pins are child's play compared to his array of electrical alligator clamps, new surgical needles, and sterile X-acto blades whose neat little slices juice up so red and well under a pair of rubber snake-bite suction cups.

Some guys tentatively try one of his tit clamps on their finger and whine. They fail to realize the proper sophistication of this man's sensual titplay foreplay. He ain't no Chopper Charlie or Jack the Ripper. He can do to tits, and have done to his tits, manstough so severe that your head kicks out all the little protective tapes, programmed into your head as a child, about PAIN. Instead, his tit action teaches a man how to take possession of adult sensuality. He takes out the old protective tapes and puts in new ones to redefine the excruciatingly exquisite pressure.

Suddenly, his partners realize that what they had once too

easily, and much too quickly, defined as pain is really not pain, but is, in fact, simply heavy sensation. Pain is something different from heavy sensation. Heavy sensation causes no damage, no marks. Pain, as an S&M label in any scene, tits or not-tits, is confined to that upper level of heavy sensation where damage is done, where trauma happens to the body.

Nice guys don't cut off your nipples with the garden shears. That only happens in Liz Taylor movies scripted by Carson McCullers like Reflections in a Golden Eye.

CELLULOID TITS

Films sneak in a lot of tit shit. In Circle of Deception, Battle of Algiers, and State of Siege, men's nipples are tortured in bondage with electrical clamps attached to a "Double E8" Field Telephone that the uniformed interrogators crank up by the handle to send the shrieking voltage into the tied-up tits.

Film: State of Siege. Set: An austere room. CIA instructors have prepared a class in interrogation. Voiceover: "Torture can be a useful technique."

"Disciplined marine, army, and air force officers hurry down the hall toward the entrance to the room. The youngest, were it not for their distinctive uniforms, would look like noisy, carefree male students rushing to a class.

"The vast room is flooded with a harsh white light. The officers take their places on benches arranged in a half-circle.

"The hubbub ceases abruptly. The room falls silent. Four muscular, uniformed GUARDS bring in a blindfolded PRISONER. They lead him to the center of the semicircle, up to a sort of rack about two yards high. They go about stripping him as the room full of military personnel observes.

"Staff officers from the three branches of the armed forces take their seats on a large platform facing the benches.

"The PRISONER is naked. His body is young, lean, and athletic. His tan indicates he is a relatively fresh capture. The GUARDS lift him up and set him on the middle pole of the rack. They bend him over backward so as to tie his wrists and ankles together. And they leave him like that, his arched, naked body strained and swaying, supported only by the middle pole of the rack, which catches him in the backs of the knees.

"A MAN in civilian clothes approaches the subject PRISONER. He is carrying a black plastic box, about two feet long, eight inches high. Three plastic-coated wires, each about two yards long, stick out of the top. At the ends of the wires are metal triangle clamps of different sizes and thickness.

"The MAN lays the box down by the rack. He presses down a red button; suddenly the silence is broken by a shrill, insistent buzz. There are close-shots of the intent young military faces observing this lesson in interrogation by torture. Calmly, patiently, meticulously, the MAN proceeds with his demonstration. He applies the electrodes, one by one, to the most sensitive parts of the PRISONER'S body.

"His ears. Gums. Nostrils. Nipples. Genitals. Anus.

"Swept over by the electrical charges, the young PRISONER'S body vibrates, stretches, contracts. His wrenching, partially gagged screams heighten the intensity in the young military faces eagerly studying the interrogation techniques."

Odd, how straight men ignore their own nipples in the bedroom and head straight for another man's tits in the interrogation chamber!

In Walking Tall II, gigantic Buford Pusser is held down by muscular rednecks who slash the bejesus out of his chest and nipples with their hunting knives. Gore Vidal's Myra novel has the world's shortest chapter. It consists of Myron waking up, shouting two sentences: "My tits are gone! My tits are gone!"

A BOY CALLED PONY; A MAN CALLED HORSE

Frederic Remington's Own West describes the Blackfoot Sundance Ritual in which A Boy Called Pony becomes A Man Called Horse: "Gaily attired onlookers watch with eager and sympathetic interest the tortured young braves who, betraying no sign of the pain they endure from the claws skewered through their chests, dance wildly, lifted time to time from the dirt floor to the roof of the wickiup by hemp ropes attached to the skewers. Songs of admiration and encouragement accompany the violent beating of the tomtom.

"The tortured young warrior is the epitome of the religion, the ambition and the heroic character of this Spartanlike people.

"The young aspirants, weakened by the previous fast, the peyote, and the ritual torture often fall faint and senseless to the ground; but they are pulled up by the bloody barbs through their chests, and they continue their sun dance until either their flesh tears loose or it is manifest that they can endure no more, in which case they are honorably cut loose.... Each, after his release from torture, receives the attentions of his relatives, who have prepared a feast for him. In after-years, the Indian braves show the scars of their ordeal with all the pride that comes from their offering a boy's chest up to a piercing and bloody rite of passage into enduring manhood."

Any man can pervert anything. As T. S. Eliot's Murder in the Cathedral poses, the greatest temptation, perhaps, is "to do the right thing for the wrong reason."

Herein lies an important attitude.

When a man's chest belong to the Sun, he knows the vast difference between slavish masochism and manly nobility.

HARDWARE

Since the brain is the main sex organ, suggestion is a sex toy's best function. With tits, the best source beyond the convenience of bars and catalogs is cruising your favorite hardware store. Reaching into bins right next to the thick-fingered general contractor come in sweaty from the job to pick up fitting needs, you can come across everything you need to stage a tit scene.

Something can be said for the authenticity of real tools turned to real tit toys: clothes pins, for anybody but a beginner, are not worth bothering with, except for the fact that to have any really good scene, the principle is to start out slow and lead your partner into not only wanting more, but into begging for more.

Clothes pins are light enough to whet the appetite for some

reality play that leads up to scenes out of the Roman Martyrology where St. Agatha had her tits torn off with redhot pincers. (Ask any guy who grew up in a Catholic school where he got his S&M start!) Clothes pins' one drawback is their color: they remind some guys of mommy's wash. Easy antidote: daub them black with boot polish.

MAIL-ORDER TORTURE

Phillips and Fein of Manhattan produce, for those who prefer mail-order convenience, a brochure called Tit-Torture: Fantasy and Function (A Catalog for All Degrees). Their "tit clamp restraints have been created to provide the sensation of being secured directly by the nipples. When the subject is bound into various positions, the added discomfort produced by struggle, resistance, or movement of any kind, is a constant, active stimulation, no matter which end of the Alligators you're on." One virtue of tit clamps, whether used for heavy S&M or for sensual fun, is that each pair is like an extra pair of hands introduced to the scene. The artful photographic catalogs of Richard Hawkins' Mr. S Leathers, San Francisco, have taken bondage, S&M, and tit toys to a millennial high.

TWO TO TANGLE

Pleasant man-to-man play can be arranged by connecting two pairs of alligator clamps together and then, chest to chest with your partner, clamping his left tit to your right one and his right one to your left one, the four clamps connected by a foot of chain. You'll stay close to each other! He'll get a direct reading of your mutuality as you lean back, because the pressure on his tits is the same as the pull on yours. Not only are you and your buddy linked directly with tit-to-tit communication and energy, but your hands are also free to conjure magic faster than the eye can see!

GUYS DO THIS TO EACH OTHER?

Phillips and Fein, besides wrist-to-ankle tit clamps, and

tit-to-earlobe clamps, and magnetic tit clamps that add weight (as magnet after magnet is added), offer niceties such as the "Tit Whip," a 7-inch handle with 3 ½-inch leather thongs designed for concentrated application; and the "Nipple Whip" with flat rubber straps having hard spiky rubber points that leave "satisfying and exciting," but temporary, marks. For the Tit Freak who has everything, including a variety of gold rings for his pierced nipples, Phillips and Fein offer a Tit-Clamp silk-screened teeshirt. Sort of like wearing your "heart" on your sleeve.

PIERCED TO THE QUICK

Doug Malloy, the piercing expert of L.A.'s Gauntlet Enterprises, said, "Piercing of the nipples is not really new. The proud Roman Centurions, Caesar's bodyguard, wore nipple rings as a sign of their virility and courage, and as a uniform accessory for securing their short capes. The practice was also quite common in the Victorian era to enhance the size and shape of the nipples. Today the lure of piercing is primarily a sexual one. It provides a mechanical 'titillation' achieved by no other means. For many, especially men into bondage and discipline, and S&M scenes, tit piercing is a tremendous psychological turn-on."

Malloy recommended: "Where possible, piercing should be professionally done as placement determines the nipple's development, shape, and esthetic effect. While difficult to obtain unless one knows a sympathetic doctor, anesthetics are available for the faint-of-heart. Healing normally takes six to eight weeks and is quickest where a retainer with a straight post is used."

Malloy was a Master Piercer: nipples, navels, cock heads, and taints. (A taint is that stretch of skin between your balls and your asshole; it is called a taint because it ain't your balls and it ain't your ass. But it can be effectively pierced and ringed.)

TIT BUDDIES

Fucking, sucking, and fisting are all-time favorites on this century's Sexual Top Ten. Titwork is next. The East Coast, longer than the West Coast, has enjoyed the pleasures of pecs. In SF, when a man meets you, he wants to shake your hand. A handshake is not so much an old American custom as it is taking the measure of a man. The Fist Cruisers care less about the size of your dick and more about the size of your glove. (San Francisco "invented" fistfucking, and it, uh, spread!) In NYC, at the Mineshaft, the Manhattan Hello is "Tits and Pits": First you grab each others' nipples, and then one man or the other, or both, lifts an armpit for a quick sniff-n-lick.

TIT PRINCIPLE
To turn a man every which way including loose, often all you have to do is go manfully after his chest. If he follows you home, you can keep him.

INTERNATIONAL WRESTLING
In Olympic Greco-Roman wrestling, "upper body techniques" score more points than a lot of diving for the legs. Globally in wrestling, Europeans easily outclass American wrestlers because of their greater skill in what Disney's ABC-TV Wide World of Sports officially calls "Upper Body Techniques." Why leave it to the sensual Europeans? Sexually and sensually, titsports are an "upper body technique" worth the learning.

TITS FOR DAZE
Mantit training falls into educative classes. Tit response can be learned: self-taught or, better, tutored. You can roll your own, or enjoy a buddy-rub. Too many guys go for the kill too fast. What good are wrecked tits? Slow squeezing in the Big City will lay down more tread faster than apelike brutalization unless you happen to be into Neanderthal sex, which is also fun when the mood strikes.

With use, tits can grow hard like a dick and bigger like a bicep. Their connections are circulatory and musculatory. In fact, among homomasculine men, big nipples have become a true sign of sensual adulthood.

Big nipples on a firm chest are definite status symbols: good mileage and heavy tread. Gynomastic little "Bitch Tits" on a bodybuilder, however, are signs of steroid use and are a source of several kinds of amusement.

Reach under a man's white cotton teeshirt. Run your hand up his furry, hard abdomen. Find the valley between the mounds of his pecs. Spread your hand like Van Cliburn stretching for the Big Octave. (Why do you think Physique Pictorial has for years given its hot models' measurements "nipple-to-nipple"? That's info for Tit Freaks!) If the mantits you touch grow hard and large like living leather, your touch can very definitely tell you all you need to know about the sundance in his butch eyes.

**The Mineshaft, the Navy, and
pissing in the wind...**

Wet Dreams, Golden Showers

Gay reality often reads like fiction. Mainly because the gay
sense of adventure, that sense of openness to experience, causes
fantasy to turn into fact and, once turned, that fact is often
so outrageous in its reality, it sounds like fiction to people too
chickenshit to pursue their fantasies. "What," they ask, "would
happen if you actualized your fantasies? There'd be nothing left
to fantasize about."

Wrong. There would be new fantasies, one-step-further
fantasies, push-the-limit fantasies. There would be bent, sick,
twisted fantasies, and new lost horizons to celebrate.

A man without fantasies is a man of the First Kind.

A man afraid to actualize his fantasies is a man of the Second Kind.

A man who acts out his fantasies is a man of the Third Kind.

BACKROOM BARS: STAND-UP SEX

The backroom bars, watering holes for night bloomers, are phe-
nomena of the Third Kind: Contact. They are native to San
Francisco and New York. They began as literal backrooms,
spontaneous, in bars like The Tool Box, The Folsom Prison
and The Ambush. They came out on their own as The Covered
Wagon, The Anvil and with increasing intensity, The Zodiac,
The Toilet, and the latest infleshtation The Mineshaft.

GREENWICH VILLAGE:
THE MINESHAFT EXPERIENCE

After midnight, after the lights go down low, a man of the Third
Kind can see what the boys in the backroom will have: fantasy

actualized a la carte. New York's Mineshaft is the current front-runner. Up a steep stairway to the entrance, and then down a steep stairway, The Mineshaft offers "The Lourdes Room," featuring a full-length white porcelain bathtub suitable for baptizing and initiating any man who dares.

Any given night, a man can climb into the tub for nonstop Golden Showers. Fairer faucets, major and minor (less than seven inches), than he ever dreamed of, turn on—literally—to him and all over him. Saturday nights, especially, on three sides of the tub, men press in, six or seven deep. Men nearest the tub unbutton their Levi's, unsnap their leather codpieces, or go for their meat by peeling down their jocks. They are the front line of the Third Kind, pressed from behind by dozens of others chugging their beers as they press forward toward the tub.

BATHTUB PISS ORGIES

A single red light illuminates the dark Italian faces of Renaissance laborers from the 15th century, the blond moustaches of Vikings, the bared chests of nippling Jews wet with the humid cellar sweat. Often, a man of no patience drops to his knees to drink the piss of a man three rows back from the tub. The pissers move around the private scene toward their target: the man, laid back in the white tub, sometimes naked, more often wearing only construction boots, athletic socks, a piss-soaked jock, maybe a USMC fatigue hat.

One night, a perfectly groomed dude climbed into the tub wearing wingtips, a Brooks Brothers dark wool suit, Ivy League tie, a white oxford-cloth dress shirt which, when he pulled open the suit coat, exposed holes cut out over his large nipples on his hairy chest. His hands found his crotch and fished his own cock hard from his white jockey shorts. On all sides, he looked up at the fifty or so piss-filled men looking down on him. A guy in full leather hawked up some deep spit and flumed it down on the dark suit. His baptism had begun.

The ritual runs nightly the same. The dozen men closest to the tub rim are in various erect stages of pissing. Some unbuttoning, some whipping it out fast. Others teasing it out slowly. One peels back his lip of heavy foreskin through his full hardon. One stands, muscular arms folded across his thick pecs, eyes closed, waiting for his piss to work its way down from inside his tight belly to his dick hanging out of his jeans: untouched, untouchable, but willing to piss down hard and heavy on the right motherfucker laid back in the tub. One by one, then in pairs, building to four and five at a time, they join together in a waterfall of piss.

Each chooses his own target. A man in the tub can study how some guys choose to piss on his boots. Others on his jock. Many on his chest. Most on his face and shoulders. The streams come thick. Some with firehose force. The hard ones piss straight down on his body. The thicker soft cocks rain down in a curved arc of beer-rich piss.

Ordinary to great bodies climb into the tub. Every body looks better hosed down with gallons of shiny piss. The look of the wet skin. The sound of hot piss splashing on warm flesh. The feeling, from celebration to humiliation, of aiming cock to piss on another man's cock and balls. The feel, to the man in the tub, of twenty streams of piss hitting him at once. The hot energy trade-off, man to man, in a communion of piss.

SIGHTS TRULY SEEN: PISS JOCKS

One dark-headed guy stands at the head of the tub with a dozen orange-and-blue Bike supporter boxes. He opens them slow and deliberate. One by one. Pulling out of each a clean new jockstrap. He opens the first box and throws the jock on the belly of the body soaking in the tub. Three dudes turn their dicks directly on to the new jock. It soaks up their piss fast. The second Bike box opens and the second jock lands in the tub. Again and again. The bearded guy tosses each box to the floor as he tosses each jock on top the man in the tub.

Another guy, one of those blonds with a thick red Marlboro moustache, sticks a finger through a small hole near the neck of his own white teeshirt. Slowly he tears the white cotton, shredding it to strips of rag, revealing his good pecs and smooth belly. He holds the rag of teeshirt balled up in his hand. His other hand pulls out his cock. He pisses long and heavy into his torn teeshirt. His cock hardens as he pisses.

The other men, except for one with a piss-load that won't quit, stop leaking to look at the big long blond. When his teeshirt is soaked, he balls it up, wrings it out over the face of the man in the tub. Then he pisses in the shirt some more. Two other guys piss toward his cock pissing into the shirt. One hits the shirt. The other hits the blond's jeans.

Nothing bothers him. Pissed out, he lobs the dripping teeshirt like a wet softball into the face of the man in the tub. He catches it in his mouth and sucks it. Loud. His eager sucking causes six or seven more cocks to piss in his face.

The dude with the dozen jockstraps stuffs one of them into the tub drain. The tub fills up fast. Pisswaves slosh side to side as the man in the tub twists and bobs for all the piss he can handle. As row after row of men moves in, the piss level covers most of his body. Once he slips. In the dripping, shuffling silence his hand makes the squeak of flesh sliding in a wet tub. For a moment, his whole head disappears under the piss and floating jockstraps.

A big fucker in full leather reaches down into the piss and dredges him up by the hair. The man in the tub gasps. Swallows. Wallows. Kneels up. Jerking off. Mouth open. Piss hitting his face. With him kneeling, the tub has room for two. Another guy climbs in for the same treatment. Both of them make gurgling sounds, mouths open, hunched back waist deep in the piss.

The guy with the jocks starts dredging them out. Fully soaked. No reason to wring them out. One at a time he pulls on the dripping jocks until his cock and balls are completely padded beneath a dozen straps soaked with the piss of nearly a hundred guys. He moves off into the darkly lit cellar and is lost in the crush. The second guy into the tub dives for the teeshirt in the drain. He comes up with it in his teeth. The men piss harder in his face. He's working for it, begging for it, drinking it, as the tub level goes down. Slowly. The last piss swirls, gurgles, and leaves the tub slick. The first man climbs out, helped by the men standing nearest the tub. He's satisfied. He's had his turn. His scene is over.

Now the tub is ready for the new guy. He's busy already sucking the piss off the thigh-high rubber boots of a man who has thrown his fireman-booted leg across the tub. A fresh dozen dicks stream into the changing scene.

Off in another Mineshaft corner, in more private spaces, other men have waded off to bridge waters of their own. Near the bar, a short muscular man pisses into his empty beer can. He hands it to his buddy. They nod. They smile. The buddy drinks.

WET REALITIES: USMC

Camp Pendleton survival training teaches the young Marine recruits that to survive they can drink their own piss twice and eat their own shit once. Navy survival training is even better. For years, in fact, naval officers and cadets have whispered about the Navy Torture Camps: beatings by guards, "tiger cages," the starvation, and especially the exotic water tortures.

The source of all this cruel, unusual, and hard-on punishment of young American males is not a foreign prison camp. It is the U.S. Navy's own hard-assed school for Survival, Evasion, Resistance, and Escape (SERE). Designed to train servicemen to survive the rigors of POW life the Navy's two SERE programs, one at Warner Springs near San Diego and another in northwestern Maine, lost their secrecy recently when an embittered SERE graduate filed suit against Navy personnel, exposing the SERE training as an S&M reality.

NAVY PISS: SEX ABUSE?

Navy Lt. Wendell Richard Young rejected the secrecy forced on every SERE graduate, telling tales of fetid tiger cages, beatings and jarring judo flips by Navy instructors he called "gorillas," and a torture device called the "water board." Young also charged, though not in his suit, that SERE students have been tortured into spitting, pissing, and shitting on the American flag, masturbating on order before Navy guards and, on one occasion at least, engaging in sex with an instructor.

The Navy denied the unsubstantiated charges of sexual abuse, but it did acknowledge the use of water torture and physical punishment in its training camps. A Navy spokesman, Comdr. William Collins, insisted that these activities were mostly "illusions of reality" that were not as dangerous as they seemed.

These "illusions of reality" done in the name of "patriotic military training" sound very close to the "illusions of reality" done nightly in the name of "sleazy sexual ritual." In America, it's not what you do, it's what you call it in order to excuse it.

DON'T ASK! NAVY HAZING TURNS SAILOR GAY

An ex-Navy officer, who was not gay at the time of his SERE training, explained that it was only after he was out of the Navy and had come out sexually that he realized the full implications of the week-long SERE training which he was forced to take on threat of disciplinary action.

He was stripped to his skivvies and boots and made to stand at attention in a line with the other young officers forced to take the San Diego training. They were hooded one by one, "sacked" the guards called it, with a heavy canvas bag tied around the neck. After that he saw no one except for contact with the guards. His hands were tied behind his back and he was locked in a kneeling position inside a small wooden box where he was left hooded, tied, and cramped for twenty-four hours. He figured the large tincan between his thighs was for his piss. Hooded he couldn't see it. Tied he couldn't get his cock out of his skivvies anyway. He held back as long as he could, hearing the muffled sounds of the other men isolated in other wooden boxes. Finally he had to let go of his piss which wet his shorts, ran down his thigh, and pooled around his knees.

He found out that his piss was to be the excuse.

When the guards opened his box, still hooded, he could

not rise from his cramped position. His boots and socks were wet with his piss. The guards, pretending outrage, lifted him bodily and dragged him across the compound, shouting at him about how even a dog won't piss in its own box. His legs were pins and needles, useless beneath him. They carried him into a room, unhooded him, and with a guard for each foot and hand, laid him out on a plywood torture board, tying him in place spreadeagled.

A hose was brought near his mouth. He was thirsty from the desert heat and the twenty-four-hour isolation. He drank. They pushed the nozzle closer to his face. He drank some more. They pushed the nozzle into his mouth. A strong pair of hands held his jaws closed. The water flooded his mouth, forced out his cheeks, ran out his nose, into his ears, down his throat. He was drowning, choking, drinking to stay alive. They knew what they were doing. Right before unconsciousness, they pulled the hose from his mouth. He thought they were finished.

He was wrong. The water torture lasted over an hour.

A tube was forced through his left nostril and fed the three-foot length to his belly. The water hose was attached to the tube. His belly filled to full distention. He admits to begging them to stop. Instead, they shoved a water-soaked teeshirt into his mouth, leaving only one nostril free for breathing.

Then a guard posing as a foreign interrogator, climbed up on the board, astraddle his bound waist, and kneaded his bloated belly until he was screaming into the teeshirt. He felt he could take no more. They knew he could. He knew he had to. They continued. The guard, kneading his belly rising and sitting, rising and pushing on his belly, then sitting back across his piss-soaked skivvies, worked him over with obvious pleasure.

Such isolation, torture, and forced feeding continued for the week. And with good reason.

AMERICAN POW'S, COMMUNIST VIOLENCE
Some facts get ignored, because American culture—confused about sex and violence—does not want to focus on the sexual

aspect of torture endured by returning American soldiers cap-
tured by the enemy. In his clinically detailed book, P.O.W.: A
Definitive History of the American Prisoner-of-War Experience, Reader's Digest Press, 1977, research-writer John Hubbell
writes of how the enemy attacks the macho American prisoner
by belittling his manhood. He exposes how in Vietnam prison-
ers were forced to crawl through enemy latrines on their hands
and knees, left for weeks tied in their own waste and sometimes
sexually tortured. Hubbell reports facts that never made the
evening news.

For instance, in a torture cell 150 miles south of Hanoi,
a Navy pilot, was interrogated in a scene of sadistic bondage-
suspension torture as an American "air pirate." Made to squat on
the seat of a chair, the young flier's arms were tied tighter than a
tourniquet behind his back. A rope, knotted through his shoulders, connected to a wood rafter. The chair was kicked out. He
swung and hung from his shoulders. Agony. Suspension. Pain.
Watching his torturer, seated behind a big desk, watching him.
Watching his torturer masturbating during the session where he
hung suspended for two to three hours. (Pages 352, 353)

The national conversation in American media—at least
before the internet—has never addressed the known sexual
abuse of American POW's from Vietnam or any other war—as
if rape, which is about power, happens only to one gender. Men
have been raped by invaders and conquerors since Cain killed
Abel and moved to Bosnia. It doesn't mean they or their rapists
are homosexual; and it doesn't give homosexuality a bad name.
Homosex like heterosex, both legit in use, can become illegit in
abuse. Can TV's talking heads explain this?

At least the American military tries to deal with this sex-
torture. Such in-your-face and up-your-ass realities cause the
military to prepare its "Ask-and-Tell" heterosexual men for
sexual abuse—and cause some civilian belief in the secret training details coming to light: the gay-seeming "Don't Ask/Don't
Tell" spitting, pissing, shitting, masturbating, and powersex
all juiced with excuse as preparation for patriotism. "C'mon,

maggot! Faggot!" Or is such institutionalized, ritualized survival training just hetero S&M in military culture? So, ironically, if homosex rape is taught as a terrible torture that can happen to a POW, small wonder the military is confused about the pleasure of consensual homosex.

THAT'S STRAIGHT PISS FOR YOU

For relief, comic and cockwise, Burt Reynolds won the Wet Oscar for Best On-Screen Piss in Semi-Tough when he inserted his dick into a rubber hose, strapped it down his leg, and pissed into a metal flask strapped inside his boot. The loud soundtrack outdoes rain on a hot tin roof. Pasolini, in his version of Something for Everyone called Teorema, films the humpy teenaged son pissing off the family balcony. In Kenneth Anger's Scorpio Rising, a classic gay version of The Wild One the lead biker stands on an altar in a church and pisses into the chalice of his helmet, and finally pisses down on all the worshipers gathered around him.

In prison plays and film like Miguel Pinero's Short Eyes or Kenneth Brown's The Brig, the piss scene is obligatory. Experienced cons usually take to shoving a new dude's head into the cellblock toilet in an initiation as time-honored as the Hell's Angels' initiation of pissing on a new member's colors. And his leather jacket. And his jeans. From then on an Angel pulls off the road strictly for a good shit. Piss just goes off like a rocket in his pocket.

What we do after midnight at the Mineshaft is a high-flying reality that has naturally to do with male animals pissing on their own territory. Richard Gere, probably feeling on top of the world at the height of his American Gigolo film career, received a citation from a New York police officer for publicly pissing on a Greenwich Village street. The omnipotent media magnate and cup-winning sailor, Ted Turner, pissed triumphantly over the side of his sailing sloop after winning a major East Coast race. No wonder the extra-ordinarily handsome daddy Ted Turner has been dubbed by the media as "Captain Outrageous."

SOME LIKE IT HOT

Ancient warriors bathed in piss. Victorian athletes rubbed
themselves down with piss before a good cricket match. Health
addicts for years have claimed piss perfect for brushing the teeth.
India's Prime Minister Norarji Desai announced recently: "For
the past five or six years, I have drunk a glass of my own urine-
-about six to eight ounces--every morning. It is very good for
you, and it is even free. Even in the Bible it says drink from your
own cistern. What's your own cistern? It is your urine. Urine is
the water of life."

Some men, always working toward versatility, often take a
liking for piss: from beer-clear to early morning thick. The range
of preference is an acquired taste; the reasons for taking another
man's piss range from the sacred to the profane.

Some guys start off early in life pissing, as little boys, into
the family john with their little brother having races to see who
will finish first. Others start later, at college bars, pissing into the
same trough. Refinements set in: going off to bars across from
police stations to give the porcelain a good lick when the cops
come in after duty for a quick beer quickly pissed out; pissing up
a guy's ass before, during, and/or after a good hard fuck; prepar-
ing the basic water sports emblem, a piss-soaked jock, tucked
into the back pocket.

RECYCLE

Variations on any theme, even Handel's "Water Music," are as
endless as the inventive mind of man. Run an ad in a sex/fetish
newsletter for "Mason Jars of Dirty Bathwater" and takers will
beat a path to your P.O. Box. You just can't out-fetish and out-
fantasize and out-actualize all of the people all of the time. But
that is The Joy of Water Sports, like the joy of almost everything
else: finding out that you as a man of the Third Kind are not
alone, and in piss, more than almost anything else, together men
sink to swim.

Fetish Noir **is a taste for something
that isn't sex itself,
but that causes your sexual response...**

Fetish *Noir*:
Alternative Sex Games
for Your Inner Wild Child
(Just When You Think We've Thought Up Everything,
We Think Up Something Else!)

Talk to me, Fetish Boy! Whatever turns you on! Sex lib goes
into the *mondo beyondo* because you need no partner but Viagra.
Forget Breeder Sex. In this brave new world, fertility clinics take
care of that messy business with turkey basters in the petrie dish.
Congratulate yourself! You are a free man. You are liberated from
providing seed and cash. You survived primitive fundamentalists'
fears of Y2K. So consider what progressive millennial eroticism
will please your Inner Wild Child. Fetish replaces sex.

Fetish noir means you are free to get your nut however you
please.

You may be gay or bi or even straight. Don't worry. Be happy.
If you turn your focus to your most *noir* fetish, you won't need
Viagra, because "wet dreams may cum" when you admit your
turn-on is beyond the old norms of insertion sex.

Since boyhood, you've always known your best sex is masturbation. Nobody does it better. That's why your Inner Wild Child
likes magazines and videos and live nude shows. Even when you're
kneeling (actually in scene or virtually on screen) before your
Master or your Mistress, you know that every caress, garterbelt,
jockstrap, whiplash, boot, and shoe is aimed at getting you off in
your hand. Every hustler, hooker, and rentboy in the world knows
that's all you want.

Fetish noir focuses on your favorite sex partner: you. And whatever turns you on.

Your human body has forty-nine miles of nerves.

So there's a lot more of you than six or seven inches of dick.

A fetish, in case you're dazed and confused, is an object that a person (you) or a culture (television, magazines, religion, etc.) invests with sexual power.

For instance, TV news made a fetish of Monica's blue dress, and TV sports made a fetish of Mark McGwire's balls. A lot of people actually would like to cum all over that dress, those balls!

Fetish noir, just so you know, is your own private Idaho of a turn-on, something so personal to you that maybe the only place you can find it is hidden in the code of magazine ads—say, where a Marlboro Man in his Calvin's with a cigaret hanging from wet lips looks hot sending you a subliminal message about sex. Try to recall the "forbidden feeling" of jerking off as a kid to the underwear/lingerie pages in the *Sears Catalog.*

Check out one of *fetish noir*'s coolest movies, *A Man in Uniform* (1996), which is legit Hollywood—very Sundance Film Festival—and not porno, unless—very much like the hero—you're turned on by a cop uniform with boots, keys, badge, and gun. (Notice all the handcuffs used to "fetish up" movie sex scenes!) One of *fetish noir*'s most shocking films, *The Night Porter*, twists on a Jewish woman fetishizing Nazi regalia. *Fetish noir* is more psychological than a Hitchcock movie. Fetish goes deeper than sex. Sex can be quite mindless. Fetish can actually satisfy the mind. Go figure!

Fetish noir involves all your senses. Some fetishes you watch, some you wear, some you smell. And some...you eat. (Don't ask!)

Sex liberation leads from breeder sex onwards to adventure. Just as controversial erotic photographer Robert Mapplethorpe fetishized black men, gay magazines (*Hombres Latinos*) and porno videos (*Illegal Alien Blues*) often make fetishes of ethnic groups, because in the truth of erotic demographic studies, progressive producers know that bored with fetishized blonds, viewers will have an appetite for fetishized Latins. Madonna herself, in the fetishistic corsets of *Truth or Dare*, traded in the "Danny Boy Fetish" of Irish Sean Penn for the Latin man who seeded

Lourdes. Rio de Janeiro's Max Julien's Marcostudio and Kristian Bjorn's entire video career make a fetish of Brazilians for Anglos bored with Anglos who can't get it up. Palm Drive Video, which fetishizes American blue-collar men, specializes in hyper-masculine fetishes: leather, body hair, tit torture, and worship of the muscles of naked bodybuilders. Videos and DVDs, stepping out beyond generic suck/fuck action, fetishize a variety of stuff, like, for instance, Samurai Video's pregnant Japanese women in bondage, or the high-concept US video, "Pregnant Trailer-Park Women's Ex-con Husbands in Bondage."

Hey! *Fetish noir* demands you be open-minded!

Fans of *fetish noir* gotta love the media for delivering by cable and satellite and internet, not only the prison fetishes of the series *Oz*, but the delights of pro-wrestling and boxing gear on battling gals and ultimate fighting guys who are living fetishes of macho in a culture that all too often censors and censures raw masculinity which the politically correct have themselves fetishized as a bad thing.

Jokester jockster Dennis Rodman popularizes fetishes of tattoos, piercing, body-shaving, and cross-dressing. The cover of *Cigar Aficionado* mag fetishizes author Ernest Hemingway, supermodel Linda Evangelista, and action-figure Chuck Norris smoking big Havanas. Sportscaster Marv Albert's once-secret sex life included a taste for *fetish noir*isms such as threesomes, women's lingerie, and biting. Actually, talk shows are the educational TV of *fetish noir*, with exhibitionistic topics like "Adult Babies in Diapers," "Vacuum-Pump Penis Enlargement," and "Lap Dance Sex Addiction." If you haven't thought of the latest kink, tune in *Jerry Springer.*

Hey, if you can jerk off to it, and it's not missionary sex to make babies, it's probably *fetish noir* sex!

Internet sex is totally *fetish noir*. You watch an image and hear a voice of someone who is not there. Even in real-time, you can't have the real person who is on screen, but you can buy their actual (used) panties, fishnets, jockstraps, whatever, to sniff and rub and stuff in your mouth. Like the sexy "Chat Rooms," Classified Ads in underground/alternative newspapers and magazines have always been more about fetishes than actual sex. If you placed a

Classified Ad offering "dirty bath water in Mason jars," by the following Wednesday, your mailbox would be full of eager players who suddenly are turned on by the *noir*-ness of your invented fetish. Advertise it and they will cum.

The British fetishize spanking. The Miss America contest fetishizes the combo of swimsuits and high heels. The tobacco industry fetishizes smoking. Detroit fetishizes cars. The NRA reveals the absolute fetish of guns. *Suck my lethal weapon, baby!* How perfect in an age when unsafe sex is fetishized by voyeurs who want to see penetration bare-back, and when another crowd of participants makes a fetish out of condoms and latex clothes!

Hey, ya gotta love *fetish noir*, because it comes from the deepest, darkest kinks of the human cortex. *Fetish noir* is recreational sex indulged in at perfection.

Culture cannot control fetish, because fetish is so personal it is not recognizeable by the Puritans who always want to control sex which they perceive as missionary procreational sex.

Fetish noir like beauty is in the eye of the beholder.

Once upon a time, leather and lace and motorcycles and bondage and watersports were the obvious fetishes. Now that everyone has Been-There-and-Done-That, you are free to rev your vibrator to everything from fisting and sadomasochism to reading porno on the toilet wearing nipple clamps, a dildo, and a French maid's uniform.

Sex, in an overpopulated world that needs no more procreation sex, has been rescued.

Fetish noir sex is now what you do to please your Inner Wild Child.

Fetish noir is that little something that always pops up in the back of your head—even when you're having sex with someone else—that's almost unnoticed but always necessarily there to make you cum—like, maybe, a buzz of bondage. You know: you're fucking and sucking, but really you're thinking about tying up your partner, or of tying up someone else you're thinking about while fucking your partner, or most likely, thinking about getting tied up yourself, and being forced to have sex with (*fill in the blanks*) _____ while wearing _____ .

Fetish noir sex is the place where, when you go there, you get to be yourself.

No man is alone. No matter how private or personal or secret or severe his magnificent obsessions, a man deserves to enjoy his own satisfactions by celebrating them man-to-man with other homosensualists.

The litany of play and pleasure is an endless list of gestures, moments, and things snapped manfully together. The layers of this *sense*-ible inventory are as meaningful as the men who take their time to savor the signals that come from deep inside a man's expressive masculine presentation of self.

"How much pleasure do you want?"

That's a question of daring, a question of focused sybaritic answer.

"As much as I can stand."

In 1979, a flyer advertising a new genre of erotic gay 'zine titled, MAN2MAN, listed fetishes the 'zine promised to cover. (As a quarterly, the very popular MAN2MAN, lasted two years,1980-1981, and was finally put to rest, publisher Mark Hemry reminisces, because of the labor-intensive difficulties of low-budget alternative magazine production before computers made independent publishing possible.) The flyer, which was also sent out with the premier issue of MAN2MAN, explained its essence as "THE JOURNAL OF HARD2FIND OBSESSIONS."

It read: You are not alone. No matter how private or personal or secret your Magnificent Obsession, MAN2MAN's network discreetly circulates your precise desire for your precise satisfaction. Life is too short for hit-and-miss bar-and-bath hopping and hoping. A man deserves an easier way to connect with other men eager to share, or open up, mutual specialties. Sure, other newsletters, ad columns, and specialty publications exist, but none covers the waterfront as upfront as MAN2MAN. If you have secret, offbeat,shameless, manly trips that you figure you're ready to share with like-minded men (if you could easily find them), MAN2MAN is the old reliable journal where the silent-waters-that-run-deep meet.

MAN2MAN is a specialty magazine for the fetish-and-sex adventurer who intends to take on the 1980's celebrating his own satisfactions by sharing them man-to-man with other sensualists. MAN2MAN folds you into the New Adult Homomasculinity of men honestly and quietly declaring their downright upright sexuality, sensuality, and mutuality. No bull. This is a partial list of some of the heavy kicks and kinks you may find in once-and-future issues of MAN2MAN. Hey, it's 1980. Any minute, some hot guy will walk up to you and ask you if you're into one of these fetishes. If all you offer him is sex, you won't get him, because he doesn't want to have suck/fuck sex without his fetish.

Just being gay isn't enough anymore.

Prepare your head, for openers, by reading the rhythms (maybe, as performance art, outloud and with drums) of this partial list of kicks and kinks playing to a man in full possession, and fuller expression, of all his senses.

Tits, pits, fists, ass, feet, boots, filth, sweat, leather, rubber, outlaws, fur, metal harnesses, bondage, restraint, discipline, sadism, masochism, sensuality, mutuality, fingers, grease, bikes, cons, excons, trash, street hustlers, freshly showered athletes, jocks, jockstraps, socks, Levi's, clean cotton, dirty cotton, jerkoff, spitting, man2man worship, bodybuilding, wrestling boxing, padding out, loincloths, chamois, headbands, rebreathing, belching, moustaches, dirty blonds, Brylcreme, Valvoline, Pennzoil, cops, gobs, firemen, mad doctors, catheters, tender loving, intensive care, gym shoes, cleats, cigars, Marlboros, chests, golashes, rubbers, tweeds, pipes, pecs, hair, DA haircuts, shaving, cocksucking, fucking, nylon sleeping bags, wool, wet wool, longjohns, raingear, inner tubes, tires, licking, soap, cubbyholes, enemas, douches, bareback riding, exhibitionism, buzzcuts, faces, snotlockers, five-o'clock shadow, cowboys, linemen, cabins, baby-trips, daddy-fix trips, occultism, flogging, inter-race trips, saliva, spit, hawkers, sniffing, rimming, voyeurism, movies, slides, video, Polaroids, foodtrips, forcefeeding, outerspace, monsterdrag, Mustangs, bicycles, wrestling masks, dirtbiking, mud, hiking, rafting, wafting, religious ritual, blasphemy, tea rooms, tea for two, swearing, military procedures, paramedics, paranoids, barbed wire, wood, wet wood, rain, nails, crucifixion, baths, electricity, field telephone titwork, water, hanging, watersports, scatology, Scat Soap, horseplay, wrists, heavy wrist watches, hairy wrist watching, swimtrunks, Speedos, piercing, Mohawks, tattooing, ritual torture, pain, rosaries, partners, chains, lassoes, outdoor wargames, beebee guns, black eyes, bushwacking, gas-line j/o, cruising straight boulevards on straight cruise night, condoms, tweezers, Greyhound bus sex, ponchos, toiletseat covers, dingle-berries, pigs, flipping the bird, giving the finger, Hell's Angels, Harley Davidsons, Arabs, plainclothes polyester private eyes, sports, cock worship, Mason Jars of dirty bath water, wingtips, Ivy League suits and Oxford-cloth shirts with the tits cut out, hip boots, scuba gear, Saranwrap, snakebite cups, X-acto knives, swords, penknives, canvas, helmets, warriors, mercenaries, downed American flyboys, sumo, Yakuza, fundoshi, chubbies, water beds, hard lean dancers, deafmutes, dentists, rollerballing, pantsing parties, kidnap fantasies, handcuffs, hoists, sweaty stakeout in open field, bike buddy, beach bum, sand, sandpa-per, alleys, dumpsters, dumpers, subways, toilets, dumps, trucks, recruits, toilet paper, brigs, trapezes, cactus, Brazilian interroga-tion techniques, CIA investigation, butch flirting, gentlemen's clubs with overstuffed leather chairs, livery, limos, referee shirts, shitkickers, men who say "Yo," Desenex, Jockey shorts stolen from straight guys' clothes hampers while they help their wives fix supper downstairs, catcher's masks, goalie masks, skates, pucks, puckers, plastic cup supporters, old copies of *Boy's Life*, flannel pennants, letter sweaters, cuspidors, snuff, chaw tobacco, humidors, sputum, smegma, cheese, goobers, fatigues, streak-ing, freaking, leaking, grease racks, Goodyear tire storage rooms, gauze, Ace bandages, Band-Aids, wens, nail clipping, foot mas-sage, choir robes, vestments, altar boys, crumbs, fleabag hotels, young bums, Ipana, foil, humanoids, quick public J/O while pass-ing for straight, canoeing, volcanoes, Coppertone, shoulder pads, Velcro, 501's, trains, upper berths, compartments, mile-high clubfucks, footlockers, blood, straight-edge razors, 747s, burials in the forest, canvas hammocks, hightop basketball shoes, ter-rycloth, professional wrestling, rechewed gum, ashtrays, firemen, the whole nine yards, hand-rolled tailormades, metal tools, chain mail knights, piss, Big Ben coveralls, bib overalls, Dickies slacks, street-fighting, long socks, elastic black garters, boxer shorts, boxing gear, wrestling singlets, poplin windbreakers, breaking

wind, farting, lighting farts, sailors, seafood, airport-USO johns,
Marines, glory holes, docks, use, abuse, whining, whipping,
spanking, pissing on trees, Lex Barker, boarding school sports,
tiger pits, shades, bifocals, ritual smashing of bifocals, goggles,
Eton suits, snowsuits, scuba, needles, guys who suck their teeth,
toothpicks, tents, parachutes, paratroopers, harnesses, erotic art,
slings, balloon-bursting surprises, disguises, pirates, fingerfuck-
ing, steam, backseats, backrows, strangers in the night, parks,
heaths, moors, caskets, dildoes, bimbos, fingercombing hair,
flashing, sticking out tongues, exchanging spit, big dogs humping
Levi's, potnpoppers, cursing, talking dirty, writing nasty, reading
in the raw, Mexicans, machetes, deerhunters, jars of pubic hair,
baggies stuffed with shaved-off beards, prosthetic devices, sutures,
Vietnam vets, beerbellies, WWII vets, ankles, initiations, brand-
ing, bruises, welders, vans, grillework, greasy spoons, cop taverns,
bowling alley bars, high-school laundry, blue collars, ring around
the collar, Bold 3, Tide, Lava, wet hair, iguanas, snakes, armor,
switches, britches, recreational barfing, moonshine, mooning,
farmers, driving naked, CB radio, reststops, guns, rodeos, Mondo
movies, gunbelts, rye whiskey, hats, caps, romance, lovemaking,
forearms, firearms, big arms, muscle contest trophies, 69, sucking, fucking, indoors, outdoors, matches, doing what you do
when you do it like you do, getting the picture, speaking your
mind, doing with your own body what you want, etc.

Afterword
The *Vice* Magazine Interview

Censorship:
Is Gay Literature Porno or Erotica?
Bruno Bayley Interviews Jack Fritscher

British journalist Bruno Bayley sat down with Jack Fritscher for a Q&A about the nasty culture war over "gay literature and censorship" for the international magazine *Vice*, published January 2010. Originally titled "Erotic Fiction, Puritan Censorship, and Gynaecological Detail," the feature, first published by *Vice*, is reprinted with permission.

Bruno Bayley: The old joke about the difference between *erotica* and *pornography* merely being a matter of the lighting, what do you think of that? Exactly where does the boundary lie?

Jack Fritscher: Boundaries are frontiers. Trapped in Bloomsbury, Lytton Strachey dared say "Semen?" and changed London. Cole Porter sang: "Good authors who once knew better words now only use four-letter words writing prose—anything goes." What was porn yesterday is literature today. *Fanny Hill, Ulysses, Lady Chatterley's Lover, Naked Lunch*, and the leather lyrics of gay British poet Thom Gunn have all become pop-culture child's play. I waffle my linguistics between *porn* and *erotica* depending if I'm talking to a sex seminar or to church ladies. I'm not concerned about labels. The endless debate about *erotica* and *porn* is an Ockham's razor important mostly to politically correct academics and to religious fundamentalists. Whether one and the same or not, *erotica* and *porn* should both be judged by multicultural literary standards.

Vice readers, living in the slipstream of fundamentalism sweeping the world, might take action that censorship does not bring back the "old school" closet of having to "read between the lines." Satirizing that difficult search for nasty bits, songwriter Tom Lehrer wrote: "All books can be indecent books/though recent books are bolder,/for filth (I'm glad to say)/ is in the mind of the beholder./When correctly viewed,/everything is lewd."

In the American fundamentalist theater of the absurd, seven of Robert Mapplethorpe's photographs were put on trial in Ohio during 1990 to determine if they were erotica or porn. I have a certain insight in that I was Mapplethorpe's bicoastal lover, and, as editor of *Drummer* magazine, I assigned him his first cover before he was world famous. While I thought Robert's content and style beautiful, I doubt to this day if for all his vaunted "porno" anyone has every masturbated to a Mapplethorpe photograph. (All seven were acquitted.) Regarding the seesaw between *erotica* and *porn*, my longtime pal, the London art critic Edward Lucie-Smith, pointed out, "A Mapplethorpe photo of a calla lily hanging in the dining room gains *frisson* from the Mapplethorpe fisting photo hanging in the bedroom."

About the impossibility of defining pornography, Justice Potter Stewart, in the most famous phrase ever uttered by the U.S. Supreme Court, said he couldn't define it, but "I know it when I see it." Porn is personal. I'm an author without borders. I write gripping tales for prehensile readers. I don't write porn. I write literary erotica that begins in the head and works its way down. In the alchemy of eros, if readers cum, it is they defining what is erotica and what is porn.

Bruno Bayley: You earned a doctorate for your dissertation *Love and Death in Tennessee Williams*. Was that the start of your interest in erotic writing, or merely the culmination of an amateur interest that then became a profession? Could you name some "classic novels" that many people might read totally oblivious to their erotic undercurrents, or importance to erotic writing?

Jack Fritscher: As the conformist 1950s became the liberated

1960s, I read Tennessee Williams to learn about sex because I was an innocent student stranded in a Catholic seminary, and I was having a nervous breakthrough. After reading five Williams plays, I ended my eleven years of study, exited the seminary, came out into the world, and met Tennessee Williams. He was an archetypal artist making sexuality intelligent and literary in *Baby Doll*, *A Streetcar Named Desire*, and *Suddenly Last Summer*. In the ironic alert inherent in censorship, when I was eight years old, a shrieking priest in a pulpit had inadvertently made me aware of *Forever Amber*, the best selling novel of the 1940s that was condemned by the Catholic Church's delirious *Index of Forbidden Books*. Growing up like most Catholic intellectuals, I made the *Index* my reading list for classic literature.

Born a writer, I was hellbent on learning how to connect with readers. Is there any writing more interactive than eroticism that seduces a reader to orgasm? Censorship, conveniently citing page references, guided me to the forbidden passages in Flaubert, Balzac, and George Sand. The *Index* condemning all works by De Sade, Zola, Sartre, Moravia, and Gide, was threatening Tennessee Williams when its Inquisitional reign of terror (1515-1966) was stopped by Pope John XXIII. Absurdly, it continues defining porn in the right-wing group "Opus Dei" outed by *The Da Vinci Code*.

Pumped up on the *Index*, the Catholic Legion of Decency listed films whose viewing would send me to hell, or at least to the library to borrow the filthy books adapted by Hollywood. When the priest who was my highschool English teacher lectured on Walt Whitman, he said *Leaves of Grass* was literature, but too dirty for boys. I immediately wrapped the book in a plain brown wrapper. Expecting a sex panic, I fell into esthetic rapture that exposed the sex hysteria in my bourgeois education. Excited in my Speedo, I was Whitman's "Twenty-Ninth Bather" swooning with lust. That shock of recognition is the heart of erotica when sex and desire validate identity with the great *Yes* of a cumshot: "OMG, I really am gay!"

I was a very aggro lad attuned to whispers about sex, and I moved on to scanning between the lines of brilliant filth by James Joyce, Genet, Nabokov, Radclyffe Hall, William Burroughs,

James Leo Herlihy, Anais Nin, and my late friend, James Purdy. These writers, and Henry Miller and Camus and Ginsberg at Olympia Press and *The Evergreen Review*, taught me the rhetorical tricks of the trade. With dick in hand, I learned how to spell *hard-on*. At age fourteen, my kickstart in erotic writing was yob masturbation. I wrote to make explicit what I found missing in the erotic undertow of novels. I wanted the pen to be as mighty as the penis. I had grown up frustrated in movie palaces during World War II when, during a love scene, the camera cut away from the kiss to waves crashing on shore, or to a train roaring into a tunnel. I didn't want to write that way. I wanted the full monty.

Bruno Bayley: In erotic literature, do you favour subtlety or directness? My dad says, "For me, some of the most erotic writing of all is in Alberto Moravia's novels and short stories. These are very subtle and tend to describe gloomy afternoons behind net curtains in apartments in Rome." What are your views on the relative merits of subtlety vs. gynecological anatomical detail in erotic writing?

Jack Fritscher: I love the extraordinary films *Two Women* and *The Conformist* adapted from Alberto Moravia's engaging novels. Enlivened on the screen, his sexual realism on the page had heat back in the day of Mussolini's Fascist censorship before sexual liberation, but now that the net curtains have parted? Born freer thirty years after Moravia and Tennessee Williams, I was the next generation. I respect that the hustler-sex of Tennessee Williams' *The Roman Spring of Mrs Stone* had to occur behind the hotel portieres. Erotic pioneers, like Joyce in *Ulysses*, Moravia and Williams slowly stripped the dance of the seven veils using six, then five, then four veils.

Since 1964 in the U.S. when the written word became protected by the Constitution, my generation hasn't had to drape the windows of sex. So: what if an author writes an erotic story and no reader cums? Teasing in sex writing can be a turnon until it becomes all talk and no action. I don't want to write the menu of sex. I want to cook the food. I want it hot. I want to deliver it. I want to fuck the takeaway customer. I'm a very direct male.

I channel sex. I write declarative sentences. I don't write twee description. I write dialogue. As an erotic stylist, I find poetry in Anglo-Saxon words. Like Moravia and Whitman, I use common words. I write with explicit nouns and verbs. Unlike academics who misspell *come*, I spell *cum*. I like to knuckle up the reader with priapic rhythms as in my Irish story "Chasing Danny Boy."

However, I can zip up my fly and write romantically, and have done in my novel *Some Dance to Remember*, and in a recent short story about two lads caught in the 1906 San Francisco earthquake published in *Best Gay Romance 2009*. I was pleasantly surprised at the critics' acceptance of that tenderness because gay readers tend to demand that I write about hard-driving homomasculine sex. To test my own agility to see if I could write as "camp" as Paul Rudnick or David Sedaris, I penned a drag style in my comic short story "Stonewall: June 28, 1969, 11 PM" which is nominated this year for a Lambda Literary Award. In my romantic short novel *Titanic*, the narrative tends toward humor and then the terrible loss of disaster. However, in my *Titanic*, before the ship goes down, all the characters go down...on each other. Priapic detail? Gynecological detail? I can do that. I have written explicit lesbian and straight erotica for major publishers like Larry Flynt.

Bruno Bayley: I take it, from what I have read, that in your opinion erotic fiction is of a totally different level of importance to the gay community than it is to the heterosexual community? What purposes does it serve in the respective communities?

Jack Fritscher: Even though I was conceived and raised by heterosexuals, my sense is that straight erotica veers quickly away from male-female intercourse to that other dimension of kinky sex whose escalating degree of difficulty is akin to Olympic skaters trying to cut a "Figure 8" backwards on an ice cube. Commercial straight erotica is not about missionary sex. It is more often about power and being fisted in bondage by the archetypal Ilsa, She-Wolf of the SS. There is a hardly a taboo left standing.

Perhaps an essential difference between the erotic fiction of straights and of gays is that GLBT folks regard erotica as an identity art form. By its essentialist nature, queer erotica puts its finger on what makes the gay community different from the straight: identity sexuality. Growing up, straight kids are, simply, straight. Without such surety, gay kids must search out defini-tions of themselves. Pop culture magazines and media indicate that straight men use porn to satisfy their alternative sex urges and fetish tastes between bouts of breedership, and not for sorting their sexual identity in the bathroom where gay identity emerges singing pop tunes into a hairbrush.

Erotic writing is as necessary to gay culture as rap is to black culture. Without sex, and, radically, without sex that makes the reader cum at the roots, gay writing has no gay soul. It is just alternative safe mainstream corporate writing. The anti-sex self-censorship in the politically correct GLBT community is a self-hating scandal, and many famous gay fiction authors who are professional homosexuals at work in the fields of academe do not even have the skill sets to write erotica.

While editing and writing the monthly *Drummer* magazine for a quarter of a century with feedback from the readers, I have noticed that the lesbigay readership is nearly 100% sexual bot-toms. Therefore, all the gay erotica I write and photograph is created to dominate the reader and viewer. I've shot nearly two hundred rather successful erotic videos all from the point of view of the voyeur-bottom lying stoned on the couch at home. Straight erotica sells the same dominance. It seems everyone straight and gay on the planet is looking for a top who will fucking control them. (That's how religion was invented. And nipple clamps.)

Without erotic literature, straight culture could arguably march on. Without erotic literature, however, gay culture would not have its essentialist training manuals. Specifically, straight culture does not need *The Catcher in the Rye* to survive, but per-versatile gay culture absolutely requires thousands of detailed coming-out and coming-of-age stories.

Bruno Bayley: In terms of erotica, how do you view the differ-ing treatments between heterosexual and homosexual erotic literature by the mainstream?

Jack Fritscher: Booksellers enforce their own "Don't Ask Don't Tell." Mainstream publishers are corporations run by conservative Puritan businessmen who marginalize gay erotic literature because they fear fundamentalist religionists might threaten a boycott as they did with the benign *Brokeback Mountain*. The children's powerhouse publisher Scholastic recently banned from elementary-school book fairs a kiddy-lit book featuring lesbian moms. My own books published by dedicated gay presses, especially the hard-core *Leather Blues*, are often confiscated when sent through Canadian Customs.

There is a double standard. The quintessential difference between perceptions of hetero and homo literature is that the mainstream thinks that specifically erotic straight books are individuated from other straight books, but in a triumph of global homophobia, the mainstream thinks that ALL gay writing, whether about sex or not, is somehow erotic...and dangerous.

As an analogy, if a straight photographer and a gay photographer identically photograph a nude male at the same time and place, the verdict is that the straight photo is art and the other is gay porn. When Gay Men's Press of London published a coffee-table book of my photographs titled *American Men* (1995), the book was considered "erotic art" and was permitted because it was a "gay" book; but when author Edward Lucie-Smith tried to include some of those photos of men with erections in his historical survey *Ars Erotica*, the photos were censored by his publishers on both sides of the Atlantic because *Ars Erotica* was a "straight" book. If Mapplethorpe had been straight, he would never have been censored, and he might have become famous for little more than fathering the children of Patti Smith.

Big-box bookstores display straight sex magazines on their racks, but their begrudged gay book section is closeted away on four or five book shelves, and features lesbian writing more than gay male writing because, insofar as lesbians are women, they are of safe fetish interest to straights. Just as the straight mainstream is twisted over gay literature, the GLBT mainstream is twisted over gender. When my publisher sent a copy of my award-winning comic novel *The Geography of Women* to *The Harvard Gay and Lesbian Review*, the editor wrote back that he did not know how to review a book about women written by a man. I sent him a note and asked him how he would review *A Streetcar Named Desire*.

The few surviving GLBT bookstores focus mostly on feminist, ethnic, and politically correct titles, heavy on the academic, the self-help, the biographies, all of which are subsidized through the sale of gay greeting cards, male pin-up calendars, and porn magazines. The best mainstream ally that GLBT erotic literature has ever had is the new breed of online book sellers who mail all titles off in discreet packages to the smallest towns. A click-and-order straight bookstore is more culture changing than a bricks-and-mortar gay bookstore. Even so, anti-gay censorship can happen quickly at a corporation. During 2009, book giant Amazon suffered an attack of "gay panic" and dropped all gay titles from its site. When GLBT customers protested, Amazon blamed a computer error, and, after nearly a week of excuses and apologies, returned to selling gay books.

Bruno Bayley: In 1968, you wrote your first erotic novel *Leather Blues*. Since then you have written countless stories, articles, memoirs, and histories. Do you feel the fiction is still as important in representing the gay community as academic writing or biography? Has the Internet undermined erotic publishing?

Jack Fritscher: Fiction is all-important. Fiction reflects soul. But fiction is sinking slowly in the west. Ninety percent of titles nowadays are nonfiction. Fiction, like scripted television, has fallen victim to reality shows and blog postings. As a humanist, I'm disappointed because the current fad of politically correct academic writing is, among some other toiletries, reverse sexism, reverse racism, and twaddle psycho-babbled by newly minted academics, who are themselves often sadly educated, and desperate to publish or perish. Most academics should be given a drink-driving test before being allowed to write anything about homosexuality.

Storytelling is important to the human psyche. It is quintessentially important to GLBT culture in its final uncloseting. In the 1970s, gay magazines worked to develop gay authors. My *Drummer* magazine helped create the very leather culture we reported on each issue. Now killed by the Internet, that fertile magazine culture that churned out new material every thirty days has been replaced by dozens of annual gay fiction anthologies of the splendid kind invented by the Canadian critic Richard Labonté and edited by, for instance, the legendary Susie Bright in her straight-and-gay mixer *Best American Erotica.*

I am an academic who immigrated from the university ivory tower to the corporate world and to the gay *dolce vita* of GLBT publishing. Those who can, do; those who can't, teach. In my hybrid career, I've written academic books and papers, biography, history, and fiction, and directed films. These days many gay fiction authors, such as Edmund White and Larry Kramer and I, are trending toward publishing autobiography, biography, and nonfiction history. In 1968, I was impelled to write *Leather Blues* as an erotic-fiction novel and send it to a publisher. In 2009, one is more likely to shoot a video documentary about S&M leather and post it on Youtube. I am dedicated to both gay fiction and gay nonfiction equally because each singularly channels GLBT voices in a way that the great gay poet Walt Whitman would approve.

As example, I have written a mix of three fiction and nonfiction books about the first decade of gay liberation, the 1970s. Each book's subtitle reveals how much the DNA of fiction and nonfiction is related. In 1984, I completed the historical epic *Some Dance to Remember* whose mixed-genre subtitle is *A Memoir-Novel of San Francisco 1970-1982.* As if to underscore the nonfiction contents of that fictitious novel, the new 2010 edition is published with an index—a research tool no novel has had built-in before. In 2008, I completed twenty-five years of work on the nonfiction *Gay San Francisco* which is virtually the same story as *Some Dance* but with real people, and an index, which can also be read—as I surrender to the Internet—free online at my site. Its subtitle is a precise thumbnail: *A Memoir of the Sex, Art, Salon, Pop Culture War, and Gay History of Drummer Magazine from the Titanic 1970s to 1999.* My personal erotic memoir *Mapplethorpe: Assault with a Deadly Camera* (1994) was subtitled *A Pop-Culture Memoir, An Outlaw Reminiscence.* As an eyewitness pioneer of the gay literary scene since the mid-1960s, I think fiction and nonfiction remain equally valid, but it is fiction that is the endangered species.

Jack Fritscher is the author

of the award-winning *Gay San Francisco: Eyewitness Drummer* and of 12 books including his nonfiction memoir of his bicoastal lover, Robert Mapplethorpe, *Mapplethorpe: Assault with a Deadly Camera*—companion to his best-selling 1990 novel of Gay History 1970-1982, *Some Dance to Remember*. He is the founding San Francisco editor in chief of *Drummer* maga-

Jack Fritscher, San Francisco 2000, by Mark Hemry

zine who, the *Bay Area Reporter* writes, "created gay magazines as we know them, inventing the leather prose style."

He virtually created *Drummer*, the first leather magazine published after Stonewall.

Hundreds of his photographs and more than 400 of his stories have appeared in 30 magazines. Chuck Renslow, founder of IML and the Leather Archives and Museum says, "Fritscher is an uninhibited tour guide of leather culture."

In 1998, his third collection of fiction, *Rainbow County and Other Stories* won the U.S. National Small Press Award for Best Erotica from a field of straight, lesbian, and gay fiction and nonfiction. In 1999, his novel, *The Geography of Women: A Romantic Comedy*, was Finalist for the Independent Publisher Award for Best Fiction in the U.S. His first nonfiction book, *Popular Witchcraft: Straight from the Witch's Mouth* (1971) followed his first novel, *Leather Blues* (1969). In 1994, 55 of his photographs, from magazine covers and photo spreads, were published in the coffee-table book *Jack Fritscher's American Men*, Gay Men's Press, London.

His third and fourth collections of fiction, *Stand by Your Man* and *Titanic: Forbidden Stories Hollywood Forgot*, were published in 1999. His fifth fiction collection, *Sweet Embraceable You: Coffee-House Stories*, and his novel, *What They Did to the Kid*, were both published in 2000. His sixth fiction collection was the Lambda Literary Award nominee *Stonewall: Stories of Gay Liberation*, 2009.

www.JackFritscher.com

Acknowledgements and History

The author expresses acknowledgment and gratitude to the many magazine publishers and editors who have framed these stories into print over the years, and to the art directors and artists who illustrated the stories. Their roles in periodical publishing are often overlooked, underestimated, or lost to history. Appreciation is also owed to the hundreds of magazine readers who have encouraged versions of these stories with letters, requests, suggestions, and edits coming from their personal desire.

"That Boy That Summer" appeared as "Anticipation: That Long Hot Summer" in *Skin*, Volume 2, #3, May-June 1981: Editor, Bob Johnson, Los Angeles , illustrated with a full-page color photograph by John Cox, Jr. The same issue contained Jack Fritscher's interview with filmmaker, J. Brian, who handled a stable of hustlers who serviced clientele such as Rock Hudson: "Boys for Hire." Also appeared in *Man2Man Quarterly* #7, Spring/March 1981: Publisher, Mark Hemry; Editor, Jack Fritscher, San Francisco; also appeared in *The California Action Guide*, Volume 1, #1, July 1982: Publisher, Michael Redman; Editor, Jack Fritscher; Art Director, Mark Hemry. *Action Guide* photographs by David Hurles' Old Reliable Studio, Los Angeles, and David Sparrow/Jack Fritscher, San Francisco.

"I'm a Sucker for Uncut Meat" appeared in *Skin*, Volume 2 #4, July-August 1981: Editor, Bob Johnson, Los Angeles. Also appeared in *Man2Man Quarterly* #2, Winter/December 1980: Publisher, Mark Hemry; Editor, Jack Fritscher, San Francisco. Appeared as well in *The California Action Guide*, Volume 1, #1, July 1982: Publisher, Michael Redman; Editor, Jack Fritscher; Art Director, Mark Hemry, San Francisco. The story provided the concept for the video, *Tom's Gloryhole: Foreskin Obsession*, Palm Drive Video. Straight businessman Michael Redman was the successful San Francisco publisher of the straight tabloid, *California Pleasure Guide*, sold in adult stores and vending machines on the streets of San Francisco. He advertised in the Sunday *Chronicle* for an experienced editor to conceptualize and start-up a companion adult tabloid, the gay *California Action Guide*. Redman and Fritscher interviewed at the Noe Valley coffee-shop and deli, the Meat Market, on 24th Street a few doors west of Castro, May 14, 1982.

"Big Beefy College Jocks" appeared in *Man2Man Quarterly* #2, Winter/December 1980: Publisher, Mark Hemry; Editor, Jack Fritscher, San Francisco.

"The Princeton Rub"appeared in *Skin*, Volume 2, #1, January-February 1980: Editor, Bob Johnson, Los Angeles; and as "Speedos, Jockstraps, and the Princeton Rub" in *Man2Man Quarterly* #4, Summer/June 1981: Publisher, Mark Hemry; Editor, Jack Fritscher, San Francisco.

"Corporal in Charge of Taking Care of Captain O'Malley" appeared serialized in two installments. The first act, published in *Drummer* #22, May 1978, was illustrated with a Bob Mizer photograph from Athletic Model Guild and a drawing created by Al Shapiro, the artist A. Jay, who was also art director; the second act appeared in *Drummer* #23, July 1978, with an opening illustration by Al Shapiro/A. Jay: Publisher, John Embry; Editor, Jack Fritscher, San Francisco. Inspiring director David Hurles, Old Reliable studios, created an audiotape of an early version of this written piece in its first performance-art origination in Los Angeles in 1977. The art of A. Jay/Al Shapiro appears in this volume at the suggestion of "the Widow Shapiro," Dick Kriegmont. A unique collection of A. Jay's art is the subject of *The A. Jay Video Gallery: Spit*, 60 minutes, Palm Drive Video.

"USMC Slap Captain" is both a pioneer story and a famously reprinted story of iconic, archetypal gay myth. It was the first story in the gay press introducing slapping as a fetish, and initially appeared as "USMC Slapcaptain: How The Corporal Came to Be in Charge of Taking Care of Captain O'Malley" in *Man2Man Quarterly* #7, Spring/March 1982: Publisher, Mark Hemry; Editor, Jack Fritscher, San Francisco. "Slap Captain" also appeared in *Dungeonmaster* #47, January 1994: Publisher, Martyn Bakker; Editor, Anthony F. DeBlase; illustrated with two photographs by

Jack Fritscher: one of actor Terry Kelly from the Palm Drive Video, *Hot Lunch* (*Dungeonmaster*, page 24), and a second from the Palm Drive Video, *Gut Punchers*, starring Dan Dufort, 2nd-Place Winner of Physique Contest, Gay Games II, San Francisco, August 15, 1986. Mark Hemry and Jack Fritscher, as Palm Drive Video, shot the only video of the physique contest at the Castro Theater for Gay Games I (at that time called "The Gay Olympics"). The same gut-puncher photograph, requested specifically by Brian Pronger, was also featured (unindexed) in Brian Pronger's *Gay Sports: The Arena of Masculinity* (St Martin's Press, 1990)."Slap Captain" also appeared in *Powerplay* #10, May 1996, Brush Creek Media, San Francisco, with illustration drawn by DadeUrsus, with color cover shot by Jack Fritscher from the cover of the photography book, *Jack Fritscher's American Men* (GMP, London, 1995), including two pages of five photographs by Jack Fritscher titled "Slap Shots." Publisher, Bear-Dog Hoffman; Editor, Alec Wagner. Confer also the Palm Drive Video, *Slap Happy*. "USMC Slapcaptain" also was featured in *Best Gay Literary Erotica 1998*, Edited by Richard LaBonté, Selected and Introduced by Christopher Bram, Cleis Press. Editor LaBonté combined "USMC Slapcaptain" with Jack Fritscher's "Cigar Sarge" under the Fritscher title, "Sexual Harassment in the Military: 2 Performance Pieces for 4 Actors in 3 Lovely Costumes." Christopher Bram is the author of the novel, *Father of Frankenstein*, upon which was based the Academy-Award winning movie, *Gods and Monsters*, starring Ian McKellen, Lynn Redgrave, and Brendan Fraser.

"Officer Mike: San Francisco's Finest" appeared in *Just Men*, Volume 1 #4, May-June 1984: Editor, Bob Johnson. Illustrated with a Rapidograph drawing by Rex. Fritscher and Rex collaborated in a Tenderloin coffee shop in San Francisco to discuss the concept, as an experiment for the gay press, so that words and illustration would match organically, rather than the usual paste-up of slapping almost any illustration to almost any text. A very early "leather" draft appeared as "Mike: Solo" in *Skin*, Volume 2 #2, November 1980: Editor, Bob Johnson, Los Angeles. Illustrated with a color photograph from Western Man Studio, San Francisco. The same issue featured Jack Fritscher's long poem, "In

Praise of Fuckabilly Butt," illustrated with a charcoal drawing by the artist Kit whose narrative cartoon strip, "The Adventures of Billy Joe"–a leathery Huckleberry Finn, appeared episodically in *Skin* (Eg.: *Skin*, Volume 2 #1, 1980).

"Black-and-White-and-Brown Doublefuck" appeared in *Just Men*, Volume 1 #1, June 1982: Founding Editor, Bob Johnson, Los Angeles.

"Hustler Bars" appeared in *Skin*, Volume 2 #5, September-October 1981: Editor, Bob Johnson, Los Angeles; appeared also as "Paying For Sex" in *The California Action Guide*, Volume 1 #6, December 1982, San Francisco, with four photographs by David Hurles' Old Reliable Studio, Los Angeles; and as the (by-lined on-cover) cover feature, "Hustler Bars: Show Me the Money!" in *International Drummer* #204, June 1997, San Francisco, which continued to list Jack Fritscher on the masthead as a continuously "Contributing Writer," twenty years after he first edited *Drummer*. This issue also featured four color pages (22-25) of photographs reproduced electronically from Jack Fritscher's Palm Drive Video feature, *Dave Gold's Gym Workout*. The issue of *Skin*, Volume 2 #5, was written by Jack Fritscher whose two other gay-history articles in this issue were "AMG's Duos: Bob Mizer's *Physique Pictorial* Studio" with 15 AMG photographs in color and black and white, and "Old Reliable: The Company That Dirty Talk Built," illustrated with a drawing by Rex and with 23 David Hurles' Old Reliable Studio photographs in color and black-and-white. Also appeared as "Patron of the Arts" in the anthology *Bar Stories*, edited by Scott Brassart, Alyson Publications, 2000, Los Angeles/New York.

"Young Deputy K-9 Cop" first appeared as "Dog Master" in the premiere issue of *Man2Man Quarterly* #1, October 1980, "The Documentary Journal of Homomasculine Gay Popular Culture": Publisher, Mark Hemry; Editor, Jack Fritscher; Cover model, Jim Enger. Also appeared as "Dog Dik" in *The California Action Guide*, Volume 1 #3, September 1982: Publisher, Michael Redman; Editor, Jack Fritscher; Art Director, Mark Hemry.

"Fisting the Selfsucker" first appeared in the premiere issue of *Skin*, Volume 1 #3, May-June 1980: Editor, Bob Johnson, Los Angeles; illustrated with a full-page color photograph of autofellatio by Richard Lyle. This story was pre-amble to a larger feature article written by Jack Fritscher titled "Solo Sex" that appeared as the cover feature in *Drummer* #123, November 1988.

"Caro Ricardo" appeared, as gift to Robert Mapplethorpe, in the first edition of *Corporal in Charge*. Transposed to a nonfiction memoir–a feature-article obituary, "Caro Ricardo" appeared as "Pentimento for Robert Mapplethorpe" in *Drummer* #133, August 1989. Publisher, Anthony DeBlase, in May 1989, two months after Robert's death in March 1989, welcomed the feature two months before the Mapplethorpe censorship controversy broke out, July 1989. The piece appeared as "Chapter Two: Pentimento for Robert Mapplethorpe" in the hard-cover nonfiction memoir, *Mapplethorpe: Assault with a Deadly Camera*, Hastings House, 1994. A similar feature- article obituary of the artist A. Jay appeared in *Drummer* #107, October 1987: Publisher, Anthony DeBlase; Editor, JimEd Thompson. A. Jay was the artist who created the original artwork for the first magazine publication of "Corporal in Charge." Robert Mapplethorpe's first cover was cast, designed, and commissioned by Jack Fritscher for the cover of *Drummer* #24, October 1978. The intended Mapplethorpe-Fritscher book was to be titled, *Rimshots: Inside the Fetish Factor*.

"B-Movie on Castro Street" appeared in *In Touch* # 57, July 1981: Editor-in-Chief, John Calendo, Los Angeles. The story is a 1981 draft of a scene for, but not used in, the 1990 novel, *Some Dance to Remember*, which was fully complete as a book manuscript in February, 1984, and first published as a whole by Tim Barrus and Elizabeth Gershman, Knights Press, Stamford, Connecticut.

"The Best Dirty-Blond Carpenter in Texas" appeared in *Man-2Man Quarterly* #8, Summer/June 1981: Publisher, Mark Hemry; Editor, Jack Fritscher, San Francisco; also appeared as the cover feature, "Fiction by Fritscher," in *The Target Album* # 3, Winter 1982: Publisher, Lou Thomas, Target Studios, New

York, with drawing created specifically for this story by Dom Orejudos aka "Etienne/Stephan," Chicago. A second drawing was created by the New York artist, Domino, posing Jack Fritscher's bodybuilder-lover, Jim Enger, as the model for the fictional story. The drawing appears also in *The Domino Video Gallery: New York Natives*, 2000, Palm Drive Video, Jack Fritscher, director; Mark Hemry, producer.

"Earthorse, written in 1973, first appeared in *Man2Man Quarterly* #3, Spring/March 1981: Publisher, Mark Hemry; Editor, Jack Fritscher, San Francisco. "Earthorse" was written the week the UPI reported one of the world's first successful human-transplant stories about a woman suing to take a body-part for herself from her institutionalized, insane brother.

"Titsports: Our Pecs Belong to the Sundance, Kid" appeared as "Tit Torture Blues" in *Drummer* #30, June 1979: Publisher, John Embry; Editor, Jack Fritscher, San Francisco. Photographic illustrations by Richard Moore, Philip Beard, Mikal Bales' Zeus Studios, and Joe Tiffenbach; line drawing illustration of "Pecs O'Toole" created for the article by Al Shapiro, the artist A. Jay, who was the art director; Al Shapiro introduced his "Pecs O'Toole" comic strip when he was art director for *Queen's Quarterly*, New York. Also appeared in *Man2Man Quarterly* #5, Fall/September 1981: Publisher, Mark Hemry; Editor, Jack Fritscher, San Francisco; also appeared in *The California Action Guide*, Volume 1 #5, November 1982: Publisher, Michael Redman; Editor, Jack Fritscher, San Francisco. Illustrated with a drawing titled "Nipples with Boot" (dated 4-28-81) created for this piece by Rex, New York. Continuing the nipple theme, Fritscher wrote, "Tits: Radical Nipples," for *Drummer* #143, October 1990, illustrations by Zeus Studio. The original story also served as the treatment for the video feature, *Tit Torture Blues*, 1988, Palm Drive Video, San Francisco.

"Wet Dreams and Golden Showers" appeared as the cover feature, "Pissing in the Wind," in *Drummer* #20, December 1977: Publisher, John Embry; Editor, Jack Fritscher, San Francisco.

Photographic illustrations by the Gage Brothers from their feature film, *El Paso Wrecking Company.*

"Fetish *Noir*" was written as the introductory editorial for the premiere issue of *Fetish Noir* magazine (Volume 1 #1, February 1998) at the request of the editing art director, Armando Aguilar, Royce Publications Distributing, Los Angeles. "*Fetish Noir*: Pansexual Pleasures for the Perverse." Also included was a review by Jack Fritscher of Japanese straight erotic-bondage video; the review was titled, "Asian Market Crisis Ties Madame Butterfly in Knots." "The List" first appeared in a 1979 brochure announcing the premiere issue of *Man2Man Quarterly,* and then in the *California Action Guide,* Volume 1 #2, August 1982, as well as in the first edition of *Corporal in Charge* with the introductory lead line incorrectly laid out at Gay Sunshine Press. The author did not submit "The List" for the Prowler Press edition in the U.K. "The List" in this edition restores the first edition.

"Nooner Sex," "By Blonds Obsessed," and "Cruising the Merchant Marines" are original to the first edition of *Corporal in Charge.* "Nooner Sex" was written as a companion piece to Jack Fritscher's cover-feature, "The Daddy Mystique," *In Touch* #56, June 1981: Editor, John Calendo. "By Blonds Obsessed" was written in October 1981 at David Hurles' Old Reliable apartment, Hollywood. "Cruising the Merchant Marines" was written in San Francisco, January 1983.

All these stories, scripts, and articles were first printed in book form in the sold-out best-seller (10,000 copies), *Corporal in Charge of Taking Care of Captain O'Malley and Other Stories,* produced by publisher Winston Leyland, Gay Sunshine Press, San Francisco, 1984. In England, in 1998, *Corporal in Charge,* with some stories transposed, was published in a paperback edition by Prowler Press, London. For further gay popular culture information and literary history, visit www.JackFritscher.com.

In This Book
Photographs by Jack Fritscher

Chris Duffy, Mr. America, cover, color photograph; from video,
 Sunset Bull

Page iv: Chris Duffy, color photograph; *Sunset Bull*

Page viii: Steve Thrasher, video capture from *Thrasher: If Looks
 Could Kill*

Page x: Lifeguard, color photograph; from video *Young Muscle*

Page 6: Larry Perry, color photograph; from video,
 Naked Came the Stranger

Page 14: Chris Duffy, cover, color photograph; *Sunset Bull*

Page 53: "Slap Happy," color photograph

Page 59: Chris Duffy, color photograph; *Sunset Bull*

Page 65: "What Wraps around a Motorcycle," color photograph

Page 68: José del Norté, B&W photograph; from video,
 Illegal Alien Blues

Page 74: Sonny Butts, color photograph; from video,
 When Sonny Turns Daddy

Page 84: Mike Welder, B&W photograph; from video,
 Uncut Muscle Mechanic

Page 90: Tom Howard, color photograph; from video,
 Party Animal Raw

Page 96: B&W photograph of poster; from video,
 Domino Video Gallery

Page 112: Donnie Russo, color photograph; from video,
 5 Guys in a Whorehouse

Page 130: Mickey Squires, color photograph

Page 156: David Sparrow, color photograph

Availability

The photographs reproduced herein are available as original prints signed by
the artist. Print types, sizes, edition sizes, and prices are also available on specific request by title.

Order and inquiries may be directed to:
Mark Hemry, mark@PalmDrivePublishing.com

For information about videos directed and photographed
by Jack Fritscher: www.JackFritscher.com

Also by Jack Fritscher

Fiction Books

Leather Blues, novel, 1969, 1972 and 1984

Corporal in Charge of Taking Care of Captain O'Malley and Other Stories, 1984, 1999, 2000

Stand By Your Man and Other Stories, 1987, 1999

Some Dance to Remember: A Memoir-Novel of San Francisco 1970-1982, 1990, 2005

The Geography of Women, 1998

Titanic: Forbidden Stories Hollywood Forgot, 1999

Sweet Embraceable You: Coffee-House Stories, 2000

Jacked: The Best of Jack Fritscher, 2002

Stonewall: Stories of Gay Liberation, 2009

Non-Fiction Books

Love and Death in Tennessee Williams, 1967

Popular Witchcraft: Straight from the Witch's Mouth, 1971, 2004

Television Today, 1972

Mapplethorpe: Assault with a Deadly Camera, 1994

Mapplethorpe: El fotographo del escandalo, 1995

Gay San Francisco: Eyewitness Drummer—A Memoir of the Sex, Art, Salon, Pop Culture War, and Gay History of Drummer Magazine, 2008

Photography Book

Jack Fritscher's American Men, London, UK, 1995

Writing in Other's Books

Gay Roots: Twenty Years of Gay Sunshine: An Anthology of Gay History, Sex, Politics, and Culture, Winston Leyland, 1991

Vamps and Tramps: New Essays, Camille Paglia, 1994

Leatherfolk: Radical Sex, People, Politics, and Practice, Mark Thompson, 1991

Mystery, Magic, and Miracle: Religion in a Post-Aquarian Age, Edward F. Heenan, 1973

Challenges in American Culture, Ray B. Browne, 1970

Best Gay Erotica 1997, Douglas Sadownick and Richard Labonté,

1997

Best Gay Erotica 1998, Richard Labonté, 1998

Chasing Danny Boy: Powerful Stories of Celtic Eros, Mark Hemry, 1999

Bar Stories, Scott Brassart, 2000

Best of the Best Gay Erotica, Richard Labonté, 2000

Friction 3, Austin Foxxe & Jesse Grant, 2000

The Leatherman's Handbook, "Gay History Introduction," 25th Anniversary Edition, Larry Townsend, 2000

Rough Stuff, Simon Sheppard & M. Christian, 2000

Bear Book II, Les Wright, 2001

The Burning Pen: Sex Writers on Sex Writing, Simon Sheppard, 2001

Tales from the Bear Cult, Mark Hemry, 2001

Twink, John Hart, 2001

Bears on Bears, Ron Suresha, 2002

Censorship: An International Encyclopedia, Derek Jones, 2002

Friction 5, Jesse Grant and Austin Foxxe, 2002

Tough Guys, Bill Brent & Rob Stephenson, 2002

Best American Erotica 2003, Susie Bright, 2003

Kink, Paul Willis & Ron Jackson, 2003

First Hand, Tim Brough, 2006

Country Boys, Richard Labonté, 2007

Homosex: Sixty Years of Gay Erotica, Simon Sheppard, 2007

Best Gay Bondage Erotica, Richard Labonté, 2008

Best Gay Romance 2008, Richard Labonté, 2008

Best Gay Romance 2009, Richard Labonté, 2009

Special Forces: Gay Military Erotica, Phillip MacKenzie, Jr., 2009

Muscle Men, Richard Labonté, 2010

Writing in Scholarly Journals

"William Bradford's *History of Plymouth Plantation*,"
The Bucknell Review

"Religious Ritual in the Plays of Tennessee Williams,"
Modern Drama

"2001: A Space Odyssey,"
The Journal of American Popular Culture

"The Boys in the Band in *The Boys in the Band*,"

The Journal of Popular Culture
"*Hair*: The Dawning of the Age of Aquarius,"
The Journal of Popular Culture

Photographs Appearing in Other's Books

The Arena of Masculinity: Sports, Homosexuality, and the Meaning of Sex, Brian Pronger, London, 1990

Narrow Rooms, James Purdy [cover], London, 1997

Ars Erotica: An Encyclopedic Guide, Edward Lucie-Smith, London, 1998

Adam: The Male Figure in Art, Edward Lucie-Smith, London, 1998

International Mr. Leather (IML): 25 Years of Champions, Joseph W. Bean, 2004

The Big Penis Book, Dian Hanson, Taschen, 2008

Writing and Photography in Magazine Culture

Jack Fritscher's fiction, essays, and photography appear regularly or variously in the following magazines: *Drummer, International Leatherman, Honcho, Thrust, Harrington Gay Men's Fiction Quarterly, The James White Review, Vice, Unzipped, Leather Times: Journal of the Leather Archives & Museum, The Leather Journal, Skin, Skinflicks, Dungeonmaster, Inches, In Touch, Checkmate, Powerplay, Bear, Classic Bear Annual, Son of Drummer, Bunkhouse, Mach, Man2Man Quarterly, Uncut, Foreskin Quarterly, Hombres Latinos, Just Men, Stroke, Rubber Rebel, Eagle* from *The Leather Journal, Hippie Dick, Gruf, William Higgins' California, Men in Boots Journal, GMSMA Newsletter, Hot Ash Hot Tips, The California Action Guide, Adam Gay Video Guide, Dan Lurie's Muscle Training Illustrated, Hooker, Expose, California Pleasure Guide*, and others.

For further bibliography and gay history, visit
JackFritscher.com